The Dog on the Acropolis

The Dog on the Acropolis

Mark Tedesco

Published in the United States of America by
Academia Publications

© Copyright Mark Tedesco 2019
Cover design by Jesus De Dios
Edited by Stacee Stricker

THE DOG ON THE ACROPOLIS

ISBN 978-0-578-21436-8

Book formatted by www.bookformatting.co.uk.

Contents

To Gina, Cindy and Ginger

Beginnings

Nobody knew just how long the large, black dog named Draco lived on the Acropolis; in fact, how he got his name was an equal mystery. It was known that he slept on the steps of the Parthenon, that he greeted visitors warmly, and that he regularly visited the Plaka area where a few shopkeepers knew him by name.

I first met Draco as I made my way up the Acropolis one night to take in the view. About halfway up, the large, black dog, a Labrador mix but with longer hair, rushed at me, then stopped, turned, and started leading the way. He didn't beg for food or demand to be caressed; he simply offered himself as my guide as if it was the most natural thing in the world.

There were other creatures who frequented the Acropolis including cats, mice, and other rodents, but Draco was the only canine who could claim this area as his home. Other animals didn't bother him. He ignored them since humans were his passion, and his mission was to guide them up to his beloved Parthenon since, without his help, they could very well get lost.

Sometimes large groups made their way up the side of the hill, following a leader who held up a flag or umbrella or even spoke into a loudspeaker. Draco kept away from such groups of humans. Sometimes the entire bunch smelled of garlic, other times of herbal scrubs and perfumes. The dog could be overpowered by a cacophony of odors and sounds so intense and diverse that he could become quite confused. No, Draco preferred to ally himself with one or two humans at the most. He could thus keep his eye on them, become familiar with their scent, and guide them to their proper destination.

The Meeting

Life in the Plaka was busy with tourists but low on profits. Full of restaurants, cafes, and tourist stores, the bustling façade often masked the reality of shopkeepers and workers who struggled to make ends meet. On the edge of this tourist area, near the base of the Acropolis, stood a shop that had been in Akil's family for generations. As a child Akil had played with his friends in this area, but now he had a family to support, a business to run, and bills to pay. His once carefree life was full of obligations and he was struggling: his son Jason was now 12 and was turning out to be a rebellious young man, store profits were down, taxes were up, and he was falling behind in his bills.

Then, one day, into his life scampered Draco.

It was a beautiful summer morning and the smell of freshly baking bread and rolls wafted through the streets of the Plaka. Akil had just put the last loaves in the oven and stepped out of his shop to sit in his chair underneath the tree. As he sat down, he looked up and saw not more than ten feet away, the large, black, furry dog. Both looked in each other's eyes. Akil had seen many strays before and had never paid much attention to them. To his son's pleadings to get a dog, his response was always the same: "When we can afford one, we will get a dog." They never did. But that morning, as man and dog now sized each other up, neither moved nor gave any indication of their intentions. The dog's gaze softened and he gave a slight wag of his tail. Akil gave a slight smile but both stayed where they were. The dog's tail began to wag wildly; at this Akil got up from his chair, retrieved a warm roll from his shop, and tossed it to the dog. Draco caught the roll in his mouth and trotted up the Acropolis to eat it in his favorite place. Akil stood there shaking his head.

It was mid-summer so the days were so hot that Draco sometimes sought relief among the bushes where few humans ventured. He much preferred to carry out his mission in the evenings, leading visitors up the side of the hill to the great monument above.

Draco avoided little humans (small children) since they were unpredictable: petting him one moment and hitting him on the nose the next, trying to ride him like a pony or teasing him by throwing a piece of food down the slope. After a few encounters the dog realized that it was best to avoid this type of human altogether. Draco did not beg, though he would not refuse a caress; he did not seek handouts, though he would gobble up a good piece of ham or bread; he only sought to be accepted as the most knowledgeable guide to the Parthenon. As soon as he finished leading some visitors to the top, he ran down the steps to seek out another tourist in need of his guidance.

Home Life

It was often after 8 o'clock that Akil arrived home after cleaning his shop and preparing the dough for the following morning. He was a strong man, medium build, with jet-black hair and dark eyes, who was used to hard work. His wife, Maria, was of Italian descent but born in Athens. Her dark hair, always worn up, illuminated her green eyes, and though her face showed some lines of worry, she was a stylish and pretty woman. Maria always had a large, home-made meal waiting for Akil, as well as many stories about the misbehavior of their son as well as their nephews and nieces. When he walked in, Akil smelled the pasta Bolognese that she was preparing. But just as he opened his mouth to tell her how delicious it smelled, Maria sighed and said: "Tonight, Akil; you must speak with him tonight! I am at my wits end. This son of yours is always in the streets; I don't know who he is with or what he is doing. His teachers tell me he does well because he is smart, but he misbehaves in all of his classes. And today, to make matters worse, I smelled *ouzo* on his breath!" Maria often raised her voice when she was excited and tonight was no exception. "Where is the boy?" Akil asked. Maria pointed to Jason's room.

The relationship between Akil and Jason had been strained for the past few years. The joy that Akil experienced when his son was a small child had been replaced by a heavy sense of responsibility, and Jason responded by distancing himself from his father and choosing the most troublesome boys in his neighborhood as his closest companions. He shared little with his

3

parents, and Maria was mystified at the direction their son was heading.

As she often did at times of stress, Maria focused on cooking as she listened to the exchange between father and son. First she heard Akil shouting, then Jason back. The bedroom door began to open, then was slammed shut. More shouting, this time only Akil. Silence. A few minutes later the door opened and Akil appeared in the kitchen, his face worn but a forced smile on his lips. It was his responsibility to be strong and hold the family together. "Thank you, my wife, for the delicious meal you have prepared. Jason will not be eating with us tonight."

For his part, Jason was angry. His father's only concerns were money, bills, and his business. His mother's woes consisted of the price of pasta and tomatoes. His cousins were too young, his family didn't understand him, so Jason preferred spending time with other adventurous boys.

After the fight with his father Jason was more careful to separate his life on the streets from his family, and he became more capable of inventing stories so that his mother would have no clue what he was up to.

Life on the Acropolis

While these events unfolded at Akil's home, Draco was joyfully making his way down the hill for his evening meal. He could always count on a nice plate of leftovers outside the back door of the restaurant owned by Alexander: Souvlaki, Moussaka, potatoes, and occasionally bananas and other fruit. Drako shied away from most vegetables and often left them on his plate. "Draco!" Alexander called, as the dog turned the corner and ran towards the chef, jumping high to try to lick Alexander's nose. "You're hungry today after a long day of work, Draco!" After putting down a bowl of water, Alexander went indoors to wait on his customers as Draco finished his meal and trotted back up the Acropolis, looking this way and that for any pilgrim that needed a guide.

Though unaware in his waking hours, Draco often dreamt of the long line of canines living on the Acropolis from which he came. When the monument was closed at night, the dog knew of a passage through the fence where he could come and go freely; tonight was no exception. Draco trotted across the ruins to his favorite place in the Parthenon, and there, under the moon and stars, he slept.

Dreams from the Past

This night was like many others. His dreams were filled with images of the past where the humans looked and smelled different, yet groups of them kept coming up the hill, talking, pointing, laughing, hiking up further. Draco's canine ancestors carried out their mission just as he continued to do so. Then there were other dreams more ancient, when the buildings on top of the hill were not yet built. This was the age of Pericles who, being the leading politician in Athens in the 5th century B.C., began the construction of the Parthenon. The sculptor Pheidias created a 40-foot-high statue of Athena, and the goddess had to be surrounded by a dignified temple.

Though Draco's dreams revealed only flashes of this ancient history, his ancestor's link to the Acropolis began during this time, when workers were offered one drachma a day to work on the constructions. Draco's first ancestor on the Acropolis was Daria; she was a small, short-haired, brown and white dog with slender legs, perfect proportions, and large, brown eyes. Daria's master was Adelino, who worked under the architect Callicrates. The mission of the architects and all the workers was to bring to realization the vision of Pericles.

Every morning the stonecutter Adelino, a stocky muscular man who had toiled in marble and limestone his entire life, would report to work at the same hour, and Daria would accompany him up the hill and stay in a shady place under some bushes until Adelino would call her at the mid-day meal. Sometimes Adelino's son Tiro, who was twelve years old, and his wife

Diana, a slender Greek woman with long, black, curly hair, would bring him food, share the meal, and Tiro would play with Daria. As they ate their bread, cheese, olives and fresh fruit, Daria would look on with her big, brown eyes. Her reward for her patience was always to get a morsel. If she was given an olive, however, she would sniff it but would shy away. She wondered why humans would eat such things.

Daria was content with her life but sometimes seemed anxious; she would creep over to the area where Adelino was working and look to make sure he was there. Once she spotted him she would return to her spot in the shade. At the end of his workday, Adelino would always find Daria waiting for him, tail wagging and barking until he reached down and caressed her. Then they were ready to go home.

It was a long walk to where Aldelino's family lived since it was in the poorer section of the city where many other workers dwelt. Once arrived, however, the neighborhood was full of life: children playing in the streets, music wafting through the air, and the smells, oh the smells! Every evening there was another delightful combination of odors that made Daria's mouth water. Having arrived at home, however, Daria had to wait outside.

If it was up to Adelino and Tiro, Daria would always be indoors but Adelino's wife would not have it. Over and over again the same discussion erupted: Daria is clean, I will wash her every day, she will not dirty the house, I will take her outside before bed. Yet the conclusion was always the same: "I keep this house in order so I say no dogs." But Diana had a good heart and though her words were strict, she said nothing when Tiro sometimes snuck the dog into his room late at night. Daria would curl up in the corner and not stir; the dog was intelligent and knew that her chances of staying all night indoors increased if she was as quiet as possible.

Every morning Adelino left for the Acropolis before the sun had risen, and Daria, after having crept out of Tiro's room, was always ready for him at the front door. They walked down the road and up the hill together. Once they arrived at his workstation, Adelino always spoke to her: "Daria, wait for me in the shade. I will be alright. You be a good girl and I will see you at mid-day." At that the dog went to her usual place, scratched the leaves to make them just right, curled up, and laid down.

Though the toil was difficult, Adelino was proud of his work as a stonecutter on the Acropolis. The plan of Pericles was to construct a series of temples, including the Parthenon, which would make the Greek city the center of the world. The Greek sculptor Pheidias oversaw the creation of the image of Athena and the temples that would adorn the Acropolis; Adelino sometimes saw him at work with his bushy, brown beard, and white robe, measuring, drawing, and meeting with the architects. Pheidias seemed extremely meticulous but not even-tempered. He sometimes walked among the stone cutters and movers, joking with them one minute, shouting at them the next.

Pericles' plan involved not only the construction of the most important temple of the ancient world, but also other important constructions, such as the reinforcement of the southern and northern walls, the monumental gate called the Propylaea, the smaller temples of Athena Nike, and the beautiful Erechtheion temple, lined with ionic columns on one side and huge female figures, or Caryatids, on the south. For this was the Golden Age of Athens[1], in which Socrates questioned the meaning of existence, democracy was being born, and Pheidias created sculptures that seemed to pulsate with life.

Like most Athenians, Adelino had been taught to read and write and he valued the education of his son. Tiro began his schooling at the age of seven; if he had been born a girl he would have had to remain at home and help the mother run the home. Education was seldom given to girls since their destiny was marriage and the family.

Tiro was the only son, being twelve years of age, and a

---

[1] 460-430 BC

decision would have to be made as to whether to continue his schooling or send him out for employment. Going to work with his father and Daria looked much more appealing to the boy, who begged his parents to allow him to leave school to labor on the Acropolis. "Yes, we are promised work for ten years or more," Adelino told his son. "But after that? Do you want to cut stones all your life?" The boy nodded as Adelino shook his head disapprovingly.

In Daria's world, such concerns did not exist. Her sole preoccupation was for Adelino; at times during his work he looked in the direction where he had told her to stay. He could see her often looking out at him, brow knitted, concerned. When they met eyes and he waved to her, she would relax, retreat back into her sheltered spot, and lie down again.

The Accident

The work of a stone cutter was difficult and could be dangerous if the task involved large blocks. Though the workers took precautions, there were sometimes accidents on the Acropolis.

It was almost midday when Adelino was working on a ledge about twenty feet from the ground. Suddenly there was a shout and a large crunching sound; as he looked up, Adelino saw a huge stone rolling down the slope. Somehow the rock had broken free of its support and plunged on to his ledge; Adelino was knocked unconscious and fell backwards off the edge. Everything went dark.

When he regained consciousness, all he could hear was Daria barking and all he could see were faces gathered around him. When he opened his eyes his coworkers clapped. "We thought we lost you, Adelino!" one said after another. Daria was vigorously licking his face. "I'm fine," he said as he tried to get up. Unable to, another gave him his hand; once he stood, Adelino took a step and fell down again. As Daria whined, four of his comrades lifted him and carried him down the long hill to his home.

Once Adelino was inside, the family was in an uproar. His wife Diana demanded to know whose fault this was; the nieces and nephews in the house were crying, the men who carried him home were trying to tell her how sorry they were. Daria was shut outside, barking continuously. Only Tiro came to his father to ask: "Papa, what can I do for you?" Adelino squeezed his hand, "Bring the doctor."

Fortunately for Adelino, medicine was a flourishing science in

Athens during this time, and when the physician showed up at the door there was great relief and expectation. All were led out of the room, including Diana, since her emotional outpour was causing distress. After spending nearly an hour with Adelino, the doctor left his room and spoke with the family. "There is good news; he can move his toes, and though his legs are numb now, he may gradually recover. He has injured his back and must move as little as possible for the next four to six months. For his future, we will see. He will not be able to work with heavy stones again, as he has done in the past."

Tiro and his cousins were frightened; Diana sensed this and her maternal instinct finally kicked in. "You heard the doctor; Papa will be fine. We just have to take good care of him," she said as she caressed her son's head. She then took a long look at Tiro and asked him to take the other children outside. Tiro and his cousins waited quietly in front of the house, wondering what was being discussed. When Diana came out, she asked Tiro to fetch his aunt to bring her children home. "When you return we need to talk." Tiro felt a lump in his stomach but didn't respond.

Once the children had been picked up and Tiro returned, Diana sat him down. "Tiro, tomorrow you will go to work in place of your father. But you will not work with the heavy stones. I will go make the arrangements for you. I am sorry, but we cannot survive unless we continue to have that one drachma each day." Tiro loved his family and he was grateful that he was old enough to help his parents through this difficult situation.

Daria was normally a quiet dog but this was too much for her; she first wined, then howled, and now was again barking incessantly outside the door. When Tiro opened to see what was the matter, the dog darted into the house and straight into the room where Adelino was lying. Finding him on his bed, she licked his hand over and over again until Adelino reassured her that he was alright. She then curled up in a corner, so as to be as little noticed as possible, and kept one eye on the man.

When Diana entered later with food and drink for her

husband, she pretended not to see Daria curled up in the corner.

It was an anxious night for the family and nobody slept well. At dawn the next morning when Tiro got out of bed, his mother was up already, preparing his lunch. "I spoke with your father's coworker and he agrees that you can do light work. If I hear that you are working with heavy stones, I will come there myself and yank you off of that hill for good!" she said. Tiro knew that she was serious so he shook his head in agreement. "As for Daria, I don't think she will leave your father until he is better, so leave her be." He was a little saddened that he had to go to work alone, but he knew he had to be the man for the family until his father could get on his feet. Daria was frightened and needed to be near his father, he reasoned. So he kissed his mother, took his meal of bread and cheese, and made his way towards the Acropolis.

Friends in the Plaka

Draco awoke with the morning sun with only faint images of the dreams of the distant past. How these memories came down to him, whether part of his ancestral line or in the stones of the Parthenon itself, was unknown. What Draco did know was that it was time for breakfast.

Down the steps of the Acropolis he trotted, down into the Plaka where his human friends could be found; he ran faster as he approached the backdoor of Alexander's restaurant. The day was already becoming warm as Alexander called out, "Dracooooooooooooo!!!" The dog leapt at him, jumping up and down. The man laughed as he put down a plate of last night's leftovers, which Draco devoured happily. Alexander stroked his back, then smelled his hand. "It's time for you to go see Cynarra," he said.

There was a flower stand in the Plaka that Cynarra, a young, green-eyed, pretty woman with dark, flowing hair, ran with her family. Her stand was near the water spout and she often gave Draco a spray on hot days. Though Cynarra didn't want everyone to know this, she also gave the dog a bath when Draco began to smell. Cynarra was afraid that others would make fun of her as she took care of a stray dog. She knew about the gossip in the Plaka, and being an unmarried woman working alone made her a target of talk. So she usually bathed Draco in the early morning or evening hours behind her shop.

Alexander knew more about the people living in the Plaka than anyone else, so it was no secret to him that Cynarra could be relied on to keep Draco clean. So he walked over to her shop with Draco, greeted her, handed her a pastry he had made that morning, and asked her to keep an eye on Draco.

Draco looked at Cynarra, head tilted, wondering what the woman was thinking, while Cynarra wondered why Alexander brought Draco by. She then leaned forward and smelled the dog and nodded. She then got out her hose, which excited Draco, then grabbed her shampoo, which she hid behind her back. Once she sprayed him down she poured the shampoo on his back before he could run and created a huge mound of suds; though Draco wasn't fond of the soap, he loved the fresh way he felt after a bath, so he stood there and allowed Cynarra to wash him down. After a good rinsing, the dog shook, ran around her shop several times, leapt up, and planted two wet paw prints on Cynarra's dress, then ran back up towards the Acropolis.

On his way, however, Draco smelled the rolls baking at Akil's shop and he changed course until he found the source. There he found Akil, just like the other time, sitting outside. Draco sat in front of him and looked into Akil's dark eyes. Akil asked him: "What do you want? Why do you come here? You want food? No food for you! I can't feed stray dogs and cats and birds! I have responsibilities!" The dog just looked at him. Draco then turned and ran up the steps toward the top of the hill.

The morning was turning hot but Draco was undeterred. He spied his first pair, an elderly British couple, who were slowly making their way up the stairs. The dog dashed towards them, surprising the couple as they froze in their steps. Draco circled them several times then preceded them up towards the Parthenon. Their unease turned into laughter as the couple pushed on ahead, following the dog all the way to the top. Once he safely delivered the couple to the steps of the Parthenon, Draco dashed down to look for another visitor.

Down in the Plaka, however, Akil was having a different type of day. As he was putting the fresh loaves and rolls on the shelves before the arrival of tourists, his wife Maria telephoned him.

"Akil, you must talk with your son again! He is up to no good. His teacher called this morning; he has been missing class in the afternoons and he has been spending time with those boys, the ones he promised not to see any more. I think that Jason has been telling us one thing but doing another..." Akil sighed; he was weary of this and did not understand his son at all. "Very well Maria. Send him around an hour before I close the shop. I will speak to him again." Akil had no idea how to deal with his rebellious son.

During the day Akil had numerous conversations with himself. "Son, why do you make your mother so sorrowful? She worries about you and cannot sleep." That was one angle, but he wasn't sure if Jason would accept the burden of guilt. "What do you think you are doing, lying to me and your mother! This is the ultimatum: if you do not keep your word, we will send you to live with your grandfather!" Anger and threats; Akil was unsure that this had any lasting effect on Jason in the past. "Son, I have responsibilities and so do you. Just as I must work every day so you can have a home and food, so you must do what your parents and teachers tell you." He wondered if he should try this last tactic and try to keep from being angry.

It never occurred to Akil to ask his son what was bothering him.

When evening came, Jason did show up, eyes downcast, awaiting the verbal bashing that he was sure would come from his father. Akil was still busy cleaning up the shop, so Jason stepped in, picked up a broom, and began to help. The boy didn't realize that his father was as uneasy as he was.

After some time, when the shop was cleaned and doors were shut, Akil invited his son to sit with him outside under the tree, his favorite spot. Akil looked at his son; he loved Jason but it seemed he no longer knew the boy. Jason looked down at the ground, awaiting sentencing. "Jason," Akil began. The boy looked up, paused, then smiled. Akil looked at his son, perplexed, then looked in the direction that Jason was looking. There was

Draco, who had quietly crept up and seemed to be eavesdropping on their conversation. "Who is that?" Jason asked. "That's Draco!" a voice from behind them said. Alexander stood there with a plate of food from his restaurant. "He comes to see me every night but for some reason he came to see you, so I brought his food." Alexander placed the plate in front of the dog who ate it gratefully. "Draco and I are friends; he lives on the Acropolis. Haven't you ever seen him?" Alexander asked. Akil responded, "I don't have time for such things!" "Well," Alexander said as he turned to return to his restaurant, "Draco apparently has time for you." Jason laughed as Draco had inched his way up and was now within two feet of him and his father. Jason reached out and stroked the dog's head. "He likes it, Papa, look!" Even Akil softened as he looked at his boy's smile as Draco's tail wagged wildly. So father and son, rather then having an argument or threatening one another, spent the evening with Draco, the dog from the Acropolis.

When it was time to go home for dinner, Draco hoped that they would follow him up the hill; when they turned to go towards their home, the dog leapt up the steps to the Parthenon where he would sleep. Father and son made their way home; before entering the house Akil said to Jason, "If your mother asks if we had our talk, tell her yes and that all is well." Jason smiled and understood.

Changes

It was late and there were no more tourists when Draco felt that his work was over and he made his way up the many steps towards the Parthenon. He slipped through the fence, trotted across the open areas, made his way through the small wall, and up the stairs of the monument. He curled up in his usual spot; before he could look at the city below and wag his tail, he was asleep.

Daria watched Adelino closely as he lay in bed; after a few hours, hearing nothing in the house, the dog crept next to him and lay down. Adelino managed to reach over and stroke her head with his fingers as he lay in pain and sorrow over what had happened. He wanted Tiro to have a future beyond heavy labor; he was just a boy and Adelino didn't want his son to become a man yet. He was sorry for his family; they were so wrought with worry. At one point Adelino tried to sit up to see if he could walk, but a sharp pain shot through his back as he moaned and dropped back. Daria sprung to her feet and looked in his eyes as a tear rolled down Adelino's cheek.

It was barely dawn on the Acropolis as Tiro arrived for work that morning. The boy was uneasy as he made his way up the hill. Though he had longed to leave school and work with his father, he had not anticipated working *instead* of his father. He could not fail at this since his family now depended on him. Tiro wondered if he would be able to see his friends, play sports, or enjoy himself again. His life now became full of responsibilities and this frightened him.

"Are you Adelino's boy?" called a large man chipping away at an unfinished column. Tiro nodded and walked over to the man who, because of his size, made the boy feel even smaller than he was. "They told me to watch out for you. Your father is my friend, a good man. You will work with me until he can return. Your name?" Tiro tripped over his words as he pronounced his name; fear and nervousness enveloped him. "Don't worry son, you will do just fine," the man said. "My name is Isidoros. I will teach you how to work with stone today; let's start with this," he said as he handed Tiro a chisel and a small hammer, leading him to a covered area where other workers were either working on various pieces of stone or setting up for the day.

Tiro watched wide-eyed as Isidoros chipped away at a stone as if it was butter. Isidoros laughed. "Don't worry, Tiro; I am at this work for over twenty years. You will come to understand and respect the stone and not simply subdue it. To do this, you have to understand its purpose and its function. Do you know what the foundations of this great building we are erecting will hold?" Tiro shook his head and Isidoros motioned for the boy to sit down.

"When I was about your age, I remember my father rushing home in a panic. He cried out 'they are burning the temple! They are destroying our work and our lives!' He then sat down and began to weep. What he was referring to was a great temple that stood on this very spot, and which he worked on as a stone cutter just like me. With the Persian invasion, his work was ruined and the partially-constructed temple with it. The gods have brought me back to this place; when I was hired here, it was if I was carrying on the work of my father." Isidoros paused as if he were watching a scene playing out in his imagination.

"Do you know what we are building here, boy?" the man asked. Tiro winced as he tried to recall what his father had told him. "A....temple....to a god?" he stammered. "Not just any god, son," Isidoros said dramatically as he stood and motioned around him. "We are creating the most beautiful building in the world for our goddess, Athena Parthenos. She is greater than you and me and all of us; she is greater than this building, and this will be clear when the temple to house her statue will be completed." Isidoros then sat down again. "Tiro, you, your father, me, all of us here are constructing a great history and we will be remembered in these stones forever..." Just then both heard a whine which Tiro recognized but Isidoros did not. "Daria!" the boy cried as the dog leapt towards him.

"This is my dog," Tiro said. Isidoros laughed, "I know Daria. Every day she waits for your father under those bushes until he goes home at night. I didn't see her after your father got hurt..." As he spoke Daria turned and ran down the hill towards the boy's home. "I guess she was just checking up on you," Isidoros said and smiled.

"Now Tiro," Isidoros continued. "Do you want to see the plans for the statue of Athena Parthenos that will fill this temple? I will see if I can bring you to the workshop of our great sculptor Pheidias so you can see the work at hand. The statue will be covered in gold and will be the largest figure of Athena that you will ever see in your life. I will show you one day soon, but now we must work." At that Isidoros took up his tools again and motioned for the boy to sit. "Today I just want you to watch. If you do not work the stone properly it will give way and be ruined. If you respect her strength and weaknesses you will create beauty and your arms will ache less!" he said as he laughed. Tiro spent the rest of the day at Isidoros' side, learning how to wet the stone, how to chip and gently sand the surface to a perfect smoothness. He was anxious to begin but waited for permission to be given. "Tomorrow, Tiro, tomorrow you will become a stone carver," Isidoros said at the close of the workday. The boy nodded and began his way down the hill.

Cynarra's Dream

Draco yawned as the images of the night before faded from his imagination. The sun was just below the horizon as the sky was blushing pink and the Parthenon glowed. Draco was lying on one of the steps and gently wagged his tail in glee. As he leapt to his feet he scampered down the hill to visit his friend Cynarra. She was always at her shop early to arrange the newly bought flowers. Reaching the Plaka, Draco made his way around the food stands and cafes, until he sighted Cynarra outside of her shop. He took off at full speed towards her, jumping over hedges and planters.Turning, Cynarra laughed and called out, "Draaaaccccc-ooooooooooo!" The dog ran even faster; reaching her, Draco leapt up and licked her nose. Cynarra wiped her face and laughed even harder; she then gathered up his dish and filled it with fresh water for Draco. As the dog lapped it up, Cynarra bent down and gave Draco a sniff. "You kept clean so far!" she exclaimed. "A bath for you next week!" she said decisively.

Draco looked up at her with his large, brown eyes, wagged his tail and drank again.

When she took over her parent's flower shop five years previous, Cynarra laid down one condition: she would never work evenings. She saw how her parents had lived in the Plaka, day in and day out arranging flowers and selling to tourists and providing for weddings. Her parents were happy with this life but Cynarra wanted something more. "I will run the shop on the condition that I can attend university classes in the evening," she had told her father. "When I complete my degree I will get a job

20

and leave the Plaka, leave Greece and make a life elsewhere." Her father shook his head; he did not understand such notions and imagined that his daughter would grow out of these ideas. He agreed, however, since he and his wife were growing too old to run the business themselves.

Cynarra had two brothers who were married and were living in Thessaloniki with their young families. They did not want a life in a flower shop either and had gone on to make careers of their own; the shop, therefore, fell into Cynarra's hands. She knew she could become trapped in this existence unless she took steps now to carve out her future. Almost every evening, therefore, Cynarra attended classes at the university. Her goal was to obtain a degree in business and accounting; she would then find an international company to work for and transfer to the United Kingdom or the United States. Nothing would stand in her way.

Work began before dawn for Cynarra; she had to go purchase fresh flowers, prepare the shop, sort through the flowers of the previous day, and make the arrangements. This left little time for socializing. In the afternoons, when business slowed down, she would devote herself to studying.

To reach her goal, Cynarra had to make sacrifices. She did not go out much, she had no husband or boyfriend, and her free time was either spent studying or caring for her parents, with whom she lived. Some considered Cynarra to be hard or unemotional, others said she was distant. In reality, she was driven by her dream of a greater life, and she gave little importance to whatever and whoever didn't fit into that dream.

It was uncharacteristic for Cynarra to make time for Draco when he first began to show up at her shop. She discovered him one morning attempting to drink from the few drops leaking from the faucet. She poured water into a dish and put it in front of the dog. Draco sat and looked at Cynarra in the eyes for a long time, tilting his head. When Cynarra smiled and pointed to the water, Draco eagerly drank. This was the first time they met and Cynarra doubted she would see the dog again.

Two days later, when Cynarra arrived at the shop before dawn, she found Draco waiting for her.

Though Draco played no part in Cynarra's vision of her future, his almost daily visits began to awaken a little place in her heart that had remained dormant. "If we are going to be friends, you need to get a bath," she told Draco after several weeks of visits. The dog, in fact, did have a strong smell and Cynarra doubted that he had ever been bathed. The next day she was ready for Draco with soap, a large tub, and a hose. Cynarra was prepared for resistance but she was determined, just as she was in every aspect of her life. If her goal was to bathe Draco, he would get bathed.

To prevent him from running away, Cynarra gently slipped a rope tied to a stake around Draco's neck while he was drinking. She then spoke to the dog, reassuring him that everything would be O.K.. Draco looked up at her with his brown eyes and Cynarra smiled. She then began to wet the dog, first with a sponge, then slowly introducing the hose. Draco didn't panic since he seemed to trust the woman. So slowly, step by step, Cynarra soaked the dog, introduced the soap, and lathered him up; all the while she kept looking Draco in the eyes, reassuring him that he was fine. After a good scrub and rinse she removed the rope. "You're clean Draco! Go!" she said as the dog dashed away, running around the Plaka, shaking the water off. He then ran towards the Acropolis and up the steps towards the Parthenon. This was Draco's first bath.

Cynarra smiled and returned to arranging the flowers for the day.

Sometimes Cynarra felt sorry for Draco; perhaps she saw herself in him. The dog was on a daily mission to guide tourists to the top of the Acropolis and was driven to fulfill this on a daily basis. But he was alone and relied on strangers for his needs and companionship. Would it always be this way? "Does working for a goal preclude loving relationships?" she wondered. Cynarra then placed the arrangements in the display and sat down outside to read a chapter for class that evening, as Draco laid down at her feet.

Many hours later, after a long day at work and class, Cynarra headed home. She made a detour towards the Areopagus, a rough hill rising in Athens where tradition holds that St. Paul preached. Cynarra climbed the hill and sat on a rock overlooking the city. The Areopagus was illuminated by the moon and stars and she felt at peace. This was her special place, where she would come to contemplate and also to prepare herself for her mother's endless questions when she arrived home. "You are a beautiful girl. You are a woman! When do you find a good man to settle down, Cynarra? Your father and I are getting old..." It went on and on. Her parents would never understand that she wanted a bigger life than what the Plaka could provide. Cynarra thought of Draco and laughed. She laughed because she thought to herself, "Draco would understand."

Friendship

It was still dark when Draco showed up at Akil's shop the next day. It was so early, in fact, that Akil was just unloading the flour to prepare his first loaves when Draco romped down the hill, ran across the Plaka, and bumped into the back of Akil's legs. The man gave a start; realizing it was Draco, he laughed. "Come for a hand out, did you?" he asked the dog. Draco sat down and looked at the man, perplexed. Akil assumed that Draco wanted something from him, just as he made this assumption with everyone he came into contact with. If his wife seemed extra kind, he prepared himself for a request. If Jason seemed meek, he would be asking for money. If Draco came to visit, it was because he was begging for food.

Akil turned and focused on his work while Draco sat in the doorway watching him. Glancing up, Akil shook his head. He was tired of everyone taking and so few giving. He began to knead the sweet dough he had prepared and turned on the oven to warm the shop so the bread would rise quickly. If the dog approached the food area, he would chase him away. Instead, Draco lay down in the doorway, his eyes following every move the man made.

After forming half of the dough into rolls, Akil kneaded a separate batch from which he would make the long loaves that European tourists were so fond of. Draco put his head on his paws and continued to watch Akil, fascinated by the work of this man. When the second batch of dough was finished, Akil put the first set of rolls in the oven and prepared the third batch, mixing the flour, yeast, salt, sugar, butter, and water. As the smell of baking bread filled the shop, even his mouth began to water. Akil smiled when he saw Draco watching him still. "You want some bread, do you?" he asked Draco. Akil turned to take the loaves out of the oven and put the second set in to bake. Then he turned, expecting Draco to have moved indoors to beg for a morsel.

Draco was gone.

It was a few days later that Jason came to his father's shop after school. His mother had insisted that the boy spend more time with his family and less with his friends. Mostly to appease his mother, Jason headed over to the family business once or twice a week.

Since it was the middle of the afternoon and there would be no more baking, Akil had begun cleaning out the oven. Customers were rare at this time a day, so he took advantage of the calm to get the hardest part of the clean up finished so that he could go home right after he closed up shop. Though Jason disliked helping to clean the oven more than any other chore, he felt sorry for his father as he walked into the shop. It was a hot day and Akil had climbed on a stool and was almost completely inside the oven, scraping the baked-on spills and charred fragments. Akil was covered with sweat as he turned to Jason who was still standing in the doorway. "I came to help you, Papa," he said and Akil smiled. "You can help me by sitting with me in the shade so I can rest." The two went to the back of the shop and sat down in the cool shade with a light breeze. Akil closed his eyes for what seemed only a few seconds when he heard Jason laughing. Akil, feeling something on his hand, opened his eyes to see Draco licking his fingers.

"Son, can you get some water and a roll for Draco? It's hot and he is tired and hungry," Akil said as he looked at the dog. As Jason got up, Draco moved closer to Akil and put his chin on the man's knee. Akil looked at him with curiosity as Draco fixed his eyes on Akil's. After a few moments Akil asked, "Draco, what are you thinking?" as he patted his head.

The dog was indeed thirsty and Jason had to fill the bowl again. Draco also devoured the roll that Jason offered to him. Once satiated, the dog laid down to rest while leaning against Akil's leg. The man smiled and looked at his son, who was also smiling. "Let's hope we don't have any customers for awhile," Akil told his son as he scooted himself into a more comfortable position. "Don't worry, father," the boy said, "I will take care of the customers. You and Draco rest. I will bring you something cold to drink." These were the last words that Akil remembered until he woke up hours later as the sun was beginning to set.

Akil opened his eyes and found Draco still beside him; the dog stood up and stretched. "Awake, Papa?" the boy called out from the shop. "How long have I been sleeping, son?" he asked. "All afternoon! But don't worry; we had a few who asked for bread and sandwiches. I took care of them. I even finished cleaning the oven. Is Draco still there?" As he said these words, Draco began to lick Akil's hand again. The dog then turned and trotted away towards the Acropolis. "He was," Akil responded.

It was a few days later that Akil was busy serving customers in the evening that Draco showed up. Akil laughed when he saw Draco sitting outside the ajar back door, staring at him. Akil threw him a morsel as he continued to wrap bread and rolls for his hungry customers. When things slowed down after half an hour, he found Draco still in the doorway, following his movements from side to side. Leaving his shop, the dog followed him to his chair underneath the tree and close to him. Akil never had time for pets; he considered them a waste of money. But looking down at Draco, whose chin was on his knee gazing up, Akil felt a tinge of compassion.

"Did Draco come today?" Jason whispered when Akil arrived home. Akil nodded, glancing over at his wife. They had decided to keep Draco a secret from her since, they thought, she wouldn't understand. "Can I come tomorrow?" the boy asked, eagerly. Akil reached over and kissed the boy's head.

That night Draco was sleepy. After visiting Akil, he ate his meal of leftover chopped meats and fruit at Alexander's restaurant, dashed over to Cynarra's flower shop to lap up the water she left for him, and then he scampered up towards the Parthenon. There were still a few straggling tourists going up the hill as evening wore on, so the dog went up and down the stairs to guide a few newcomers to the top. By the time he scooted under the fence and lay down on one of the Acropolis' steps, he was exhausted.

The Workshop

It was several weeks now that Tiro was working the stone on the Acropolis; the boy was allowed to sand but not allowed to chisel the rock. Daria also had developed her routine: the dog would accompany Tiro to work every morning, then return to stay at Adelino's side for the rest of the day. Diana, Adelino's wife, had become accustomed to the arrangement since the dog brought a smile to the faces of her husband and son. Daria had become part of the family.

Adelino was still in great pain but he was not one to sit around for long. His injuries were so severe that he could not walk without help, but the man was determined to get his strength back. When Diana came into the room and scolded him for moving himself out of bed, Adelino turned to Daria. "So much fuss for nothing. Why is everyone making so much fuss?" he asked the dog. Daria strove to understand, tilting her head. Adelino sat down on the bed; as soon as his wife left the room, he raised himself again, holding onto the wall, and moved himself across the room, albeit with great pain. Daria followed him and whined, perhaps sensing her master's discomfort. "Three more times," Adelino said out loud, as he struggled to keep himself erect. He then sat himself on the bed and slowly raised his legs to take the strain off his back. Daria nuzzled her head under Adelino's hand as the man panted from the effort.

When Tiro arrived home and kissed his mother, he looked in on his father, who was sleeping. Daria, however, leapt up and jumped on the boy, whining in excitement. Fearing to wake his father, Tiro backed out of the room, followed by Daria.

"How is he, Mama?" Tiro asked. "He was walking today," Maria said, shaking her head. "That is good, no?" His mother looked at the boy for a moment before answering. "I no longer know what is good, son." At that she rose to begin to prepare dinner. "Come tell me about your day, son," she called out.

When Tiro rose the next day, Daria was waiting for him at the front door. In a house of sadness, the dog made him smile. Together they walked to the Acropolis to begin the day's work. As he reflected on his father's injury and his mother's anxiety, Tiro said a silent prayer to Athena, on whose temple he was honored to labor. "Hear my prayer, O Pallas Athena. You who protect your people with power and might, look at my father and heal him. Give him some of your strength, goddess, and send your healing rays. Oh, and help my mother too." He had stopped while sending up this prayer and Daria had stopped also, looking at the boy. She then barked to let Tiro know that they had better be on their way.

When he arrived at the workshop, Isidoros was already there; he stood with a big smile on his face. Tiro looked at him inquisitively. Isidoros laughed and said, "I have arranged a great treat for you today, Tiro. And if you wish, for her highness also," as he bowed to Daria. "We are going to the workshop of Pheidias to see the progress on the statue of Athena! This is a rare event and few are allowed inside. Are you pleased?" Tiro nodded while saying a silent prayer: "Thank you, goddess."

Pheidias was admired as the greatest sculptor in Greece. Under Pericles, Pheidias was in charge of all artistic aspects of the city's building program. As they made their way to the workshop, Tiro felt uneasy about meeting the renowned sculptor, whereas Daria expressed no concern at all as she trotted at the boy's side.

Isidoros stopped Tiro as they approached the workshop and asked him, "Do you know the story of Athena?" The boy nodded.

"Tell me what you know before we enter." Tiro stated that

29

Athena was the protector of Athens. When Isidoros continued to look at him, the boy realized he had not told him enough so he looked down at the ground, thinking. "Have a seat," Isidoros said as he motioned to two rocks under a tree.

"Can your father cut stone?" Isidoros asked the boy. "Yes," Tiro replied. "If someone asked you to describe your father, and you replied that he is a stone cutter, have you left anything out?" The boy nodded; "Yes, a lot of things. He is more than a stone cutter." Isidoros smiled. "Yes, now you understand. And Daria here, who is looking at me now. If I said that Daria is an animal that eats meat, have I stated the truth?" Now the boy shook his head as Daria looked this way and that. "Yes, but she is much more than that!" Isidoros was pleased with the boy's understanding. "So if you tell me that Athena is the protector of Athens, this is true and praiseworthy. But the goddess is more than that."

Isidoros scooted towards Tiro. "It all started at her birth. Did you know that Athena was not born of woman? She actually leapt right out of the forehead of Zeus," he said as he touched the boy's forehead with his thumb and made a flying arc. "Now the title with which we honor her here is Athena Parthenos, 'Virgin Athena,' since neither man nor god was worthy to have the goddess. Because of her origin and purity, the ways of the goddess are wisdom and courage, justice and strength. The greatness of our patroness Athena is not measured by coin or weapons but rather by the mind, the intelligence. She is the wisdom having leapt forth from the head of Zeus, and in her greatness is ours." At this, the two sat silently as Tiro contemplated the words. "Can Athena make my father well?" he asked Isidoros. "She can do all things if you ask," was the reply.

With this the two rose, followed by Daria, and entered the workshop of Pheidias.

The first thing that struck Tiro was the bustle. The stone work on the Acropolis was strenuous, but calm and focused. Here, there were dozens of workers running all over. Some were pacing and arguing, some were studying a drawing, others were building a scaffolding, while still others were working with gold and ivory. It was not difficult to spot Pheidias, a larger-than-life bearded man in a white robe, waving his arms and shouting directions to those erecting the scaffolding. "Master, we cannot build any higher. The whole statue will collapse!" shouted a man on the scaffolding, looking down at Pheidias. "It will not, I tell you! We will build it from within; this statue will not fail!" was the sculptor's response. But the man above him persisted: "Master, with respect. Gold and ivory are weak materials. They cannot sustain such height. We can only build as high as the materials permit us!" With this, Pheidias motioned to the man to come down and they walked over to the drawing and proceeded to argue as Tiro, Isidoros, and Daria backed off.

"You must be the stonecutters!" exclaimed a slightly built man in a white tunic as he walked towards the group. "And who is this?" he said, as he bent towards Daria. "She wants to be a stone cutter too!" said Tiro. After a chuckle, the man introduced himself. "My name is Mikkos and I work with the ivory and the gold, keeping track of every spec at the beginning of the day and at its conclusion. Welcome to our workshop!" he said, gesturing to all the activity surrounding them. They slowly turned and surveyed the entire workshop. "What is the first thing you notice?" the guide asked. "The scaffolding," answered Tiro. Mikkos nodded. "Yes. What does that tell you?" The boy smiled and replied, "How tall the statue will be!" Daria was watching this scene with her tail wagging, since she knew something important was being discussed.

As all three men looked up at the scaffolding, it was Isidoros who asked, "How tall will she be, Mikkos?" At this the guide smiled. "If there were seven of you, each one standing on the head of the other, Athena Parthenos would still be taller," he replied. "This is what is being discussed. Some say it is not possible and the statue will collapse. Others are trying to influence Pheidias to reduce the size of the statue to avoid the risk. Still others wish to change the materials used to construct the statue to assure its stability. So this is the discussion occurring today as the work continues," he said with a sigh.

"The statue will have a wooden core and will be covered in ivory and gold," Mikkos continued. "For this reason, your work is so essential. The temple you are constructing, in fact, is more important than our work, because without you we would not be here discussing a statue. Rather, we would be arguing with a vendor about the price of olives or sweeping a floor to earn a few coins. But your work has taken us to another level, my friends. This temple that you are raising will protect the statue and ensure that the cult of Athena will last for eternity, and so our city will be protected and our people will be guided in all wisdom. This is your work and we are at your service," he said, bowing. Tiro felt goosebumps at this and even Daria remained still, watching Mikkos. "On another day I will show you each one of our stations, and I invite you to return here when you wish." As he walked ahead, Isidoros took his arm and stopped him. "Mikkos, may we meet Pheidias?" he asked. At this Mikkos grimaced and shook his head. "I have worked with Pheidias for several years, and I can tell you that today is not a good day to meet the master." With this, the tour concluded.

The boy felt exhilarated as they left the workshop and headed towards the Acropolis. Daria trotted alongside him but when she recognized the area they were in, she turned and trotted in another direction. "She is going to spend the rest of the day with Papa," he said, and Isidoros smiled.

"Where have you been?" Adelino asked as a dust-covered Daria used her nose to push herself into his room. She wagged her tail and put her chin on the bed, looking at Adelino with a fixed gaze. "An adventure that perhaps my son can tell me about," he said. Daria then curled up in the corner for a well-deserved nap.

Home

Draco never recalled the details of his dreams but he remembered the workshop, the faces, and the feelings. The images were disconnected as he opened his eyes as the sun came up, which bathed the Parthenon in a golden hue.

Draco was hungry and he knew where food would be waiting for him, so he scampered down the Acropolis and dashed through the Plaka to Alexander's restaurant. Alexander, a middle-aged man with greying hair and slightly built, was already peeling potatoes and preparing Stifado, a delicious beef stew. When he heard a slight whining outside of his back door, Alexander called out loud, "Draaaaaccccooooooooooooo!" The dog barked excitedly and started to jump up and down. He was beside himself when Alexander presented him with a plate of last night's leftovers. On his plate there was Keftedakia: meatballs seasoned with oregano and mint. There was also a big square of Pastitsio: a delicious baked pasta dish with ground meat and bechamel sauce on top. To top it off, there was a generous helping of Moussaka, made with layered eggplant and spiced meat. "Slow down, Draco," Alexander said as he petted the dog's back.

Alexander's life was simple. He ran the restaurant in the Plaka that had been in his family for generations; his adult son Alex helped in the mornings and his wife Sapphira in the evenings. They were not rich, neither were they poor, but they worked hard and mostly kept to themselves.

When Alexander once spoke to his wife about Draco, and the possibility of bringing the dog home to live with them, Sapphira laughed. Alexander did not bring up the topic again. This saddened him. Perhaps he was feeling an emptiness, knowing that someday Alex would leave home and then it would just be the two of them. The dog reminded him how his son, nieces, and nephews used to play on the living room as toddlers, and Alexander used to laugh and play with them.

"What plans do you have today, Draco?" Alexander asked as the dog finished his meal. Draco sat and looked at the man. "Oh, a day of work I can see, just like me. Bringing those lost tourists up the hill, I've seen you! Why don't you lead some of them down the hill to this restaurant to eat?" Draco cocked his head, not quite getting the meaning. "Oh, go on, you! I know you have things to do!" With that, Alexander turned and entered the kitchen. Draco dashed off to see his other friend in the Plaka, Cynarra.

She was filling up vases and spraying off plants when Draco crept up behind her and licked her leg. Cynarra gave a start and then turned the hose on Draco. Rather than fleeing, the dog tried to bite the stream of water. Cynarra laughed as Drago leapt at the water flowing, trying to capture it in his teeth. She said out loud: "Draco, you always remind me to have fun!" She laughed again as the dog barked at the water.

"Now I have to finish my work," Cynarra told the dog firmly. "You come and drink." Draco followed her as she poured water into his bowl; he drank and drank, his tail wagging. When he finished, he leapt up to try to lick her face, turned, and dashed back across the Plaka. "Be a good guide today, Draco!" she called out just before the dog turned the corner.

As the weeks and months passed, Draco began to show up almost every evening at Akil's shop. As the attachment between the man and dog grew, Akil had an idea. "Jason," he asked his son one evening, "Do you like Draco?" The boy smiled and nodded. Akil knew his wife and realized that this matter had to be handled diplomatically. "Tell your mother you want a dog. But don't tell her it is Draco! She will say to ask me. Then we will bring Draco home. What do you say, son?" The boy nodded. Akil and Jason had grown closer lately and bringing the dog home seemed to be the next logical step, but Maria would need convincing.

It was a few days later that Jason approached his mother and asked: "Mama, can we get a dog if I take care of him and he can stay at the shop all day?" His mother looked at the boy as if he was crazy. Believing that Akil would never hear of such a thing, she said: "It's up to your father." Jason smiled.

The next day, father and son waited for Draco at the shop with a leash.

That evening, since Draco had never been on a leash before, he dragged Akil behind him. Rarely having been outside of the Plaka, the dog was curious; he stopped to sniff every two or three feet. "Papa, we're never going to get home if Draco keeps stopping," the boy complained. At this, Akil pulled on the leash and led Draco towards his new home.

"So this is the dog," Maria stated, arms crossed, as the two walked up to the house with Draco. "Maria, this is Draco. Draco, this is Maria," Akil started with a smile. Maria shook her head and went inside. Akil and Jason looked at one another and rolled their eyes.

"Do you think Mama will let us bring Draco inside?" Jason asked his father. Akil thought a moment. "Eventually. But now we must be a little sneaky. Why don't you take him for a walk, show him the neighborhood. I will go and spend time with your mother. After about an hour you return and bring Draco into your room without your mother seeing. I think once she sees how well behaved Draco is, she will accept him." The agreement was made and Jason and Draco trotted off.

Jason snuck Draco quietly into his room, but once he left to sit down to dinner with his family, he could hear the dog whimpering across the house. Maria shot a glance at Akil, then at Jason; both looked down as she shook her head. "I can already see that I will not win this one," she said. "O.K., but I am not responsible for cleaning up after that dog! You keep him clean and your room clean; and he doesn't stay here with me during the day. Akil, you bring him to work!" Father and son smiled broadly and began enjoying their dinner.

When he returned to his room, Jason found Draco at the door, eager to leave. He put his leash on to take him for a long walk in the neighborhood, but once outside, the dog pulled towards the Acropolis. "Draco, you live with us now," Jason said to the dog, who looked at the boy without understanding. Jason pulled him and Draco followed, through the unfamiliar streets and smells, passing houses and people and streets he never imagined before. He walked very close to Jason.

That night, curled up in a corner in Jason's room on a blanket, Draco didn't dream of the past. He was uneasy since this was the first time that he had not slept under the stars.

When Akil was getting ready for work the next morning, Draco was jumping and wagging his tail, exceedingly excited. When Akil managed to put Draco's leash on, the dog practically leapt out the door as the two directed their steps towards the Plaka. "Draco, Draco," Akil said. "Now you have two homes and I hope you will choose mine." The dog dashed ahead, pulling Akil behind him.

When they arrived in the Plaka, Draco continued on towards the Acropolis but Akil pulled him towards the shop. The dog seemed confused, but followed Akil. But when they arrived at the shop and Akil tied his leash onto a pole while he went into the shop to work, the dog began to whine. It seemed to Draco that he was being punished but he didn't know what he had done wrong. He whined and whined until Akil came up, pulled up a chair next to him, and patted his head. "I want you to stay here with me, Draco. I want you to be part of my family. Jason wants you too. Maria….well, that's another story. But the fact is, Draco, if I let you go, you will race up that hill and I may not see you for days. So here you are, tied up…" Akil was feeling bad when Jason turned the corner. "Are you talking to Draco again, Papa?" the boy asked, smiling. "Son, can you sit with him while I open up the shop? I think he is confused." The boy willingly sat with Draco, who lay down at his feet.

Days went by as father and son attempted to transform Draco into a house dog. They played with him, fed, and walked him. But in the evenings, as Akil watched Draco sit at the front door waiting to be set free, the man's heart sank. Though he and the boy were happy to have the dog around, Draco seemed increasingly unhappy. After a week of this, Akil began to doubt his decision.

"Son," Akil began as father and son sat together at home that following Sunday, "What do you think is best for Draco?" Right away Jason realized where the conversation was going and tears welled up in his eyes. The boy looked down as Akil continued. "It seemed the perfect solution. Draco comes to visit us at the shop almost every day; you want a dog; Draco needs a home. What could be more simple? But he seems unhappy to me. What do you think, son?" Tears rolled down the boy's face. "This is my fault. I have caused you pain and Draco is unhappy. What should we do son?" He waited for Jason to regain his composure as he put his hand on Jason's shoulder. "We should let Draco live the life he wants," said the boy. At this Akil smiled and hugged his son.

The next day, when he arrived at the shop with Draco, Akil unfastened the leash. At first Draco stayed right behind the man, following him as he went about his morning chores. Then Draco seemed to discover that there was no longer a chain that bound him. After licking Akil's hand, he turned and ran with all his might towards the Acropolis. After all, he had neglected his work and he had to find anyone lost or lagging behind to lead them up to the Parthenon.

Freedom

Draco's other friends in the Plaka, Cynarra and Alexander, had no idea what had happened to the dog during the days that he was with Akil's family. Cynarra feared that Draco had been injured or worse and she had even climbed the Parthenon to search for him. Alexander, with a plate of food in hand, went searching for Draco in the Plaka, but never passed by Akil's shop. But when Draco returned to the Plaka later that evening on the day that Akil had released him, he went to Alexander's restaurant for his dinner. Alexander chuckled when he saw the dog. "Draco! Where were you, Draco? Did you find a better dinner somewhere?" he asked. But the dog continued to eat his food, then looked at Alexander with his head tilted to one side as the man continued to ask him questions. Then he licked Alexander's hand and pressed against his leg. Alexander went inside to peel potatoes; when he turned to look out the back door later, the dog was gone.

Cynarra was closing up shop when Draco came upon her at lightning speed and once again leapt up to lick her nose. She wiped her face and laughed at the dog's prank and out of joy that Draco was back. The dog's tail waggled wildly as she petted him and asked him question after question. Then Cynarra bent down and smelled Draco's coat. "Freshly washed," she said to herself. When she questioned him more Draco wagged his tail and eventually was able to lead her to the water hose; Cynarra realized that the dog wanted to play, so she turned on the water and tried to spray him as Draco dodged the stream of water in one direction, then ran right into it on the next run around. He was happy to be free and Cynarra was happy he had returned.

A few days later, it was getting dark as Akil and Jason began to close up the shop before heading home. The same thought was on both their minds as they silently washed down the countertops and carried out the garbage. From inside the shop Akil heard his son say: "Draco?" Dropping his sponge, Akil stepped out of his shop and spotted the dog, crouched down some distance away, partly hidden by a shrub. "Come on, Draco," the boy called, but the dog didn't budge. "Wait, son," Akil advised as he sized up the situation. "I think Draco is frightened. He was probably confused by us bringing him home. Perhaps he thought he was being punished. Let's not scare him off. Let me handle this," he said as he crouched down. Draco put his chin on his paws as Akil knelt down on the gravel to be on his level. Then he spoke to the dog: "Draco, we missed you and we won't hurt you or put a chain on you. We just want to see you again," he began as he slowly moved towards the dog. Draco watched him with big, round eyes as Akil moved closer. When he was about ten feet away, the dog began to whimper and slowly scooted towards him, still crouched down. So man and dog moved towards one another on the ground, and once united, Draco timidly licked Akil's hand as the man soothingly spoke to him and patted his head and his back. Then the dog stood up; as did Akil, who gave him a treat. Realizing that he wasn't in trouble, Draco ran to Jason and jumped on his leg. The two sat down on the chairs outside the shop as Draco stood before them, looking first at one, then at the other. When Akil beckoned him by patting his knee, Draco jumped up and licked Akil on the cheek.

It had been almost a week since Draco had dreamt or even slept well, but tonight he was happy as he trotted up the Acropolis for his rest. After being reconciled to Akil and Jason, his little dog heart was at peace.

The stars were bright as Draco curled up on one of the steps of the Parthenon, and soon he was transported to that ancient age when his ancestors dwelt on this hill.

The Boy and the Man

When Tiro arrived home from work that evening, he spotted Daria looking at him from Adelino's room, partially hidden behind the wall. Perhaps the dog was still afraid that Diana might put him out. "Daria!" Tiro called, and the dog ran to the boy. "Is that you, Tiro?" his father called. Boy and dog went into the room; when Tiro saw his father in bed, his heart sank. The once strong and powerful man now seemed so feeble. "Sit here, son, and tell me about your day." So Tiro sat on the bed, Daria curled up at his feet, as he recounted his visit to the workshop of Pheidias. His father's eyes grew wide as the boy told him of Pheidias' vision and the bustle of the stone cutters in his workshop. "I am so proud of you, son," Adelino said with tears in his eyes. Daria looked up and whimpered.

Daria was at the door when Tiro left for the Acropolis the next morning. It was still dark as the dog darted in front and around the boy. "Daria!" Tiro called, and the dog stopped in her tracks and looked at the boy. Both froze; then Tiro ran at full speed, Daria chasing behind him to catch up. When he could run no longer, Tiro walked towards the hill with Daria beside him. "Do you like coming to work with me?" he asked the dog. "I think you want to be with me and Papa. I understand how you feel." He glanced down at Daria, who looked up at him as she trotted alongside of him. "Today I am going to cut stone, but I also want to learn how to cast bronze and help create the beautiful things I saw yesterday. Wasn't Pheidias' workshop unbelievable, Daria? Don't tell Papa, but I am going to ask if I can one day work for the great Pheidias. That is my dream, Daria, but it is our secret," he said as the dog cocked her head, straining to understand. The boy bent down and patted Daria as they continued up the Acropolis together.

As the days and weeks passed, Daria and Tiro began their day the same way: up at dawn, walking together to the Acropolis, Tiro set to work carving stone, and Daria, always midmorning, ran back home to stay with Adelino. The boy was content, Daria seemed happy, and Adelino began to improve. The man was now able to rise from bed and walk around while bracing himself for balance. Life seemed good until one day, making his way home, Tiro sensed something wasn't right.

It was a day like the others; Tiro' ability at chipping at the stone was improving to the point that he no longer needed supervision. Daria trotted beside him at work that morning; the boy set out his tools and as he prepared to chip his first stone, he looked up at Daria, who returned his gaze. The dog then dashed off. The day was hot as Tiro chiseled away and he was grateful when the sun started to set and he could set off for home.

By now Daria knew what time Tiro arrived and she waited for him outside the front door. When he turned the corner she would run towards him to greet him.

This day, however, as he neared the house, there was no greeting. Walking in, Adelino stood in the small kitchen, propping himself up, concern written across his face. He reached out for Tiro and caressed the boy's head. He then looked at Tiro in the eyes and asked, "Where is Daria, son?" The boy's heart fell. "She left me as she always does to come stay with you. Is she not here?" Tears began to well up in the boy's eyes. At that moment, Diana walked into the house and stopped in her tracks. "What is wrong?" she asked, looking at the one then the other. It was Adelino who answered: "Daria is gone."

Heavy Heart

Draco awoke startled while the sky was still grey. He stood and tried to shake off the dreams of the night before. He then slowly walked down the steps of the Parthenon and made his way, continuing his slower gait, down the Acropolis towards the Plaka. Akil was opening up his shop when he felt a nudge against his leg. Draco was pressing his head against him. Akil crouched down and looked at Draco in the eyes, holding his head. "What's wrong, Draco?" he asked. The dog whimpered and licked Akil's hand. The man looked both ways, to make sure no one was watching, then kissed the dog on his head. As he got up to continue his morning chores, Draco followed him and remained no more than an arm's length away.

In the afternoon, Jason stopped by the shop to see how his father was doing and he noticed that Draco was always at his father's heels. "What's wrong with Draco, Papa?" he asked. Akil looked at his son, then looked at the dog as he patted Draco's head. "I don't know, son. Something has upset our little friend here and he doesn't want to be alone. I wish I knew what it was. When I finish up here, we will give Draco the choice to come home with us or return to the Acropolis." Jason nodded in agreement.

When the last customer had gone and Akil, with Jason's help, had finished cleaning the shop, they sat under a tree to relax. It was that time between afternoon and evening, when the wind was still and the sun began to set. Draco put his chin on Akil's leg and seemed content with the man's hand resting on his head. Akil looked at Jason. "Son, I appreciate your help; I appreciate you coming to see me every day, and I appreciate you not causing me to worry as I did so much in the past." The boy smiled and replied, "Can you tell Mama what you said?" Akil laughed and said, "Yes, I will tell Mama!" After a long silence, Jason asked his father: "Papa, can we keep Draco as part of the family?" Akil looked in his son's eyes to grasp his meaning. "Son, he is already part of our family. Don't you see who Draco comes to in difficulty? But he has a free spirit; he cannot be kept at home without killing his spirit. His home is this hill and we are his family. Do you see that, son?" Jason nodded.

When it was time to go home, father and son rose from their chairs as Draco sat down and looked first at the one, then at the other. The dog then jumped up and leaned on Akil with his front paws, looked him in the eyes, then turned and dashed towards the Acropolis.

As the sun set, Draco lay on the steps of the Parthenon drifting off into a fitful sleep. He felt closed in and scared…

Taken

Daria was shivering, not from cold but from fear. She found herself in a small wooden crate, next to other boxes, each with a dog imprisoned inside. The crates were bouncing and rattling, as they were on a cart being pulled down a road. Athens was shrinking in the background; Daria looked out a crack at her beloved Acropolis and sniffed the smells of her beloved city. As it all faded into the distance, she curled up in the corner of the crate and whimpered quietly.

A day and a night the cart was pulled; it seemed like an eternity for the dogs, having been given no food or water. When the crates were finally unloaded and pieces of meat were thrown to each animal, Daria was too frightened to eat. She remained curled up, hoping the nightmare would end and Adelino would appear to bring her home.

Daria was more comfortable with humans than with other dogs, so when she was let out of her crate within a fenced area with other barking animals, she was out of her element. She looked this way and that, not understanding what situation she was in, or how she got here; she wondered where her family was. Suddenly, she heard human voices nearby.

"These are hunting dogs. They will get you a good price. My friend raises all types of hunting dogs and I am doing you a favor by bringing them to you. Make me a good price and they are all yours," one voice said. Another answered: "I have to feed these animals so they better make money for me. Let me take a look..." After a pause, the voice continued, "You have to be kidding me.

These are street dogs. You just rounded these up and are trying to unload them. What kind of idiot do you take me for?" and an argument ensued. In the end, a few dogs were left, while Daria and the others were forced back into their crates, loaded back onto the cart, and driven down the bumpy road once more.

Daria smelled the scent of farm animals when the cart next stopped. A long conversation ensued between two men; one was the man who captured her and the other was unknown. "Yes, I will take three of them. They better know how to herd the animals as you promised!" A few minutes later, Daria's crate was picked up and placed on the ground. She crept out when the little door was opened. The unknown voice said: "This one is too small! How can she herd my sheep?" Another argument followed and Daria was allowed to stay. Though the dog was terrified, when food and water was offered this time, she eagerly devoured both.

It was evening when Daria and the two other dogs were put into a room with a horse, a cow, and a pile of hay. The door was closed and Daria stood there, wide-eyed, wondering where there would be a safe place in these unfamiliar surroundings. She slowly crept over to the hay and buried herself so as to remain unseen. Then, out of sheer exhaustion, she fell into a deep sleep.

Searching

Adelino was walking through the streets of Athens, using a stick to prop himself up with one hand and holding on to any available fence or wall with the other. Running at him from behind was his wife Diana. "Adelino, you cannot do this! You will fall. The dog will come back! Come home, husband," she implored. Adelino shook his head. "No, my wife. Daria will not come back unless we find her. Something has happened to her; she would never have run off. She doesn't know how to survive on her own. We must find her soon." Seeing her husband so upset, Diana stopped trying to convince him to return home. "I will send Tiro," she said. Adelino was fighting his fatigue and his injury as he crisscrossed the streets looking for Daria. He stopped at all his neighbor's houses one after the other, seeking information about the dog's disappearance. No one saw anything, no one heard anything, but each one promised to keep an eye out for Daria, and several of the children offered to help Adelino search the next day.

When Tiro caught up with his father about an hour later, Adelino had barely the strength to walk. Tiro was about to question his father about what he found out concerning Daria's disappearance, but he noticed how upset his father looked. At this the boy gave his father his arm and they both walked home in silence.

Feelings

Draco awoke by his own whining as he was dreaming. He stood and shook himself, then headed straight to the Plaka.

It was early and the shop was still closed, so Draco lay down at the step to wait. After nearly an hour he heard, "Dracooooooooooo!" The dog ran to Akil and leapt up to greet him. "Why so early, Draco?" This new behavior was strange and Akil was concerned. "Tonight I will go up the hill with you to find out what is going on," he said. Draco tilted his head to one side. Akil began opening the shop with the dog following close behind.

The residents of the Plaka knew one another by sight, sometimes by name, and they would often say hello to one another but rarely would venture into one another's business. So Akil was surprised to hear a female voice greet him that morning as he washed the counters and prepared his baking area. "Kalimera! Good morning! I am Cynarra; my family owns the flower shop near the entrance of the Plaka," she said. Akil smiled as he recognized the girl and recalled seeing her parents work in their shop year after year. As he offered her a coffee, Draco ran from his side, jumped up to Cynarra and licked her smack on the lips. "I see you know Draco," Akil said laughing as Cynarra wiped her face with a napkin. "Oh yes, I know Draco," she said. "In fact, he comes to me regularly, to drink water, to get sprayed with the hose and, when I can manage it, to get a bath. But I haven't seen him much lately and I was hoping that nothing had happened to him. But now I see he is safe with you."

Akil motioned for Cynarra to sit down while he took a coffee also. "Draco is safe and I believe he is fine, but the last few days something has changed. He has a free spirit and he loves his home on the Acropolis, but lately he seems less free, as if he is worried about something. So he comes here and doesn't leave my side. It's a mystery, Cynarra. But tonight I want to find out what is going on. I'm going to go up the Acropolis with Draco; I want to make sure no one is hurting him." Cynarra paused for a moment, looking out into space, as if she were seeing something. "I would like to come with you, Akil." As Cynarra rose to say goodbye, they agreed to meet after they closed their shops.

Akil didn't recognize the voice when he heard someone calling "Draco!" so he was unsure if he should respond. Draco stood fast by Akil's side. As the voice approached, Akil made a split-second decision and replied, "He is here!" From around the corner came Alexander, a full plate of food in hand. Draco licked his chops and trotted over to him as Alexander put the plate down near Akil and stood to formally introduce himself.

"I didn't realize that Draco had made so many friends," Akil said as he shook Alexander's hand. Both men chuckled. "Let me see if I know the story: Draco was coming to visit you but you haven't seen him in a few days. So you came to look for him to make sure he was alright." Alexander paused then responded: "And how did you know that, Akil?" He then explained Cynarra's visit that same morning, as Alexander smiled and chuckled. "I see our little friend has made an impression on each one of us. To me he comes for dinner, to Cynarra for baths and water, and to you, Akil, for what does he come to you?" Akil thought a moment, then responded, "For friendship."

Akil told Alexander about his and Cynarra's plan to follow Draco up the Acropolis that evening to see if there was someone on the hill bothering the dog. "My wife will scold me, but I want to make sure our friend is safe," Akil said. "Jason," he said as he turned to his son, "Tell your mother that I will be home late and not to worry. Tell her that I have something to take care of, but do not tell her more than that." The boy smiled and Akil knew he understood. "Tell me what you find out!" Alexander said. "Return tomorrow for a coffee together," Akil said and shook Alexander's hand.

Akil and Cynarra were prepared to follow the dog up the hill later that day. Jason promised to clean up the shop that evening, whereas Cynarra closed early. When the sun was setting, Draco grew anxious and Akil knew that he would soon run up the hill so they had to be ready. He tried to keep the dog at the shop as long as he could but the time was growing near; Draco began to whine, he licked Akil's hand, then turned and trotted towards the edge of the Plaka. Just then, Cynarra rounded the corner and she and Akil ran to catch up to the dog.

Having his friends on his heels on the stairs of the Acropolis was something new for Draco and this excited him as he turned around and barked for his companions to keep up. When he got too far ahead, Draco returned, barked at them, then led them up once more. "Draco!" Cynarra called out. "We don't have four legs like you!"

Once they reached the top, Draco wanted to play and he kept jumping up at the two, who had sat down to catch their breath. When he got close, Draco licked Cynarra's nose, then circled around and leapt at Akil, licking his cheek. This became a game and the two humans laughed. "I don't think we will discover anything by climbing up here with Draco," Akil said. "But he certainly is happy that we came." Cynarra laughed.

The two made their way down the hill to let Draco settle down and hoped that whatever was bothering the dog was in the past.

The Farm

When she heard the door open, Daria peered out from under the hay. She was frightened and didn't understand what was happening, so she didn't move a muscle in the hope that the hay would keep her hidden. The man in the doorway started to shout and clap his hands; the other animals grew restless, and the two other dogs began to bark. "Where is that mouse of a dog!?" the man who had made the purchase mumbled. He starting clapping his hands again and shouting: "Come out! Come out or I will thrash you!" and he began to kick the hay which was scattered around the floor. He was heading straight towards Daria and would have kicked her also if she had not darted out just in time. "There you are! Now out with you! You have to earn your keep too!" he shouted. Terrified, the dog ran between the other dogs and found herself in an enclosure containing sheep.

Little Daria was confused as the man was shouting, the sheep were baaing, and the other two dogs were barking. This was too much and she crept back into a corner for safety. "No you don't!" she heard as a quick kick sent her flying into the middle of the sheep. She ran to be free of them as the mean man opened the gate and the sheep poured out, with the two dogs running behind and Daria trailing.

Suddenly, there were two other dogs who ran behind the sheep and kept them moving up the hill towards the meadow. The new dogs soon followed the example of the more experienced ones and began chasing the sheep, running beside and behind the flock. Daria, however, trotted behind the others. She had never been around other animals before and she relied on human companionship to feel safe. Lacking someone whom she could trust, Daria was scared and couldn't cope with these new circumstances.

In the evening when the mean man brought the sheep and dogs back to the enclosure, Daria buried herself in the hay, just like the night before. She hoped that when she awoke she would find herself at Adelino's side.

Seeking

Adelino would not give up. Every morning, despite his wife's objections, he would leave the house and, using a stick to prop himself up, would make his way through the streets of the city. He suspected that Daria had gotten injured or been taken, since she knew the neighborhood and could always find her way back. He knocked on every door, one street after another, talking with every friend and stranger about the disappearance of his dog. He felt sick about the loss of Daria, because he knew she would find it difficult to make her way in the world alone.

Days turned into weeks and there was still no hint about what happened to Daria, until one day a stranger on the other side of the city told Adelino about some men who buy and sell dogs. "Where can I find these people?" Adelino pleaded. The man shrugged, "Come back tomorrow. I will ask around." The men separated. Adelino returned home with hope in his heart.

"Did you find her?" Tiro asked his father as he entered the house. "Not yet, but I might have a clue. Tomorrow I will find out if she has been taken and sold; I pray the gods little Daria is safe." The boy nodded, then asked Adelino, "Can I come with you tomorrow? We have two days without work while some deliveries are made. I can help you search for Daria." His father smiled and made his way across the room to hug his son.

Diana walked in and asked if there was any news. She had grown very concerned about her husband suffering from the loss of Daria. The glimmer of hope in Adelino's eyes heartened her. "I hope our Daria will be home by tomorrow," Tiro said. His mother kissed the boy on the forehead.

Dreams and Plans

While he was washing down the counter that morning, Akil had the sensation that he was being watched. He looked over the counter but saw no one. As he focused on his work he heard whining from Draco, who was sitting behind him, wagging his tail. "Oh, my friend," Akil said. "Is my Draco back to his normal happy self?" he asked. Akil put his his hands on his hips and waited for an answer. Draco barked and tried to jump on Akil, who backed up and patted him on the head. He then found half a sandwich in the refrigerator and handed it to Draco. When he finished his breakfast, the dog followed the man around as he completed his chores.

When Jason came a little later, he realized that Draco wanted to play, trying to get the boy to chase him. "Papa! Draco seems well again!" he called out as his father smiled. "Go and play for awhile. Draco has been so depressed that he needs some fun. Then, bring him to Cynarra because I need your help this morning," he said. Jason and Draco ran off.

For some, the Plaka was a vacation destination; for others, it was a place to earn a living, but for Cynarra it continued to feel like a prison. Since she was a little girl she was considered to be a little odd. Cynarra was not satisfied with things that contented others and she had little patience for those whom she considered to be small minded. She wanted a bigger life than anyone she knew. If she did not set a goal and strive to reach it, she realized that the Plaka would be her destiny.

She was studying from one of her textbooks when Draco ran

up with Jason trying to catch up. The dog stopped in front of her little shop and began to bark from excitement, urging Cynarra to come out. Knowing Draco so well, she first hastily put on her apron in case he jumped up on her; she had heard enough customers comment on the paw prints on her clothing. As she came out the door, Draco jumped high to try to lick her face. "Dracoooooooo!" she scolded him, but she also laughed as the dog started running around her in circles. "Does somebody want a bath?" she asked. Draco stopped in his tracks and began to run from her. Jason smiled and said, "He is so smart he knows what you said!" Eventually Draco crept up to Cynarra, who rubbed his ears. "Can you watch Draco today, Cynarra?" Jason asked. "Papa is busy and Draco wants to play. He has been so down lately that he seems to need attention. I can come back for him in a few hours." Cynarra looked at Draco and asked him if he would like to stay. "You have to be quiet since I have to study," she said. She then coaxed Draco to lie down in the shade next to her shop and handed him his treat. When she went inside the shop and opened her book, she leaned over and noticed that Draco was laying down taking a nap.

"Do you want a bath now?" she asked the dog a few hours later. Draco sprang to his feet. He was wide awake in an instant and wanted to play again; he ran from her, daring her to chase him. She chased him for a few minutes, then caught him and brought him over to the hose. A few minutes later he was full of suds; looking up, Cynarra spotted Alexander the restaurant owner. "Kalimera! Good morning! He has gotten to you also, eh?" he said. Cynarra responded, "Kalimera! Is there anyone in the Plaka who doesn't know this dog?" Alexander laughed and bent down to give Draco a small piece of meat he had brought over.

"How are the studies, Cynarra?" Alexander asked. He continued. "Don't be surprised! I know your parents and they have spoken to me about you!" Looking up from the sudsy dog, she replied: "The university is my ticket to see the world and to leave this place." Alexander sat on a nearby bench, obviously in the mood to chat. "You have a job, a business, family here. That isn't enough?" he asked. Draco stretched in pleasure as Cynarra scrubbed his back. "For my parents it was enough; in fact, there are those who would envy me. But the Plaka was never the place I wanted to live my entire life. Even my brothers moved away to live far from here. Now for our canine friend here, the Plaka is a huge world; he has many friends and he loves this place. But for me, Alexander, no, it is not enough." There was silence as Alexander reflected.

"When I was a boy I dreamt of being a pilot," he began. "Every time I heard an airplane I would look up and watch it until it was out of sight. I even thought of joining the military to get training. But then my father needed help at his restaurant and my responsibilities grew from there. Now I rarely think of being a pilot, but sometimes I do long to be free. Free like Draco." The dog looked up at Alexander and wagged his tail. "Can you help me rinse him?" Cynarra asked Alexander. "He doesn't like that part so much," she said. So Cynarra, already wet, held Draco firmly while Alexander sprayed him with the hose. The dog shook and shook but only got wetter. When they had finished, Draco took off running at high speed and zigzagged through the Plaka to dry off.

Cynarra went back to her work, cutting flower stems and setting plants out for tourists to buy. Alexander went back to his work at the restaurant and Draco, eventually, returned to Akil's shop. "Somebody smells good!" he told Draco as the dog wagged his tail. Draco then lay down on a mat placed outdoors for him and watched Akil's every move.

"Are you going to your hill now?" Akil asked that evening. Draco wagged his tail and barked. Akil gave him part of a roll and the dog hastily ate it, then ran across the Plaka and up the Acropolis. The stars were already out so the dog went directly to the steps on the Parthenon where he loved to sleep.

The Escape

Daria escaped. She didn't know where she was going but she knew she couldn't stay in such a scary place full of strange animals, cruel humans, and bad food. She had never been in a situation before where nobody cared for her, where it didn't matter to anyone whether she lived or died. She had to leave.

She set off down the nearest road, trotting along to distance herself so as to not get caught. She would be more careful to avoid humans this time.

As she made her way down the road, Daria searched the air for familiar scents. She kept looking back to make sure the mean man wasn't on her trail. Feeling safer, she stopped to eat a piece of fruit that had fallen on the ground from someone's cart. She whined in loneliness then kept running along the road, until she picked up a scent that was vaguely familiar. There were trees and a small creek; the smell of the water and the woods reminded her of passing this way before. She was on the right road! She started to trot faster.

As the day grew longer, Daria grew tired and thirsty. She no longer trusted humans, so as evening approached, she crept off the road in search of food. She was not a hunter; Daria was afraid of other animals. Fortunately, she had a taste for fruit and she soon found some apples that had fallen from a tree. Still hungry, she curled up to rest, hidden by the grasses growing amid the trees.

Adelino and Tiro set out at dawn to follow their lead on Daria's whereabouts. It took them several hours to arrive at the stranger's house from the day before. The man, who introduced himself as Antiochus, invited them into his small home. "There is a man in the next village," he began, "who looks for dogs to sell. The scoundrel even takes dogs that belong to others! He is driven by money. I think he may know where your dog ended up. But let me caution you: if you ask him a favor, he will shut the door in your face. If you offer him money, he may help you." Antiochus paused and looked first at Adelino and then at Tiro. They all rose to their feet. After thanking him, father and son left.

"Papa, where will we get money?" Tiro asked once they were on the street. Adelino paused and looked at his son. "I will go back to work. We can make an agreement to pay this man a little at a time." Tiro objected, "But Papa!" Adelino caressed his son's head and said, "It is the only way." The two set off, following the directions given by Antiochus.

After nearly an hour of walking, as the sun rose towards midday, the two spotted an isolated house in a field. It looked neglected but they heard dogs barking in the back. "Remember son," Adelino said, "This man will do us no favors. Let us not accuse him but rather make a deal, for Daria's sake."

"Who are you?" asked the short, middle-aged, disheveled man as he opened the door. "I am Adelino, and this is my son Tiro, and we are looking for a dog." At this the short man smiled, since he sensed money was at hand, and he introduced himself. "My name is Georgios and I am certain I have the right dog for you," he said as he motioned them inside. "What are you looking for?" he asked Adelino. "A farm dog, a work dog?" At this Adelino looked at his son and said: "We are looking for a small dog, female, for a house dog. I would like her to be brown and white, gentle, even timid. Not a puppy, but a fully grown dog, from two to three years old. Do you have such an animal?" Adelino asked. When Georgios stood up to look out his window at his dogs, Adelino winked at his son. "Of course, if you do not have such a dog, we can look elsewhere. If you referred us to where we could find such a pet, we would even pay you a referral fee." Georgios reached up and scratched his head.

"Come with me," he said. Adelino's heart leapt at the prospect of being reunited with Daria in minutes. As he led father and son behind his house, Georgios motioned to the enclosures containing dozens of dogs. "You can have your pick and I will give you a good price," he said. The dogs were not being taken care of: they were thin, dirty, and they were all whining and barking. Adelino shook his head. "No, there is no dog here who fits what we want. If you have seen or sold such a dog we will pay you a referral fee once the dog is found," he said. Georgios scratched his head again. He did not want to miss this opportunity and he knew that if he sent the two away he would probably never see them again. "Can you come with me?" he asked "I may know where you can find a dog that fits this description." The three left the house and started down the road, Adelino using a stick for support.

It was over an hour later that the three came within sight of an old farmhouse. Wandering around were a few chickens and the smell of farm animals was heavy in the air. "He isn't here if you're looking for my husband!" a woman called out from the window. Georgios approached the window and spoke in a low voice to the woman, glancing back at Adelino and Tiro. He then returned. "I sold a dog to this man which fits your exact description. The woman doesn't remember it, but her husband is pasturing the sheep. If you can manage it, we can meet him in the pastures." The three set off again.

Daria, meanwhile, had not eaten that day and since there were many people on the road, she hid and waited. Humans made her feel unsafe. So she continued to watch until the road cleared, though she was growing weaker from lack of food.

Belonging

"Draco!" Akil called out as he arrived at work the next morning, the dog already waiting for him. Draco ran up to the man and leaned against him. "What's up, Draco?" Akil asked. Akil put his supplies inside the shop, only to find Draco right behind him, leaning on his leg again. So Akil sat down. "What happened, Draco?" he asked the dog. At this point the dog started to climb into his lap. Akil laughed: "Draco, you are too big for me!" and the dog stopped. He then put his head under Akil's arm to snuggle. "You are safe here with me, Draco," Akil said. Now his smile was gone and concern was written on his face.

When Jason showed up at the shop he found his father with his arms around Draco, the dog with his front legs on his father's lap. "What's wrong with Draco?" the boy asked in alarm. "I wish I knew, son. Can you set up the shop this morning? Draco won't let me move." Jason happily helped his father. "Papa, can we take Draco home with us tonight? Perhaps someone is hurting him up there." Akil immediately thought of the fuss his wife would make, but then he looked down on Draco's hidden face. "Yes, son," he replied.

When evening came, the two prepared to head home. "Let me talk with your mother," Akil said as put a leash on Draco. This time the dog seemed excited to be heading somewhere with Akil and Jason. "Finally Draco seems happy!" Jason exclaimed.

By the time they reached the house, Maria had already seen them coming down the road, and she was standing outside with her hands on her hips. "I can explain," Akil said as he handed her some flowers that he had obtained from Cynarra before leaving the shop. Maria accepted the flowers but her expression did not change. "Jason, can you take Draco while I speak with your mother?" The boy took the leash and walked Draco down the road, where the dog seemed intrigued by the sights and smells.

"What is it with you two and this dog?" Maria asked in exasperation. "He's a good dog; Jason no longer spends his time in the streets. He comes to the shop every day now; the boy helps me out and spends time with me and Draco. This is just for a few days; we won't keep him. He wants to be free. But he doesn't seem to be feeling well..." Maria looked at her husband and her stern look faded. She loved this man, with his dark eyes, wavy black hair and gruff nature on the outside hiding his tender heart on the inside. She approached him and hugged him. "Thank you, Maria," Akil whispered.

By the time Jason returned with Draco, Akil and Maria were sitting at the table eating some bread and olives. Jason was perplexed, looking first at his mother, then at his father. When Akil winked at him, Jason knew all was well.

Draco seemed content to stay indoors that night and when Jason fell asleep, the dog was lying down, head on paws, next to his bed. The dog had no dreams that night.

When morning came, Akil almost tripped as he got out of bed, for there on the floor, with one eye open watching him, was Draco. Akil smiled and, glancing at his wife, motioned for Draco to follow him out of the room.

Jason soon joined his father in the kitchen and sat down as Akil made the coffee. Akil whispered: "Son, can you buy a red collar for Draco today? Perhaps he will be safer if it is known that he belongs to us." The boy nodded and smiled as Draco lay in the corner, watching both of them.

With his new bright red collar, Draco spent the next days mostly at the shop. Occasionally he ran up the Acropolis, but after a few hours returned to Akil, who brought him home every evening where he began the night in Jason's room, yet Akil found him every morning next to his own bed. Draco slept peacefully here, but after a week he began to feel the call of the Acropolis.

It was on a Monday when Akil woke up and, not finding Draco by his bed, looked into Jason's room. The dog was not there. Growing alarmed, he went into the kitchen and found the dog next to the front door, anxious to exit. "What, Draco?" he whispered. "Are you not happy to stay here with us?" The dog looked at him curiously. "Yes, I understand. Your heart is free and you must be free. But wait until I go to work. I will bring you to the Plaka before letting you go in case you get lost. The city is dangerous." Draco laid down at these words and Akil prepared for the day.

Draco resumed his life as before; he ascended the Acropolis and greeted tourists climbing the steps; he showed up at Akil's shop, occasionally scampering off to see Cynarra and Alexander, but always returning to Akil. There was a special bond between the two that many, including Jason, noticed. "Papa, why is Draco always looking at you?" he asked a few days later at the shop. Akil looked down and smiled as Draco looked back up at him. Akil then leaned over and kissed his son's head.

Undaunted

"That useless mutt! Yeah, I had a dog like that. Good for nothing! Didn't appreciate anything I did for her. She would just stay in the corner and shake. In fact, she ran off some four or five days ago. Useless!" said the man in the field. Then, turning to Georgios, "You need to pay me back! You said that dog was a herder. You cheated me!" and the two began to argue. Adelino and Tiro looked at each other with sadness, then turned and walked away.

"Papa, are we going to give up?" Tiro asked. The man shook his head. "Son, Daria is family. We can't give up. But you have to get back to work. I will take it from here," he said as they made their way down the road towards their home.

Diana met husband and son as they approached. She could read the disappointment on their faces and was sorry for both of them. It seemed that both Adelino's body and heart were broken. She said nothing as she first embraced her husband and then kissed the head of Tiro. She then took her husband's hand and walked inside. "We will find her," she said to Tiro as tears ran down the boy's cheeks.

Diana was aware that Adelino slept little that night and wondered whether it was the physical or emotional pain that weighed on him the most. When she found him absent from their bed before the sun was out, she rose and found him staring out a window, deep in thought. She approached him and took his hand in hers. "What do you think our Daria is doing right now?" she asked, knowing his thoughts. "I hope she is safe, wherever she is.

You know how frightened she can become..." Diana kissed him and returned to bed.

"Keep her safe and bring her home," Adelino whispered towards the Acropolis before he returned to bed.

Daria opened one eye and looked around her. She had been rolled in a tight ball all night in an effort to keep warm. She had learned to sleep in the brown weeds which hid her well since her coat was brown and white. She was hungry and thirsty so she lifted her head to sniff the air, but she smelled nothing like food. As she got up and headed towards the road, she stopped and looked and sniffed again. There was something vaguely familiar, almost like a dream. This gave her little heart hope that she was heading the right way.

"Look at that little dog! It looks like it is starving," said a woman passing by as she saw Daria along the side of the road. She and her friend stopped as she tore off a large piece of bread she was carrying. She put it on the ground but Daria stayed where she was. "The poor little thing is scared. Here, let's back off," and as they distanced themselves Daria approached the bread and sniffed it. In a flash she had eaten the whole piece. "I wonder who she belongs to?" the woman asked. "Maybe we should take her home," she said as she approached Daria. Knowing her thoughts, the little dog scampered out of reach and down the road.

Two things played in Daria's favor: she had a good sense of direction and she had an extraordinary sense of smell, even for a dog. As she moved down the road, her certainty grew that she was traveling in the right direction. If only she could keep up her strength. Though she felt weak and her ribs were protruding, Daria kept moving, since she knew her salvation lay in arriving at home.

Now that Adelino knew where Daria ended up, he planned to cover that area, street by street, until he found the dog. Though walking was painful, every morning he set off after greeting his wife and spending time with his son. As he walked through the streets, he stopped strangers and approached houses, asking if anyone had seen a dog of that description. None had seen her, and none would have, since Daria was captured and hauled away in a crate. But Adelino did not know this.

It was discouraging, day after day, to find no trace. "Husband, perhaps Daria has been taken in by another family. Perhaps you should let her go and trust in the gods," Diana said one morning before her husband left. Adelino looked at his wife; Diana saw both the fatigue and determination in his eyes. Without any words they understood each other. Diana kissed her husband; then Adelino left for another day of searching.

"Daria! Daria!" Adelino called out as he walked through a field. He knew that she would seek the protection of vegetation if she had been harmed by humans. Daria was a fragile creature and Adelino knew she could be far away and starving. She didn't know how to forage on her own, since she had been treated as one of the family. "Daria!" he cried out. At times, Adelino's emotion got the best of him. He stopped while tears filled his eyes. He then lifted his arms in prayer to the great protector of Athens. "Athena, you are the goddess who watches over us, great and small. Watch over my little Daria until I find her." After he said these words, he stood there for a long time and closed his eyes. It was as if he could then see the little dog, making her way home with the same hope that he had.

Draco's Day

It was a sunny, cloudless day when Draco woke up with renewed energy. He jumped to his feet, sniffed the air, and ran down the hill.

This morning Draco was driven by thirst, so his first stop was Cynarra's flower shop. When he arrived, she was already at the faucet filling up her watering containers. Draco crept up to her, not wanting to get wet. When Cynarra turned around his nose was almost at her leg. "Draco, you scared me!" she cried out. The dog looked up and wagged his tail. "Are you thirsty, Draco?" she asked, as she went to get his dish. He drank it all up, so she filled his dish again. While he was drinking, Cynarra gave him a sniff; she then crept away to prepare his hose bath. When she returned with a rope, she noticed his red collar. "Akil," she said at once, knowing the man's attachment to Draco. This made it easier for Cynarra: she attached the rope to the collar and when Draco was finished drinking she led him over to the hose and got out the shampoo. Though Draco tried to pull away, she knew he was always happy once he was clean. She sprayed, then sponged him down as he stood there powerless.

"O.K., Draco," she said as she untied him. The dog shook, getting Cynarra completely wet. When she began to chase him, Draco ran in wide circles just beyond her reach. When Cynarra grabbed the hose again, he ran off to his next friend, Akil.

"Dracooooooooooooooo!" Akil called out as soon as he caught sight of the dog running towards him. Within a few feet of him, Draco leapt up with perfect timing and licked Akil's nose. Akil chuckled. "You're all wet, Draco! How did you get so wet?" he asked, as he sniffed. "Shampoo. It was your friend Cynarra, no? And now you come to see me. Here, I will give you something to eat while I finish opening the shop," he said as he patted the dog's black, damp head.

"Papa!" Akil heard as Jason turned the corner. Draco bolted towards him and became so excited that he started to run in circles around the two. "Draco got a bath," Akil said chuckling. When Jason began chasing the dog and playing with him, Akil went into the shop to get ready for his first customers.

"Kalimera! Good morning, Akil," a voice said outside the door. At first Akil didn't recognize it until the man stuck his head into the shop. "Alexander!" Akil called out, as he reached out to kiss him on both cheeks. "How is the restaurant business?" he asked as he handed Alexander a freshly baked roll. "Oh, the bakers are putting me out of business," he said as he bit down into the warm, sugary crust. Both men chuckled as they went outside and sat in the shade. Suddenly Draco zoomed by, followed by Jason. "Draco is coming to see you more and me less," Alexander complained. "He must like the food better here!" Akil said and both laughed again.

A few minutes later, both boy and dog came around the corner panting. Jason went in to get water for himself while Draco went to Alexander and began licking his hand. "Either Draco likes you, or you have sugar all over your hand!" Akil teased him. "Maybe both," Alexander replied as he patted the dog's head.

Draco spent the rest of the day following Akil around wherever he went, though not setting his paws inside the shop. Akil sometimes felt sorry for the dog; he understood the feeling of attachment to those he loved yet longing to be free.

Draco had neglected the day's tourists and, as the sun began to set, Akil saw that Draco was restless. So he sat down and bade Draco come sit next to him. With his chin on Akil's knee, Draco looked up and listened to Akil's words: "Now I know you are about to return to your mountain, Draco. You love it there but I worry about you, all alone. Your collar should let everyone know that you have family, but I wish you would consider coming home and living with us. That way I know you would be safe. But Draco, I know your heart is free and that you love your mountain. So I am just asking you to be careful and to come see me first thing in the morning. Can you do that, Draco?" The dog looked in Akil's eyes, licked his hand, then dashed across the Plaka towards the Acropolis.

There were still tourists walking up and down the stairs. Draco immediately set to work, meeting an elderly couple who were moving very slowly at the first set of steps. The dog brushed the man's leg and walked slowly in front of the couple, turning every few steps to make sure they kept behind him. About halfway up the steps the two were too tired, so they found a place to sit while Draco sat in front of them. "Look! We have our guard dog," the woman said. "I think he is our guide," the man replied as he took a drink from his bottled water. A few minutes later they rose to continue and Draco led them to the top. Once his mission was completed, he trotted down to the bottom of the hill to find others in need of his guidance.

Draco was tired by the time he reached the Parthenon that night and immediately fell asleep under the starry sky.

Hope

There was a mist hovering above the ground as Daria opened one eye as she lay hidden in the field by the road. She was tired and weak but she immediately smelled something different in the air; she hurriedly got up and lifted her nose to measure the direction. Yes, it was something she smelled long ago. It was not the smell of food but of a place, something in her past that was warm and comforting. Her little tail wagged for the first time in many days. She trotted out to the road and followed her nose as the sun was barely rising over the horizon.

Daria was dehydrated and hungry but she pushed on; she was too tired to care as people started to pass her on the road. Rather than hiding, she trotted past them, ignoring everything but that vaguely familiar smell. At times she lost it, but now she had a direction that she would follow until it returned. It was around noon that she lost the scent completely, but she pushed forward on that road.

For his part, Adelino was already searching for Daria since dawn. Every day he made his way in the direction that Daria had last been seen, calling her name, asking strangers and approaching houses. Diana stopped objecting and rose with her husband every day, packing him a lunch, and making sure he had his walking stick. For her husband's sake, Diana hoped that Daria could be found.

Family

Draco woke up with a start; dawn was still an hour away but he trotted down the hill and curled up outside of Akil's shop.

"Draco!" Akil called out, and the dog came running towards him. Draco leapt up to try to lick his nose. Akil laughed as the dog jumped up again and again, trying to lick him. "Draco! What is it with you, Draco?" Akil asked, noting the early hour and unusually affectionate behavior. Setting down his things, Akil sat in the chair under the tree as Draco licked his hands and attempted once more to lick his nose. "Oh, you need affection. Don't we all my friend?" he said as he put his arms around the dog. Draco closed his eyes and savored the embrace, and Akil held him for several minutes. "You are family, Draco; don't worry about that. And your collar lets everyone know that. You can stay with me today if you want," he said. Then, looking this way and that to make sure no one would see, he kissed the dog's forehead.

"Papa!" Jason called out. Akil looked up with a start to see his son turning the corner. "I thought you were going to sleep in, son," he said. "I wanted to come with you but I didn't hear you get up. Can I spend the day with you and Draco?" the boy asked. "Sure, son! That would be wonderful. Can you and Draco help me set up?" he asked, and the two went to work with the dog following closely behind.

"Papa," Jason asked once the shop was set up. "Can I take Draco with me today on the leash? I will bring him home to Mama and take him around the neighborhood and then return."

Akil smiled and nodded. "That's a great idea, son. You and Draco spend some time together."

A few minutes later Draco was pulling Jason down the street.

Dog and boy took turns dragging each other.

When he picked up the scent of the boy's neighborhood, Draco pulled even harder, eager to arrive at the house. Maria spotted the two coming down the street and went outside. Excited to see her, Draco broke free and dashed towards Maria with all his strength. Maria was more detached from Draco than the others, but even she could not help laughing as the dog was jumping up and down to try to lick her face. Jason ran up after them, and the two bent over laughing as Draco kept leaping up.

"Mama, come for a walk with us!" Jason asked. Maria was taken aback since her son had not invited her into his life in years. Thinking of all her chores waiting, she hesitated; then, looking into the eager faces of Jason and Draco, she smiled. A few minutes later the three were walking down the street, Draco happily wagging his tail.

"Son, are you getting along with your father? You know he loves you," Maria began. "Yes Mama. I go to the shop almost every day now to help him. We never have any problems. Why do you ask, Mama?" Maria paused as they continued to walk. "Because when you were running with your friends in the streets, your father suffered much. As did I," she said. "I'm sorry, Mama, for both of you. But now that is in the past," Jason said. Maria stopped in the street and asked: "But what made the difference? We talked with you, we punished you, we pleaded with you, and you wouldn't change. I am grateful that now you are different. But what changed?" she asked, perplexed. Jason shrugged.

After a long silence, Jason spoke. "Mama, why did you marry Papa?" Maria stopped; she was surprised at the question. "Son, why do you ask me such things?" Jason was silent as Maria looked in his eyes and realized that the boy meant no harm. She took her son's arm as they walked. "When I met your father, I thought that there was no man in the entire world like him," she said. "Do you still think that, Mama?" the boy asked. "No, Jason. I no longer think that. I KNOW it. You father has a tender heart that not everyone gets to see. And he would do anything for those he loves. And I do mean anything. Do you see that, son?" Jason thought before responding. "I am beginning to, Mama." The two walked on as Draco enjoyed the slower pace and the calm conversation.

"Would you like an ice cream, son?" Maria asked. "Yes, but what about Draco?" the boy asked as the dog looked up. "We can get something for Draco also," she said. So the three turned and headed towards the park.

Draco, in the meantime, was fascinated with all the new sights and smells. Though he would never venture this far out of his territory alone, he was grateful that Jason and Maria were exploring with him. He often felt his collar tugged since he wanted to stop at every new smell and investigate. When the tugging stopped, he looked up at Jason inquisitively. "Draco, we are going to stop for an ice cream and we will get something for you," Jason said. The dog sat down and waited as Maria ordered two ice creams for them and an empty cone for the dog. When Jason lowered the cone to him, Draco's tail wagged wildly. "Son, give it to him one piece at a time, otherwise he will eat the whole thing in one bite."

"Mama, why do you think Draco is so attached to Papa?" Jason asked, looking at the dog who was crunching on his last piece of ice cream cone. "I don't know, son. It is peculiar, isn't it? Maybe they are a lot alike." Maria reached down and patted Draco's head. This was the first time that Maria had touched Draco and Jason smiled. "This is a beautiful day, son. Let's enjoy it a little more together; later on you and Draco can go check on your father," she said as she rose. They continued their stroll through the neighborhood park as Draco trotted ahead of them.

Akil wondered where Jason and Draco were since it was late afternoon, and there was no word from them. "You worry like an old man!" he reproached himself as he cleaned the counters. A few minutes later he found himself gazing into the distance again, wondering what had become of them. "Ahhhhhh!" he said out loud in frustration with himself. He picked up the phone and called his wife Maria. "They're fine!" he said to himself, after the fourth ring. Though he returned to cleaning his shop, his concern for Jason and Draco grew.

It was sunset when he heard a bark; leaving the shop he saw Draco at a distance, running full speed towards him. Jason was trailing, trying to keep up. "Dracooooooooooooo!" Akil called out, as the dog leapt towards him and, this time, succeeded in licking his nose. When Jason arrived, Akil hugged him as Draco jumped up and down towards the two. "Son, are you alright?" he asked, his hands on his son's shoulders. "Sure Papa. Why?" Akil laughed. "Ahhhhhh, I was worried son. No word from you; then I called your mother and there was no word from her. I started to think….." "No, Papa," Jason answered. "We had an incredible day. Draco, Mama, and me." Akil smiled. "Tell me about it, son," he said as they sat down. Draco, however, was thirsty and nudged Akil's hand. "But first, our friend needs a drink and a snack," he said as Draco wagged his tail.

"Mama talked with me like an adult. She told me about you and her and how she feels about you, Papa." Akil was surprised as he petted Draco's head, whose chin was on his knee. "And what did Mama say?" Jason laughed. "You have to ask Mama!" he said.

The Scent

Daria woke up with a start; the day was still gray but her senses were alerted. She stood and smelled. She sniffed with all her might because she was picking up....something... With her nose held high, she made her way down the empty road as the invisible odor on the gentle breeze beckoned her forward.

Adelino awoke while it was still dark; he had been restless all night, so he decided to start out early again. He crept out of his bed, so as not to awaken his wife, and placed some bread and cheese in a cloth bag. Before leaving he said a prayer in front of the house shrine, glanced in the direction of Diana and then Tiro, and made his way out into the darkness. He would take the same road he always took, in the direction where Daria was last seen. His heart was always the same: a mixture of hope and sadness. When he was in sight of the Acropolis, Adelino turned and asked Athena to watch over his steps this day.

An hour had passed and Adelino was now in the area where Daria was last seen. It had been many weeks now; this morning he carried with him a drawing of the dog that Tiro had made. Adelino was a driven man and he was convinced that he would find Daria sooner or later.

He began to call her name, keeping his voice low since mostly everyone was still asleep. He stopped to think: "If I were Daria, where would I go at this hour?" Was she free to move? Was she in somebody's home? Was she lost in the fields? "She would go somewhere safe, somewhere familiar. She would stay near the roads but hidden by the grass," he concluded. So he began to walk through the neighborhood out onto the road in the direction of the farm where she had been held.

Daria froze in her tracks. There was an unmistakable scent so familiar that it was part of her. She could not yet place it, but it came towards her on the gentle morning breeze and drew her forward. She whimpered from sorrow and hope as she trotted ahead.

"Daria! Daria!" Adelino called as he made his way down the road, which was still covered with the morning fog. He could see little through the mist so he kept calling the dog's name. "Daria! Come home, Daria!"

Adelino heard a whimper in the distance. He called louder, "Daria!" The whimper turned into a whine. Adelino's heart practically jumped into his throat. He called again: "Daria!" Then through the mist he saw a little white face coming towards him. On seeing Adelino, Daria began to whine loudly as if in pain. As she now ran towards him, Adelino could see how thin and emaciated she was. Notwithstanding his pain, he used his walking stick to get down on his hands and knees as she approached. She leapt at his face, whining and crying from excitement and sorrow. Adelino lifted her up as Daria licked the tears from his face. The man began to sob, and turning in the direction of the Acropolis, he gave thanks that Daria had been delivered safely. He got to his feet and found a place to sit as Daria leapt onto his lap.

"I have been so worried about you my little girl. Diana and Tiro too. We all missed our little Daria but I didn't give up hope. Now you're safe, my little Daria. Do you want something to eat?" he asked as he pulled out some cheese from his pocket. Daria was too excited to eat, and she kept whining and jumping up to lick Adelino's face. "You are alright my little girl. You stay here with me and rest; then I will carry you home," he said as he held her close. The little dog, though, could not relax, and was whimpering and whining the whole time. "Come Daria, eat something," he said as he pulled off a tiny piece of cheese. She nibbled it while staring at Adelino with piercing eyes.

"Are you ready to go home, Daria?" Adelino asked her after a few minutes. With that he stood up, Daria in one arm and his walking stick in the other, and started down the road.

Affection

Draco woke up before dawn whimpering. He went directly to Akil's shop to wait for him.

A few hours later when Akil turned the corner, he found Draco sitting at the door outside of his shop, looking towards him. "Draco! Why so early today again?" he asked, as he put down his things on an outside table. The dog came up to him and leaned against his leg. "Draco, I will sit a little bit with you," Akil said as he took a chair. Before he could stop him, Draco, a large dog, had jumped up into his lap. Akil laughed. "You are too big, my friend!" he said, puffing for air. Since Draco didn't budge, Akil spoke to him. "You are safe here, Draco. You don't have to be afraid. You are family; even Maria admits that now! So why are you scared? You won't lose me, Draco. You can stay here all day if you want, and tonight you can come stay with us and remain as long as you like..." As he said these words he was petting Draco's head and the dog seemed to calm down. Akil gently lifted him to the ground and went to the shop to find something to give him to eat, while the dog followed at his heels.

After awhile Akil was tripping over Draco, since the dog wanted to stay so close. He called his wife. "Maria, good morning! Can you send Jason down to the shop this morning to help me? Thank you, wife. Oh, and Draco is coming home with me tonight. Bye!" and he quickly hung up before Maria could say anything. He looked down into Draco's longing eyes. "Don't you worry, my friend. Jason will be here soon and tonight you can spend time with us," he said as Draco cocked his head to one side.

When Jason showed up he asked, "Papa, are you O.K.?" since it was rare that he would call home and ask Maria to send him. "It's our little friend again; I can't get my work done, son. Can you stay with me this morning?" he asked. The boy nodded. "Should I take Draco for a walk?" he asked. Akil nodded. But when the boy put the leash on Draco and tried to pull him away, the dog refused and insisted on remaining next to Akil. Perplexed, Jason called Draco, coaxed him, even offered him half of a roll, but to no avail. "Why don't I finish opening the shop, Papa, and you can spend some time with Draco to see what is the matter with him." Akil agreed and the two switched places.

"Come on, Draco. Let's go see your other friends," Akil said as he led the dog in the direction of Cynarra's flower shop.

"Good morning, flower lady!" Akil called. Cynarra was inside setting up for the day but immediately came out, a frightened look on her face. "Akil, are you alright? Is everything alright?" Akil laughed. "Yes, my friend. Do not be shocked at my visit. Jason is setting up the shop and Draco wanted to come see you." With that she looked down at Draco, who stayed by Akil's side, but wagged his tail at the sight of Cynarra. "You are both acting strangely today. Usually Draco is jumping up and down on me by now. What is going on today with you two?" she asked, hands on her hips. "O.K., I will tell you the truth. Our little friend has a world of his own. Some days he is happy, some days quiet, other days he seems upset and needy. Today he is clinging to me as if he is going to be abandoned. I thought it would do him good to see his other friends. I do not know what upset him but sometimes he comes down the Acropolis like that. We will take him home to sleep at the house tonight, but this morning we are on a little walk in the Plaka." At this, Cynarra smiled.

"I know what will help him snap out of it," she said to Akil.

When she walked over to the water spout and turned on the water, Draco began to run to dodge her. "He always wants to be chased before he gets his bath," she said as she walked towards Draco, who then ran in the other direction. "Akil, you go that way," and they had the dog surrounded. But he dodged Cynarra's grasp and even brushed Akil's leg as he ran by them. "Draco! Bath time!" Cynarra called out. At this Draco was even more determined to not get caught, but he tried to dare them both to catch him. He leaned down the front part of his body and barked as if to say: "Come and try to get me!" Akil laughed as he stepped towards Draco and the dog began to run in wide circles around the both of them. "It worked! But how do you capture him when you really want to give him a bath?" Akil asked. "Just watch," Cynarra said. At this she crouched down to Draco's level and the dog, ever so slowly, made his way to her, crawling the last few feet. Then Cynarra petted his head and whispered in his ear, "Bath time, Draco." At this point the dog didn't resist and walked to the water spout with her. Akil shook his head; he had never seen anything like it. "Can I help?" he called out. Cynarra nodded and they both proceeded to suds the dog up as Draco's tail wagged wildly.

 "Should we see if Draco wants to stay with you today?" Akil asked as they were rinsing the dog. "Certainly. Now when we release him he is going to run all around the Plaka. Where he ends up, only Draco knows. Often he returns here to spend time with me outside the shop. If he comes back he can stay with me." It played out just as Cynarra predicted except for where Draco ended up. Back at his shop about half an hour later, Akil heard a bark. He leaned over to find Draco outside, who continued to bark. "O.K. Draco, you can spend the day with me," Akil said, as he exited the shop. Draco ran to his side while Jason took his father's place in finishing the food preparation. "What am I going to do with you, Draco?" Akil asked, looking into Draco's eager brown eyes.

Draco seemed happy that evening to come home with Akil and Jason; even Maria didn't complain. She was laughing when the three came up to the house. "Two men and a dog! As content as could be!" she said as she kissed her husband. Draco barked. "Are you jealous now, too?" she asked the dog. Draco followed her into the house as she got a scrap of meat for a treat.

When Draco laid down that night, at the foot of the bed next to Akil, he felt like the luckiest dog in the world.

Fear

Diana was washing vegetables in preparation for dinner but her mind was on her husband. She worried about his physical and emotional strength as he searched for Daria every day. Diana loved the dog also, but had concluded long ago that they would never see Daria again. But she felt she could not discourage Adelino from his search.

The gods ruled their daily lives and Diana also prayed that little Daria would be found. She could not imagine how Adelino would feel when he realized that the dog would not return. Her eyes welled up with tears as she turned her sorrow into a prayer to the goddess Athena who ruled their city.

Wiping her hands, Diana went outside to sweep in front of the house. She looked up at the Acropolis where Tiro was working. "I will bring him lunch today," she resolved, missing her son. She was sad for her husband, who was distraught, and sad for her son, who had to take on a man's work while still a child. Her task, she thought, was to make their lives easier and to bring some joy into the house. She didn't know how to do this, however, other than preparing their favorite meals.

At midday Diana set off for the Acropolis with cheese and olives, vegetables and wine. She would surprise her son with a good meal and brighten his day. "Diana!" someone called out down the road as she turned a corner. "Diana! Come!" It was her neighbor who was calling out. "Come, Diana! It's your husband!"

Fear gripped Diana's heart as she began to return to her home; she began to run at full speed, olives spilling on the street. "Look,

Diana!" the woman called out, pointing down the opposite street. Diana turned to see Adelino, hobbling down the street with his walking stick, Daria in one arm, tears running down his face. Diana dropped everything she had been carrying and ran towards her husband as Daria squiggled to get free to greet her. Man and wife embraced one another; they began to sob while Daria made a gallant effort to lick up all of their tears.

As neighbors gathered around, one of the boys asked Diana, "Do you want me to go get Tiro?" As soon as Diana nodded, the boy took off towards the Acropolis.

By this time Tiro was doing a man's work: chipping away at the stone, hauling heavy loads, and even transferring measurements from the drawings to the rising temple. He felt like a man but sometimes longed to be a carefree boy again. But his duty lay here, and there was no one else to take care of the family. His father was broken in body and spirit and his mother worked hard to make their wages last. He worked with determination, though sometimes he felt an ache in his heart.

This was a day when Tiro was working on the base of a column with another stone worker as his guide. "You're a good worker, son, but I miss your father," his companion said. "How is the old man?" he asked. "He is better but he still needs a stick to walk. He wants to come back to work but Mama won't let him," Tiro said. "Watch for the stone chips now," the man said as they both began to use chisels on the column. There was so much noise, and so many stone flecks flying, that Tiro didn't hear his name being called. "Tiro!!!!!" the small boy called, tapping on his back. "Your mother says to come home at once. It is your father." Fear ran down Tiro' spine as he dropped his tools and began running down the Acropolis.

Serenity

Notwithstanding Akil's effort to bring him home, Draco had made it clear that he wanted to sleep at the Parthenon, so Akil relented and the dog ran up the hill.

His tail was wagging wildly when he woke up the next morning. He stood on the steps of the Acropolis and stretched his long legs. He couldn't wait to see his friends in the Plaka and he barked with joy as he jumped off the steps and plunged down the side of the hill.

Akil was setting up his shop when he heard the jingle of Draco's collar; he had barely turned around when the dog leapt at him. Draco was so excited that he ran circles around Akil, barking and brushing his leg as he ran by. Akil laughed. "So you had a good night my friend!" he said. Since Draco wanted to play, Akil chased him around the shop twice before he stopped, panting. Draco took advantage of the pause and leapt up once more to try to lick Akil's face. "You are too much for me, Draco! Come, let's get a treat," he said as he headed into the shop to look for some sliced meat.

"Draco is so funny this morning," Jason remarked as he arrived at the shop at about 9 o'clock. The dog was running circles around the area. When Draco heard Jason's voice, he ran full speed towards him and jumped up to greet him. "Someone wants to play today!" The two ran off into the Plaka towards Cynarra's flower shop.

"I will be home at three o'clock," Cynarra told her father as she left the house. "Good luck on your exam," he said as she closed the door. Since Cynarra's parents were retired, if she had to be absent from the shop it either had to be closed or one of her parents had to fill in. This time it was her mother: a woman in her mid-sixties with gray hair and a stern face.

When they arrived at the flower shop, Draco began to whine. "Kalimera! Good morning! Is Cynarra here?" Jason asked. The old woman shook her head. "She has it in her mind to go to the university and leave us all alone. But she will be back this afternoon," she said. As the dog continued to whine, Jason turned to him and said: "Draco, Cynarra will be here later so we will come back," and the dog looked up at him inquisitively. "Good day," Jason said and the two continued their walk towards Alexander's restaurant.

Alexander knew who was outside his door as soon as he heard the barking. "Have you come to see me or do you want the food in my hand?" he asked Draco as he stepped outside. "How are both of you?" he asked. "Draco is in a very good mood and he wanted to see all his friends in the Plaka today," the boy said. "Well, I am glad to see both of you too!" When Draco finished eating he sat down and stared at Alexander. "Has Draco not been in a good mood lately?" Alexander asked the boy. "It depends on the day. Papa has been trying to figure out why. We were afraid someone was being mean to Draco on the Acropolis so we put this collar and tag on him to let everyone know he has a home. But Draco prefers to sleep on the hill and he comes to see us during the day," Jason said. "Yes, I thought of bringing Draco home as my pet but ..." Draco knew they were talking about him and started to whine. Alexander bent down to pet his head. "Don't worry, Draco. You are the most beloved dog in the Plaka!" he said.

"How is your father?" Alexander asked Jason as they sat down outside. "He is good. He is better. He seems to be in a good mood all the time now," Jason said. Alexander smiled. "How is the restaurant going?" Jason asked. "Could be better, could be worse. I am surviving. Life could always be better, Jason, but it could also be worse. I have my health, my family, my business. What more could I want?" he said. Jason could see a sadness in Alexander's eyes but dared not ask, out of respect. "Why don't you come by the shop after lunch? Papa would love to see you!" Jason offered. Alexander smiled. "I will come." Looking down, Draco was on his back next to Alexander, begging for his chest to be scratched. Alexander laughed and obliged him.

Draco grew restless and Jason understood that he wanted to run up Acropolis. "We hope to see you later, Mr. Alexander," Jason said as he got up. "Draco has to begin his day on the Acropolis and I have to see if Papa needs help." Alexander smiled. "Thank you son, and thank you Draco! Tell your father I will stop by later to say hello," and they parted ways.

Draco dashed across the Plaka, leaving Jason behind. As soon as the dog arrived at the base of the Acropolis he realized that his help was needed. There were a few Spaniards looking around as if they didn't know where to go. He ran up to them, barked, and led them towards the steps up the hill.

It was late afternoon by the time Draco returned to Akil's shop. It seemed like the whole Plaka was there, sitting in a circle, enjoying coffee and Baklava. When he turned the corner, at the site of his friends, Draco ran towards the group barking. Cynarra had returned from the university and called out, "Look out! Draco is here!" as the dog leapt in the middle, turning this way and that, looking at Cynarra, Alexander, Akil, Jason and Maria, and two other shopkeepers. Draco was so excited that all he could do was bark. "Draco!" Maria scolded, and the dog, wagging his tail, went over to her and sat leaning against her leg. "Draco, you stay by Mama," Akil said. "If you do, I will give you a treat." At these words Draco began to bark again and ran to Akil. "Draco knows that word!" Jason pointed out. Maria turned to him: "Son, can you get Draco a t-r-e-a-t please?" Jason got up and went to the shop as Draco followed him. "Does he know how to spell now too?" Alexander asked, laughing.

Hours passed without anyone realizing it until Alexander leapt up. "I have to go help at the restaurant! I've had such a nice time with you all that I forgot!" With a wave, he ran off towards his business. At this Cynarra groaned. "My mother is going to kill me! She has been stuck at the flower shop all day! I have to go too," and she fled. Maria kissed her son's forehead. "Dinner will be late tonight. I forgot too!" she said as she left. Draco sat there, gazing at Akil and Jason. "It's just the three of us now," Akil said as he got up. "I should clean up the shop area. Son, why don't you stay with Draco?" he said. Jason smiled and sat with the dog, as Draco stared in the direction of Akil.

Even Draco stayed later than usual, and when Akil was closing up the shop at the end of the day, the dog was still there, following him around. Akil turned to him and asked: "Draco, do you want to come home and stay with us tonight?" As if he understood, Draco barked, walked over to Akil, licked his hand, turned, then trotted towards the Acropolis.

It was a star-filled night as Draco arrived on the steps of the Parthenon. He sat down on the stairs and looked over the city. Then he sniffed around the building before he found the perfect place to lie down and rest.

Rescued

Tiro burst through the front door of their house, breathless and afraid. "Mama!" he cried out. "Son! Daria is back!" When the boy turned and saw Daria, exhausted and asleep on Adelino's lap, he broke down crying. All the fear of this day and the pain of these months bubbled to the surface at once. He began sobbing as Adelino motioned him over and brought the boy's head to his shoulder. "Thank the gods for listening to our prayers. I love you so much son," he whispered in the boy's ear. At this Daria woke up and, recognizing Tiro, whimpered.

Adelino handed Daria to Tiro and got a piece of meat for her. She ate it but immediately threw it up. When Diana heard Daria coughing she came into the room to find out what happened. "What did you give her?" she asked Adelino. "Just a piece of meat, wife," he said. "You gave her meat when she probably hasn't eaten in days?" she asked, incredulously. She turned to Tiro: "Son, can you take Daria into the other room?" The boy obliged. With the door shut, Tiro could hear his mother raise her voice; his parents never argued in front of him. After a few minutes of raised voices and emotional outbursts, the two emerged. "Son, neither you nor Papa will give anything to Daria to eat until she is well. I will take care of feeding her. Alright, son?" The boy shrank under his mother's piercing gaze. "Yes, Mama," he said.

Diana went to make some broth. "Daria is to have only broth and bread for three days!" she said. The woman looked determined as Adelino and Tiro looked at one another, neither daring to object.

Though she was wobbly, Daria was able to come to Diana when she called. She had prepared a small cup of warm broth in which she had soaked some small pieces of bread. The dog showed no interest in the food, however, and went to the corner to lie down. Diana shook her head. "You have to eat, Daria. You are too weak!" Something in her tone frightened the dog, who began to shiver. "Now it is my turn, my wife. She is just afraid. Son, can you help me please?" Diana looked shocked when her husband began to lower himself to the floor. "What are you doing? You will hurt yourself! Please!" Adelino responded, "I know what she needs, my wife. Can you bring me a cup of broth also? And, son, hand me Daria's bowl." At this, the man scooted himself besides Daria and stroked her head to calm her. He then put Daria's food in front of her and took his own cup of broth. He let Daria smell his. He then began to sip on his bowl. "Son, can you hand me some bread?" and Tiro did so. "I think this is the best broth I have ever had!" he said to Diana. As he continued to sip his broth and eat his bread, Daria slowly got up to sniff her bowl. Looking first at Adelino, then back at her bowl, she took a lick. Looking up at Adelino again, who continued to sip his broth as loudly as he could, she took another lick. "It is very, very good!" he said to Tiro and Diana. Daria, then, began to lap up the liquid and chew on the bread. In the end, she even licked the bowl. "You look better already, Daria!" Adelino said as he patted her head. The warm broth did do her good and she was ready for another nap next to Adelino. "Son, can you help me get up?" When he was on his feet, Adelino kissed his wife and son.

Before he could sit down, Daria was waiting for him next to his chair. As soon as he picked her up, she was asleep in his lap.

"We should make an offering to the goddess," Diana whispered as Daria slept. "It should be something special. What do you think, husband?" she asked Adelino. "I think you are right. We should make an offering at her greatest temple on the Acropolis, but it is not yet complete. Son, how long until the temple will be finished?" Tiro scratched his head. "Mama, I think it will take years. But I heard that the head of the statue of Athena is completed. Perhaps...." As he trailed off, Diana had an idea. "Son, when can Papa go with you to work? Can you get him into the workshop of Pheidias?" Both father and son looked at Diana as if she was crazy. "Oh! Leave it to me!" she said. Both men decided to stay out of the way of her plan.

It was a few days later when Diana announced: "We will go to the workshop of Pheidias at night and honor the goddess in thanksgiving for the return of Daria. I have arranged it." Father and son were stunned. "Wife! You do not know how Pheidias is. He will not accept this!" Adelino objected. "Pheidias will never know. My friend, the wife of one of his workers, has arranged that her husband will bring us into the workshop. Pheidias will never know we were there. We will honor the goddess with prayers and flowers, which we will take with us. Can we not make this sacrifice since the goddess has listened to our prayers?" she asked. Put in this way, neither Tiro nor Adelino could object.

It was only a few days later that Diana put her plan into action. "In two days time," she told Adelino and Tiro, "we shall go to the workshop; there we shall behold the face of the goddess, well, at least a carving of her face. I shall bring flowers to offer her, but we shall not leave them. We will offer up prayers in thanksgiving," she announced. "Can we take Daria with us?" Tiro asked. Diana shook her head. "Daria is still too weak, son. Plus it will be at night. No, she should stay safely at home. We won't be gone long." The plan was set, though the two men felt uneasy. Pheidias could be a volatile man and they feared his reaction should he discover them in his workshop.

Tiro felt like a thief as they made their way to Pheidias' workshop a few nights later. "We will act as if we are going out for a stroll. My friend and her husband will wait inside the workshop for us. They will let us in for a few minutes to say our prayers. We will honor the goddess and then return home," she said. Then she looked at Adelino and Tiro. "You both look so guilty! Everyone will wonder what we are up to! Come now, smile. We are out for the evening," she said. The two men feigned a smile and followed the determined woman. Daria, in the meantime, was curled up on Tiro's bed.

The workshop was dark; Diana knocked lightly on the door. When it opened, a smiling woman about Diana's age stood there. "Welcome to the temporary home of Athena," she said, beckoning them inside. When the door was closed her husband Herodotos appeared, holding an oil lamp. "Adelino! I didn't know this was your family!" and the two men warmly greeted each other. Diana, however, was focused on her task. "We will not take much of your time nor will we put you at risk. We will offer prayers and offerings to the goddess, then we will leave you to lock up the workshop. We are so grateful for your goodness to us, enabling us to thank the goddess in a special way. Now if you would show us to the head of the goddess..." The lamp led the way.

As the group approached the sculpture and the light fell on the head of Athena, Adelino gasped. "She seems alive!" he said in wonder. As the face of the goddess peered through the shadows, her translucent flesh reflected the candlelight. "What is she made of?" Diana asked. "It is ivory from the tusks of elephants," Herodotos replied. Noting their perplexed expressions, he continued: "They are animals that live in far-away lands that grow larger than any animals you have ever seen. Out of their faces grow ivory, which was removed and formed into the statue of Athena." Adelino shook his head. "It seems like a fantasy. Such things cannot be true!" He then turned towards the statue. "But her face glows! Her head is larger than all of us! She looks as if she is about to speak!" The worker intervened: "Now you see why Pheidias wants to keep the statue a secret until her unveiling. Now we should say our prayers and creep away so we will not be discovered." The others agreed.

As the group turned to go, Diana didn't notice that one of the flowers she had brought as an offering had detached itself and fluttered to the ground. When they closed the door and secured it, there the petals sat in the middle of the floor.

Healing

It was mid-morning when Akil called Jason. "Can you come to the shop now, son?" "What's wrong, Papa?" Jason asked. "I will tell you when you get here," Akil replied.

When Jason arrived an hour later he saw that his father was upset. "Papa, what is wrong?" Akil replied, "Probably nothing, son. Draco is always here when I am setting up the shop. But he didn't come down the Acropolis this morning and nobody has seen him. Can you climb the stairs, son, to see if he is alright? And lead him down, please. Oh, and don't say anything to Mama!" The boy agreed and headed up the hill, also worried that something had happened.

"Draco! Draco!" Jason called out. The boy reached all the way to the top and approached the area where Draco slept. He heard a bark and spotted Draco, who was limping towards him, favoring his back foot. "What happened, Draco?" The dog wagged his tail and leaned against Jason's leg. "Can I look at your foot?" he asked. Draco snatched it back as soon as Jason touched it. "O.K., Draco. We are going down the hill to see Papa. He will know what to do. We will go slowly." At that the boy hugged the dog and led him down, step by step, towards the Plaka.

It took a long time for Jason and Draco to descend, and by the time he reached the Plaka he spotted his father coming towards him. Draco limped towards Akil with his tail wagging. "What happened, son?" the man asked, reaching down to pat Draco's head. "I don't know, Papa. Draco was near his usual place and I found him like this. What should we do?" the boy asked. Akil looked at his son, whose eyes had filled with tears. He pulled Jason towards him and kissed his head. "Draco will be alright, son. Let's call Mama; she will know what to do." With that, Akil picked up Draco and the three returned to the shop.

"Maria, Draco is hurt. I think we need a doctor here. It's his foot; he cannot walk on it..." Before he finished his sentence, Maria interrupted. "Do not call any doctor. Wait until I get there. I know about these things. I kept you all in good health, haven't I?" With that, Akil turned to Jason, who was sitting next to Draco petting his head. "Mama says she will cure Draco. You stay here with him, son. Don't let him walk. I have to finish making the sandwiches." When Draco tried to get up as Akil walked away, Jason stopped him. "Draco, you have to stay with me now. Mama will be here soon and you will be better, you will see." With these words Draco lay back down next to Jason's chair.

It was about half an hour later that Maria arrived with a bucket full of supplies. Draco tried to get up to greet her but Jason held him in his place. She put the bucket down, put her hands on her hips, and said, "Draco, what have you done?" The dog looked up at her, his chin on his front paws. "Son, hold him there while I get some warm water. Where is your father?" she asked, as Jason nodded towards the shop.

It was a few minutes later when Maria and Akil came out of the shop. Jason could tell that his mother had a plan. "Son, can you take over the shop while we take care of Draco?" The boy willingly obliged while Draco watched all of them. Akil placed the bucket of warm, soapy water down next to the dog and comforted him while Maria stirred in a mixture of baking soda and mild disinfectant. Draco smelled it and turned away. To calm him, Akil explained to the dog that they needed to soak his foot before inspecting it and if he could let Maria have his leg to put it in the water, it would be so much easier. At this, Maria lifted his leg and put it in the bucket. "He must soak it for at least half an hour. The trick will be to keep him standing all that time." Akil said to Maria, "If you sit over here next to me, behind Draco, we can keep his foot in the water." So the two sat there with the dog, chatting about the morning, while keeping one eye on Draco.

Maria had a way with those who were ill or hurting and this was not lost on Draco. He actually let her lift his leg so she could examine his paw. She found a thorn lodged and realized immediately what to do. "We need to soak his paw in warm water one more time. Then I will need your help," she said to both Akil and Jason. When Alexander stopped by a little later to say hello, she enlisted his assistance also. "I can pull it out with my fingers but Draco is going to struggle. Jason, you need to distract him. Akil, you need to comfort him. And Alexander, if you please, can you hold him tight? But we must have fresh warm water with disinfectant ready to immediately soak the foot." She sighed. "Are you all ready?"

Draco struggled, Akil spoke to him, and Jason held his leg while Alexander held his body. Maria reached in and pulled out the thorn while the dog yelped. Jason immediately put the foot in the warm disinfectant water while the group relaxed. Akil smiled at Maria, who held up the long thorn for all to see. "Husband, that dog must not go up the Acropolis until his foot is healed. I don't care if he doesn't want to; he is going to sleep at the house! Jason, you are in charge of making sure he doesn't walk on that foot. It must be soaked every day. Can you do that, son?" Jason nodded. "Remember, no walking!" she said, looking each one in the eyes. Then glancing down on Draco, she added "Now you do what Papa and son say, O.K., Draco?" The dog wagged his tail.

Over the next week, while Draco stayed at their house, Jason noticed that Maria and the dog grew closer. Akil and Jason spoke to Draco as if he was human and soon Maria began to do the same. "I know you want to go up to your hill and run around outside and be free, but if I let you do that, your foot will not heal. So, like it or not, you have to stay home with me. Now you can see what it is like to be with Maria!" she said and laughed. At times Draco sat by the front door, longing to be outside. Then

Maria would approach him. "Draco," she said as his ears perked up. "It's no use standing by the door. Come with me and I will give you a treat." Understanding the word, he willingly followed Maria into the kitchen. Though he limped, it was less severe and he no longer struggled when Maria soaked his paw.

Draco dreamt little in those days and he longed to be back on the Acropolis. Though he enjoyed the growing bond with Maria, his little dog heart yearned for freedom. Maria kept finding him waiting at the front door.

When Jason got home one evening, she explained the problem. "He wants to go out and run and be free, but his foot is not healed. Just like you when you were little, I had to do what was best for you, even if it made you angry..." Jason perked up. "Mama, do you still have the wagon I used to have?" Maria paused to think. "I believe so, son. Why?" Jason got up. "I have an idea. Will you help me find it?"

The next day, as he left the house, Akil and Maria were laughing so hard that Maria was bent over. Jason had coaxed Draco into the wagon, who was enjoying the experience immensely, as Jason pulled him down the sidewalk. "Don't let him get out and run on that foot!" Maria called out between chuckles. "See you at the shop, Papa!" Jason said, as he headed towards the Plaka, Draco in tow.

Over the next week Draco seemed to enjoy the pampering, but he was also growing restless. Akil started bringing the dog every day to the shop to give Maria a break. "I know how you think, my friend," he said to Draco one afternoon. "I wish we could change places and I could be free and you stay here at the shop." The two seemed to understand each other. "Perhaps in a few days, if Mama sees that you are healed, you can return to your mountain. But for now you have to stay with us. I'm sorry, Draco," he said as he patted the dog's head. "Jason, can you distract Draco for me? He wants to scamper away; maybe you can help him be more content here while I make some dough." The boy agreed, loaded the dog in the wagon, and pulled him through the Plaka.

After ten days living with the family, it was clear that Draco was getting more restless than ever. Maria was the first to say it. "I think Draco is ready to be let free, but I will come check his foot at the shop this afternoon." Akil looked at Draco and was sad. But he knew that the dog would be unhappy if he prevented him from going to his beloved hill. Jason was more emotional. "Mama! What if he gets hurt again? What if we don't know about it?" The boy had tears in his eyes. "I know, son. But if we take his freedom away, will Draco be happy?"

It was a few days later when Draco was back on the Acropolis after the sun had set. As he lay down in his usual spot on the steps of the Parthenon, his tail wagged gently in contentment.

Children's Adventures

"What is this?!" Pheidias bellowed, as he held up a wilted flower he had picked up from the workshop floor. The workers grew silent and looked towards him, confused. "Who has been in my workshop last night?" he asked, turning in a full circle, holding the flower even higher. No one dared speak.

Herodotos, the worker who had allowed the family of Adelino in the workshop, stood frozen. A flower could have ended up on the floor any number of ways, he thought; if he said nothing, this would pass. "See if anything has been taken; if we have thieves on the loose, we will deal with them!" Pheidias continued. Several men began to take an inventory of supplies while the rest returned to their work.

"Pheidias is angry; he found out that someone was in the workshop last night. Have you told anyone of our visit?" Herodotos asked his wife that evening. "No one, husband," she responded. "After dark let us go together to visit Adelino and Diana, to make sure they too have spoken to no one." There was fear in his voice because losing his position would be disastrous for his family.

"Last night we offered prayers to Athena for returning Daria!" Tiro confided to his friend Kallias. "We went to the workshop of Pheidias after dark, with just a lamp! But you must keep it a secret; nobody is supposed to see the statue before it is completed!" Kallias shook his head. "I don't believe you! Only the workers get to see the statue!" Tiro replied, "I can prove it. Meet me tonight after sundown here."

After dinner Tiro slipped out of his house and found Kallias already waiting for him. "Do your parents know where you are?" Tiro asked. Kallias shook his head. "This has to be our secret. Do you promise to die a thousand deaths before you tell anyone what you are about to see?" Tiro asked. "I promise," Kallias replied.

It was dark when the boys arrived at the workshop. "We went in through this door and saw the head of the goddess inside," Tiro said. "Now do you believe me?" he asked. Kallias shook his head. "I will only believe you if I see the goddess too. Let's go inside!" Tiro shook his head. "It's dangerous. If we get caught…" Kallias shook his head. "We won't get caught. Come on!" he said, and the boys circled around the workshop as Kallias looked for another entrance.

Spying an opening in an upper window, Kallias called to Tiro. "If you lift me up, I can get in. Then I will pull you up. Come on, Tiro!" The boy was reluctant; this was going way beyond what he intended. "This is an adventure that we won't ever forget!" Kallias said. "O.K.. But we can only go in, take a look, and leave. No snooping around! Agreed?" Kallias eagerly nodded his head.

Shortly thereafter both of the boys were inside. It was pitch dark as they stood in the middle of the huge workshop, unable to tell where the statue might lie. Tiro took Kallias' arm and pointed him in the direction of the head of the statue. As their eyes grew accustomed, the face of Athena began to appear out of the darkness. Kallias held his breath, as if the goddess herself were appearing to him. "What is it made of?" he whispered.

First the ivory face appeared, followed by the golden crown. "Papa says she is made of the tusks of a thousand elephants," Tiro said. "I want to touch it!" Kallias exclaimed as he moved forward. "Noooooo!" Tiro said. "It is the goddess. It is bad luck to touch her!" but these words rung hollow on Kallias. "Her skin is so cold and smooth," he said, stroking the jaw of the statue. "Tiro, I want to climb up here," he said, pointing to the scaffolding surrounding the head of the statue. "Give me a boost!"

"Are you crazy?!" Tiro replied in a loud whisper. Just as

Kallias took the first step up the scaffolding, the two boys heard a door opening in the shop. The two froze. As the door closed, they heard footsteps. The two boys tiptoed behind the head of Athena. Peering out, they glimpsed a tall man with a lamp, followed by a shorter man, entering into the central work area. "Let's make sure that nothing has been moved since the workers left. There are so many valuable materials in here that it's a wonder that nothing was robbed last night. Let's check the storage where the gold and ivory are kept. I have a list of what should be there; it is our job to check it when we arrive, watch over it all night, then check it again in the morning. Come!" and the two went into a side room.

"What should we do?" Tiro whispered to Kallias. Kallias pointed to the door; Tiro nodded. Just as the two boys were about to make a run for it, the two men entered the sculpture room again. "Why don't you stay here awhile while I make the rounds outside," the tall man said to the shorter one. Fear crept up the spine of Tiro as the shorter man sat down, across the room, facing the head of Athena. They were directly in front of him. In fact, if he bent down, he would see the boys' legs. They hardly dared breathe as the shorter man leaned back in his chair. In a few minutes he closed his eyes and put his head back. When they heard a quiet snore, the two boys knew this was their chance.

Bonding

Akil arrived at the shop early that morning, having brought supplies to make the morning rolls. The man had both hands full when, suddenly out of nowhere, Draco jumped and licked his cheek. "Draaacccccooooooooo!" Akil called, as the dog continued to dance around him in circles. "What's up, Draco?" he asked, stopping to look at the dog. Draco barked, then followed Akil to the door of the shop.

When Jason arrived a few hours later, he laughed as he saw the dog clinging to his father. "I will take Draco off your hands, Papa." The boy attached the leash but had to drag the dog away from Akil; but once out of sight, the dog and boy began to run across the Plaka. "Draaacccooooo!" they heard as they passed in front of Cynarra's shop. "And good morning to you also Jason!" she called. "Draaaaaacooooooo!" they heard as they came within sight of Alexander's restaurant. But the two kept running out of the Plaka, down the street and towards the park.

After nearly an hour of running Jason was panting but Draco was ready to keep going. "Draco, let's rest here," Jason said as he sat down on a bench. The dog hopped up and sat next to him. "We will catch our breath here, Draco, then go to the house and see Mama. Would you like that?" he asked the dog. Draco looked at the boy.

"Why aren't you helping your father?" Maria asked as Jason entered their yard. "I am! I took Draco because he won't let Papa get his work done!" Maria put her hands on her hips and looked down at the dog. "We had one of those nights again, did we?" she asked Draco. The dog put his head down, thinking he was being scolded. Maria smiled. "Draco, do you want to spend some time here with me?" she asked. His tail began to wag. "Let's start out our morning with a treat," she said as she went to the kitchen to get a dog biscuit. Draco followed behind her, took his biscuit, and munched on it in his corner in Jason's bedroom.

"Mama, can I leave Draco with you? I need to go to the store for Papa," Jason asked. "Yes, but only until lunch time. You can come back home to pick up some food for you and your father and then bring Draco with you." The boy set out as Maria returned to her chores.

It was about half an hour after Jason left that Maria noticed that she had not seen Draco. She found him in the bedroom, curled up in the corner with his chin on the ground, looking up at her. It seemed as if the dog thought he had done something wrong. Maria sat on the bed looking at him. "Now Draco, you haven't done anything wrong. I am glad you are here with me; you don't have to stay in the room alone. We can have a nice morning together. Why don't you come into the kitchen with me while I prepare Papa's lunch?" When she stood Draco also stood and followed her, wagging his tail.

A few hours later Jason returned home and kissed his mother. "How was Draco?" he asked, as the dog looked up at him, expectantly. Maria laughed. "He follows me wherever I am going. I don't know if it is because he likes being next to me or if he just wants a treat!" Jason smiled. "He likes you, Mama," the boy said. "Son, I made lunch for you and your father. There is something for Draco inside also, but don't give it to him until after you have eaten, O.K.?" The boy nodded. "Now use the leash for Draco. There are too many cars out at this hour, and I don't want him running into the street," she said. Then the boy and dog set out.

After a few steps Draco knew where they were headed and began to bark in excitement as he pulled Jason behind him.

As they entered the Plaka, Jason released Draco who ran at

full speed around the shops, through the tourists, across the roads, leaving Jason far behind. Akil was outside his shop; seeing the dog from afar, he called out, "Draaaaaccccccooooooooooo!" The dog bolted, jumping up and down as if he hadn't seen the man in years. Akil laughed. "I missed you too, Draco," he said. "Where did you leave Jason?" he asked the dog. It was a few minutes later that Jason, leash in hand, rounded the corner. Akil greeted his son with a kiss on the forehead as Draco circled around them. "I have lunch, Papa. And Mama included something for Draco, but she said to give it to him after we eat." Akil put his hand behind his son's neck, and father and son returned under the tree in front of the shop with Draco leading the way.

As they sat down to eat, Jason turned and called out, "Mama!" Sure enough, Maria turned the corner. "I forgot the dessert!" she said. "And, I decided to eat lunch with my favorite men," she said, laughing. "You too, Draco," she said as the dog stood up to greet her.

The afternoon turned out to be one of those golden moments, unexpected and unplanned, which Jason would reflect back on into his adult life. During that afternoon together the whole world seemed to be right: Akil and Maria talked and laughed; Jason shared stories from school that made them cringe; and Draco, all the while, leaned up against Akil's leg, feeling safe in the world.

The lunch break had lasted hours; Maria looked at her watch and gasped. "We have spent the whole day here! I think we will have a cold dinner tonight!" Draco stood up and yawned. "I have to sell some more food! Jason, do you want to help me?" Akil asked. The boy nodded. Maria set out towards home, Akil and Jason towards the shop with Draco following behind, curling up outside besides the steps. The dog gave a deep sigh of contentment.

Business was slow and a few hours later the two decided to begin cleaning up. Draco usually ran up the Acropolis around this time, but he lingered. "Papa, do you think Draco wants to come home with us?" Jason asked. Akil shook his head. "You never know with these free spirits, son. He can come if he wants," he said. But soon the dog set off. This time, however, Draco kept stopping and looking back as father and son washed tables and counters. He then scampered up the hill.

The stars were out and the moon was full when Draco laid down on the steps of the Acropolis. The city was glimmering below as he drifted off into sleep.

Troubles

Daria woke up with a start. It was night, but she sensed something was wrong. She was sleeping in the corner of the bedroom of Adelino and Diana; the dog stood up and looked to make sure they were both there. After stretching, she trotted out into the main room and looked around; it was completely silent and dark. She then made her way to Tiro's room; standing at the door, she sniffed for his scent. After listening for the boy, she pushed her way in and hopped up to look into his bed, which was empty. Daria let out a little whine, then returned to Adelino. She began to lick his hand, which was hanging over the bed. The man stirred as Daria grew more persistent. Using her nose, she began to lift his hand. At this Adelino woke up. "You need to go to the bathroom, little girl?" he asked her as he got out of bed. Grabbing his walking stick, the man pulled himself up and followed Daria out. But rather than going to the front door, the dog led him to Tiro's room. "What do you want, Daria?" Adelino asked. The dog went over to the bed, showing Adelino that it was empty.

Diana was deep within a dream when she heard Adelino's voice. "Diana! Wife! Wake up!" he said, holding her hand. Opening her eyes, she sat straight up. "What's wrong?" She looked at her husband and saw the alarm in his eyes. "Tiro is not in his bed. Where could he be?" Before he finished the phrase, Diana was up, heading to Tiro's room, followed by Daria. "He said he was going out with his friends," Diana said, turning to Adelino. "He came back and went to bed; you saw him yourself. Did he leave again without us knowing? Why would he do such a thing? Where could our son be?" she asked.

Tiro and Kallias were half way across the workshop floor when the man stopped snoring; they froze in their steps and waited. Tiro felt his legs shaking and held his breath. Minutes seemed to pass and still no snoring, but it was too dark to see the man on the other side of the room.

Suddenly, without warning, Kallias took off running, making enough noise to fully rouse the guard, who shouted, "Who is there?!!!" Kallias was out the door in a second; Tiro ran after him, tripped over a stone, and slid onto the ground. Before he could get to his feet, the guard grabbed him by the neck and held tight as the boy struggled to escape.

As the sun began to rise, transforming the night into gray and pink sunshine, Adelino and Diana were frantic. Neither had any idea where their son had gone or with whom. "Did he say who he was out with earlier in the day?" Adelino asked his wife. "No, husband. He just said he was going to meet his friends," she replied. "Let's think of his friends. Which boys would most probably get into trouble?" Diana thought, the faces of the neighborhood boys flashing through her mind. "There is that new family. They have a son; there is something about him I didn't like. Tiro was spending time with him. What was his name? K...Kal...ummmmm...Kallias! His name is Kallias. Let's go pay his family a visit," she said, rising from the table.

The parents of Kallias were surprised to find early morning visitors at their door: Adelino, Diana, and Daria. Though they had never met before, both mothers, on seeing each other, realized something was wrong. "Good day. I am the mother of Tiro, a friend of your son Kallias. My son did not come home last night..." Diana broke down. Adelino stepped in: "Is your son at home? Does he know where our son is?" he asked. The parents of Kallias looked shocked. "Let me check. Please come in," they said, opening the door further. The three entered as Daria, following from behind and whimpering, sensed something was wrong.

"Kallias is in bed sleeping, just as we left him last night," his mother said. "Can you wake him, please? Our son is missing and I know that they are friends..." Diana said. The father of Kallias went to wake him and brought him to the front room. The boy yawned as he looked first at Diana, then at Adelino. "Kallias," his mother began, "Do you know where Tiro is? He has gone missing." Kallias shook his head. This wasn't good enough for Diana. "Did you see him yesterday evening?" she asked. The boy shook his head again. "But did you not say that you were going to meet Tiro when you left after dinner?" his mother asked. Kallias paused, then said, "He didn't show up." His father broke in: "Why didn't you tell us this last night? Why did you stay out if Kallias wasn't there?" The boy again paused, thinking. "I met up with my other friends." At this Adelino broke in: "Please give us the name of these other friends so that we can see if they know where our son is." Kallias shook his head. "I don't remember," he said, and turned to go back to his room.

When Adelino and Diana looked at the boy's parents pleadingly, the mother stopped her son. "Kallias, come here and sit down." The boy, head cast down, reluctantly returned and sat next to his mother. "Son, this is very important. These parents cannot find their son. If you know anything, please tell us..." The boy looked up, first at Adelino and Diana, then at his own parents. "Last night...we went to Pheidias' workshop." There was silence in the room as the shock set in.

Guilty

Tiro was terrified as the workmen began to arrive that morning. Held in a separate room with a guard standing by the door, he shrunk into the corner. He had been interrogated most of the night by the guard who caught him, but the boy was too afraid to speak and gave up little information. Tiro looked at the guard, then looked at the door; if only he could escape. But the guard was big and the door was small. Tears welled up in the boy's eyes as he thought of his parents and how distraught they must be.

There was a knock at the door; the brawny guard opened it and leaned out as someone outside whispered in his ear. The door then opened widely; two other big men entered and stood on either side of the boy. Then, in a long robe with a longer beard, entered the man himself: Pheidias.

Tiro took a deep breath, hoping that Pheidias would not recognize him. The boy was a worker among many and he hoped nothing about him would stand out in Pheidias' memory. His hopes were dashed when the first thing that Pheidias said was: "You are one of my workers! Tell me what you were up to and who else was involved, or I will notify the authorities and have you and your family punished for your crime." At this the boy began to cry.

Pheidias remained unmoved. "Who are you? Who is your family? And who was with you last night?" It didn't take long for Tiro to tell him everything: how Kallias had coaxed him to climb through the window, how his parents didn't know he had snuck out, and how the other boy had fled. "Get the family of Kallias, and this boy's family, and bring them here," he said. The workers obliged as Tiro sat cowering in the corner. "What does your father do?" Pheidias asked. "He was a stone cutter for you, but then he got injured. I took his place to help my family," he said. "You work for me and you dare break into my workshop! You will work for me no more!" he bellowed, turning on his heels. The door slammed shut.

Daria was barking when the messengers from Pheidias arrived. "You are all to come to the workshop of Pheidias at once" was the message. "We must be accompanied by the family of Kallias," Diana stated firmly to the messenger, fearing that the other family may slip away. "We will drop off the dog, then come back for you; we will go together to the workshop," Adelino said firmly to Kallias and his parents.

Having arrived at the workshop, Adelino and Diana were frightened when they were led to the great Pheidias himself, standing in the main workroom. The parents of Kallias, as well as the boy, were behind them while Tiro was nowhere in sight. "Where is my son?" Diana burst out. "You will see your son once I discover what he came here to steal" was Pheidias' reply. "My son is not a thief. This boy Kallias can give the answers you seek, but he is reluctant to speak," Diana said. Adelino looked over at his wife, impressed by her courage in front of such a great man.

"Boy, step forward!" Pheidias bellowed. Kallias, accompanied by his parents, moved to the front. Diana noticed that Kallias' legs were shaking. "Tell me why you came here last night," Pheidias demanded. "And if anything you tell me is a lie, or even a little bit from the truth, I will have you arrested. Remember, I have already heard the entire story from the other boy." Kallias swallowed hard.

Kallias recounted the story, even including the part that it had been his idea to enter the workshop, that Tiro was reluctant and that, when caught, how he had left Tiro behind. "Wonderful friend you are," Pheidias said, sarcastically. "Very well," he continued. "Bring in the other boy."

After having been locked in a room alone for hours, Tiro was led to his parents. "I am so sorry, Mama and Papa," he said and burst into tears. "I do not have time for this," Pheidias said. "Bring both boys home and punish them yourselves. But this boy cannot work for me any longer," he stated. At this Diana could no longer keep silent. She approached Pheidias and looked him in the eyes. She paused, assessing the man. "He is a boy. My husband has worked for you for many years and look at him now. He can barely walk because of being injured on your mountain. My son works for you now and he provides for our family. It is easy for you to say..." At this Adelino touched her arm; the woman turned, but then continued to speak. "It is easy for you to say: 'you no longer work for me,' but do you know what these words mean for our family? We will lose everything. He is a boy, master Pheidias, a boy, just as you were. He is a human being, who makes mistakes and learns from them, just as you are. He is young, unlike you and me and all of us here. And this other boy, who instigated the whole affair, is to receive little or no punishment. I do not stand before you begging to keep my son employed. But I do stand here before you to ask you to do what is just." When she had finished she stood there, looking into Pheidias' eyes. He looked at her, this poor peasant woman full of confidence. "Oh very well! He can stay. But he better never try something like this again!" he said, then turned and left.

There was silence in the room when Pheidias departed.

Adelino had tears in his eyes when he turned to his wife and son; opening his arms, he held them both close. "Come, son. We have to get you ready for work," Diana said as they turned to leave. Walking in front of the family of Kallias, she said in a loud voice: "You are never to see that boy Kallias again." In a moment they were in the morning sun, making their way home.

When they approached their house, Tiro could hear Daria barking inside. The dog was excited and distraught, not understanding what was taking place. "Daria!" Tiro called out, as he opened the door. The dog leapt up repeatedly at the boy until he sat down. She jumped into his lap and proceeded to lick his face until Tiro could hardly breathe. "I will make you something to eat, son. We will talk tonight. Your father and I will walk with you today to the base of the hill. Please tell no one, and I do mean tell nobody at all, about what has taken place," she said with a serious tone. Tiro nodded.

Priorities

Draco awoke with the morning sun, partly in this world and partly in his dream. The dog stood up and yawned, then stretched his back legs, which felt a little stiff. He made his way down the hill, meeting no one along the way.

Akil heard the bark from the distance. "Wait till I get into the shop, my friend!" Akil called out, but his words fell on deaf ears as Draco ran and jumped up and down and around him.

When Jason arrived at the shop a few hours later, he found his father working inside and Draco curled up outside, sleeping.

"Akil! Jason! Draco!" Alexander called out, as he rounded the corner. "Kalimera! Good morning, my friend!" Akil called out. Draco stood up, stretched, then trotted over to Alexander to lead him to the shop. "Come visit with us," Akil said. "We just finished making a pot of coffee," he continued, winking to Jason so that he would put the coffee on. "Time is too short to not make time for friends," Alexander said, taking a chair outside under the tree. "It has been too long, my friend," Akil replied. Draco sat next to Alexander, looking up at his face. "How are things, Alexander?" Akil asked. "You may regret that you asked me that question," Alexander replied. "I am listening," Akil said.

"The last time I saw you," Alexander began, "I was working ten or twelve hour days; sometimes even more. At the restaurant there is rarely a calm moment. I have been doing this for months. For years, in fact. I was feeling like a machine, like a robot. But I have to work," he said, raising his eyebrows. "I haven't been very happy and have had little time for others. I blamed my wife for seeing each other so little. I blamed my son for not working enough. Then..." Alexander said, swallowing deeply, "I went to the doctor, because I was feeling weak. And he found a problem in my heart." Akil broke in: "I am sorry, my friend." Alexander continued, "The doctor told me that if I don't change my ways I will die before my time..." Draco sensed Alexander's emotion and started to whine. This made both men laugh, and Alexander said, "Not yet, Draco! Not for a long time!"

At that point Jason brought the men their coffee. "No sugar," Alexander said. "The doctor says: no sugar, so salt, exercise, no fried foods and watch my weight. I have to get a procedure in my heart; the doctor said that, if I follow his instructions, I could live a long time. If not, I may not live long. So here I am" he said. "For exercise, Draco is going to help me. I am going to climb the Acropolis with him every day. He keeps fit that way! Look at him! No fat!" Draco was wagging his tail, his tongue hanging out. "So tonight, when Draco leaves you, I will go with him and see how he lives. After that I will go home. The others can work the restaurant until late" Alexander stated.

"See, Draco is going to help you!" Akil said, chuckling. Alexander continued: "I have realized, my friend, that life is short, that God gives us just a little time on this earth and that work is not the most important thing. Over the years I have made little time for friends, little time for my wife and family, little time for anything that lasts. Now I want to change that..." Akil broke in: "Alexander, you are welcome here any time. Your story sounds like mine. But things began to change...." Alexander looked at Akil. "You will laugh," Akil said. Then he continued: "Things began to change when Draco started to come visit. Then my son started to come spend time with me. Then I realized that my life was just about doing my duties as a father and a husband, but there was no happiness or laughter. Now that is different," he said. Jason sat down next to his father as Akil reached over and put his hand on Jason's shoulder. "Why don't you and your wife come over for dinner this week?" Akil asked Alexander. "We don't cook like your restaurant but we could grill some meat," he said. Alexander smiled, "We will be there on Friday, if that works for you."

During this conversation Draco sat in front of them, looking back and forth between Akil and Alexander. At this point the dog barked as Cynarra turned the corner. The dog ran up to her as she said: "What's the party about?" Akil winked at Jason, who got up to make more coffee. "Come sit with us, Cynarra. Life is too short to rush through it," Akil said. Cynarra nodded and took a chair in the group, as Draco licked her hand. "There will be a bath for you later!" she said; Draco's tail went between his legs.

All three of them, Akil, Alexander, and Cynarra, were late for work that morning but none of them regretted it. "Come by for lunch sometime," Akil said, as they began to go their separate ways. "You come for lunch sometime next week!" Alexander responded. "Lunch with Akil this week, lunch with Alexander next," Cynarra said. All three nodded. "A very good idea only if I can come too," Jason said from over at the shop. "Yes, you can, son!" Akil said. "Jason, can you bring Draco by later? He needs a cleaning," Cynarra asked. Jason nodded while Draco looked at both of them, wondering what they were saying.

After getting his bath from Cynarra later that day, getting fed by Alexander, and stopping to visit Akil that afternoon, Draco was ready to head back up the Acropolis. "Draco, wait," Akil said. "This evening you will have company. Wait for Alexander," Akil continued, sitting down and patting Draco's head. Knowing the dog's schedule, Alexander appeared a short time later. Draco didn't seem to understand until the man began walking across the Plaka towards the hill. Once he realized that Alexander would accompany him, Draco grew excited and ran circles around Alexander. "Yes, I will come with you every evening Draco," he said. "But I cannot stay," he continued, as the two took the first steps up the Acropolis, with a few tourists milling around.

Alexander was huffing and puffing by the time they reached the top. The sun was setting by now, streaks of yellow and orange illuminating the Parthenon. "Where do you sleep up here, Draco?" Alexander asked. Both man and dog stood, looking at each other. Then Draco ran along the fence, through some bushes, and appeared on the other side, where the Parthenon was enclosed. "There you are my friend! Here are some treats before I go home," Alexander said, handing Draco some chopped meat and bread through the fence. "Until tomorrow, Draco," Alexander said and proceeded down the hill.

Draco found his favorite place on the steps of the Parthenon and soon dozed off to a sound sleep.

Sorrow and Guilt

A worker in Pheidias' workshop wondered if, after all the commotion about the boys breaking into the shop, he should remind Pheidias about the flower found on the floor. He didn't want to start something but he didn't want to be blamed for anything either. He confided in his coworker who urged him to speak. "You should protect your own job by telling the one in charge. Then leave it to him" was the advice given.

Herodotos, who had let Akil and his family into the workshop at night, was within earshot when he heard his coworker explain the mysterious flower. He listened attentively while continuing to build the scaffolding. "...I didn't tell you beforehand because I didn't think much of it. But in light of the break in, I thought I should let you know," he said. Herodotos strained to keep silent. "You did well to tell me. There may be others coming here at night to steal our materials. I will consult Pheidias," he said. At this Herodotos could keep quiet no longer. "Can we not increase our security at night? I would volunteer one evening a week. The flower could have entered the workshop some other way. If Pheidias is alarmed by this, he could dismiss us all. You saw how angry he was with the boys. Please consider this before approaching him," Herodotos pleaded. The supervisor stopped and thought. "I will reflect on your words," he said and turned away.

After work Herodotos went directly to Adelino's house. "Did you or your boy tell anyone that I let you into the workshop?" he asked. "I did not. My wife did not. I will ask my son when he gets home. He may have told the other boy. What shall we do?" Adelino asked, understanding the risk they were now all in. "I hope that they will not look into this further. But if your son did tell that other boy, who is a dishonest boy also, we should deny it. They found a flower on the ground; this is their only evidence that someone was in the shop," he said. "I will speak with Tiro," Adelino said, and Herodotos bid him goodbye.

When Tiro got home, his father was waiting for him. Daria, standing at Adelino's side, had her tail between her legs. "Son, I have to ask you something very important. Did you tell anyone that we went into the workshop after hours?" Tiro looked down as tears welled in his eyes. "Son?" Adelino repeated, as gently as possible. The boy nodded. "Did you tell that boy that you got in trouble with?" The boy nodded again. "Did you tell anyone else?" he continued. "No Papa," Tiro responded. Adelino looked off into the distance, playing out the possible scenarios in his mind. Daria was waiting to go indoors, shaking. "Thank you, son," Adelino said and led them into the house.

The next day Adelino told Herodotos that the boy Kallias knew they had entered the workshop. "Perhaps this will come to nothing," Herodotos said. "I will keep my ears open. I am hoping the manager realizes that no good will come from speaking to Pheidias of this." The two men shook hands and Herodotos turned to head home. Then he suddenly turned around and said: "I hope you speak with your son about the danger he has put us all in." Herodotos then continued on his way.

"How did honoring the goddess bring us to this point?" Adelino asked his wife later that day. Diana stopped her husband. "It is not the fault of Athena that our son brought that boy into the workshop. Our intentions were pure; look at our blessings: we have a home, we have a son, and you found Daria," she said motioning towards the dog. "I think that we need to speak with our son about these things. The family of Kallias may try to do us harm and we do not want to give them any cause," Diana said.

In the days following, Tiro walked to and from work with his head down. He spoke little during the day and, when he returned home, he could not look his parents in the eyes. Adelino and Diana knew that their son regretted what he had done but they had to speak with him about the danger he could put them all in if he should tell others about their secret visit, or if Kallias should. The boy's spirit seemed already broken, so his parents waited for the right moment.

A week passed and no such moment arrived. So when he got home one evening, Adelino asked his son to sit down next to him. Daria hopped up between them and curled up. "You are carrying a great weight on your shoulders, son. You are supporting the family. I hope to get back to work, but in the meantime it is all up to you. I am grateful to you for this, son. I want to also speak with you about what happened in the workshop and what could happen in the future. Can we talk about this, son?" Adelino asked. The boy looked up and nodded, but Adelino saw that there were already tears in his eyes. He put his hand on his son's shoulder, who began to cry. "I am so sorry Papa," he said between sobs. "Son, it will all be alright. I think the goddess will protect us," he continued.

Adelino knew that his son's actions had put them at risk, but he also knew that the boy was broken. He decided to wait until the next day to continue the conversation.

Despite the objections of his wife, the next morning he insisted on walking with his son to work. "Your leg! You might hurt yourself!" Diana said, but Adelino replied, "This is more important. I will accompany our son every morning that I am able." So with Daria at his side, excited for the early morning walk, father and son set out for the Acropolis.

"Papa, do you want to talk with me about something?" the boy asked after they had walked a while in silence. "First, I want to repeat to you how grateful your mother and I are for you going to work every day and supporting us. When I am better things will be easier, but for now you are supporting the family, son. The second thing, Tiro, is this: it is extremely important that you never

ever speak about us going inside of Phaedias' workshop. If anyone accuses you, say nothing in reply. Also, you are not to speak to the Kallias boy, or his parents, ever again. Do you understand, son?" Tiro looked at his father. "Yes, Papa." The two continued on in silence.

Daria was happy to be out with Adelino and Tiro, but when father and son parted ways, she tugged on her rope to continue up the hill with the boy. Adelino shook his head. "Daria, we have been through this before. It's too dangerous for you to be left there. Come home with me and we will see Tiro after work." Adelino then turned and walked back home with Daria alongside him.

Unexpected Encounters

Akil was at work early that morning to receive a food delivery. After putting bowls of food and water out for the dog, Akil looked up and spotted Draco from afar, so he called out "Draaaaacccccoooooooooo!" The dog turned his trot into a run and rushed at Akil; on arrival, he jumped up as high as the man. Akil chuckled. "Come here and eat, Draco, while I finish with the delivery." The dog understood and went to his dish.

It wasn't long before Alexander and Cynarra showed up to have coffee with Akil; they were meeting at Akil's shop almost every day now to start their day together. When Draco spotted Cynarra he immediately grew excited and started running circles around her. "Don't worry, Draco. You will be getting washed later today." Draco scampered off and the three of them laughed.

When Cynarra returned to her shop she found her parents waiting for her. "Why is the shop not open? Where have you been?" her mother asked. Cynarra knew that tone of voice so she evaded the question. "Mother! Father! What a surprise! Everything is good." When her mother asked again where she had been, Cynarra remained silent. So her mother began her usual monologue with her daughter.

"Your brothers went away and left this business to us. Now it is your responsibility. I don't know why you have gotten in your head to go to the university. Your life is here. You have to open the shop at dawn and keep it open until evening. This idea you have of traveling somewhere, of living outside of Greece....these independent girls, my mother would say!" She then paused and looked at her husband. "Say something!" she insisted. Cynarra's father said: "Just what your mother said" and, when his wife wasn't looking, he winked at Cynarra. "Yes, mother. Thank you for coming by. The shop is open now. We don't want to drive away customers, do we?"

It was difficult for Cynarra to navigate between her mother's expectations and her own goals. Her mother would never see things from her point of view so she stopped trying to convince her. Cynarra had a dream and she knew that no one would hand it to her.

When Jason arrived with Draco hours later, Cynarra was deep in these thoughts. "Hello Cynarra! Papa said that Draco needs a bath today!' When Draco heard the word "bath" he pulled away. "It's not so bad Draco," Cynarra said, "especially today when Jason can help me." So she went and grabbed the soap, got a towel, and went over to the hose; Jason dragged Draco over. Cynarra bent down and said to the dog, "You know you will feel better once you are clean. Come on, Draco. This won't last long." Draco relaxed and sat down.

"I wish you could keep Draco at home. He wouldn't get so dirty all the time," Cynarra said as they soaped up the dog. "We tried. Papa said he wasn't happy there. He wanted his freedom. But we keep a close watch on him. And now Alexander walks with him up the Acropolis every evening." Cynarra looked the dog in the eyes. "I want my freedom also, Draco."

Cynarra spent the rest of the day studying; she sold a few flowers and one plant but her heart was not in it. She knew, however, that her mother would ask her that evening how much money she had made and she wanted to avoid an argument. Before leaving for her class she had an idea, and made her way over to Akil's shop. Draco, surprised to see Cynarra at that hour, barked and ran towards her; he leapt up and licked her cheek. "Dracoooooooo!" she said, as she wiped her face. "Cynarra! Welcome! Sit down and I will make you a coffee!" Akil said.

"Hello Akil! I can't. I am on my way to class. Is Jason still here?" she asked. "Jason!" Akil called, and the boy came out of the shop. "Jason, can I ask you a favor? Of your father also? I have to sell some flowers tonight after class; I will go to the restaurants to sell them to tourists. Jason, can you come with me?" he asked. "Can I Papa? Please?" the boy asked. "Yes, but you must not be home late," Akil said and winked at Cynarra. "Meet me here at 9 o'clock" Cynarra said, turning and walking away, while Draco sat and looked at her, wondering where his friend was going.

"Where shall we start?" Jason asked Cynarra later that evening. They stood there thinking for a moment, flowers in hand. "What about Alexander's restaurant?" Jason asked. "Excellent idea!" Cynarra replied, and the two set off across the Plaka.

"Welcome, my friends! And who might you be?" a young handsome bearded man asked as they approached Alexander's restaurant. "We are friends of Alexander!" Jason blurted out. Cynarra glanced at Jason, making him understand that she should do the talking. "I am Cynarra and I run the flower shop in the Plaka. This is Jason, the son of Akil, who runs the sandwich shop. We were wondering…." The young man interrupted them and bowed: "And I am Alex son of Alexander, who runs this establishment of fine Greek cuisine." "Well, Alexander never mentioned…" Jason began, until Cynarra nudged him. "It is very nice to meet you. Your father is a good friend," Cynarra said. "Now, how can I help you?" Alex asked, focusing on Cynarra, who wore her long black hair down that day, which made her face glow and her eyes sparkle in the evening light. "Can we sell some flowers to your customers? I haven't sold hardly anything today at the shop," Cynarra said. Alex replied as he kept looking in Cynarra's eyes, "Only if I can buy your first flower." "I will give it to you," she said. "No," he said, shaking his head, "That is my condition. I must buy the first flower." Cynarra conceded and accepted the money. Then Alex, taking the flower, handed it back to her. "This flower is for you. Please come back here any time.

Where is your flower shop again?"

While Draco rested on the steps of the Parthenon, Cynarra and Jason made their way to the second restaurant. Jason couldn't resist teasing Cynarra about Alex. "Cynarra has a boyfriend! Cynarra has a boyfriend!" he sang. She laughed. "I have no time for such things," she said. "But what if he shows up at the flower shop?" Jason asked. "So what if he does? I will sell him a plant!" she said. After a pause, Cynarra asked: "Why doesn't Alexander talk about his son?" Jason shrugged.

The next morning, while Draco was making his way down the Acropolis, Cynarra was already at the flower shop, putting away a new shipment of plants and flowers. "Kalimera!" she heard outside. "Kalimera, Cynarra!" the voice repeated. She came to the front of the shop to find Alex outside. "What are you doing here?" Cynarra blurted out. "It's a beautiful morning, I met a beautiful woman last night, so I came to wish her a beautiful day," Alex said. Cynarra paused. She didn't know whether to be flattered, on her guard, or dismissive. "I didn't want to interrupt. I just wanted to know if you would like to take a coffee with me to start the day," Alex said. Cynarra nodded.

More Changes

When Draco arrived at Akil's shop, it was still closed. So he sat and waited at the door, looking down the road from where Akil always arrived. When Jason approached, the dog ran up to him and barked. "Papa isn't coming today, Draco," the boy said. "He isn't feeling well," he continued. Draco sat and looked at the boy. Then he began barking again. "Come with me to the shop, Draco," he said. Draco followed him, barking along the way.

Draco stayed with Jason at the shop the whole day. The dog sat outside, looking down the path that Akil usually took. Jason tried to distract him, but Draco was determined to not miss the man should he approach. "What's wrong with Draco?" Cynarra asked, as she arrived at the shop to have a coffee with Jason. The dog greeted her, but then took up his place in front of the shop, looking down the path. "Draco is worried about Papa. He is sick today; he had pains in his chest and Mama made him stay home," the boy explained. "Why don't you take Draco home with you tonight? He isn't going to sleep, not knowing where Akil is," Cynarra suggested.

That evening, when Draco usually returned to the Acropolis, Jason attached a chain to his collar until the last customer came and he could close up the shop. He let Alexander know that the dog would not be going up the Acropolis that evening. "We will go see Papa afterwards and you can stay with us tonight," the boy told the dog. So about an hour later the boy started for home, with Draco pulling him ahead.

Akil was on the sofa when boy and dog entered; Draco ran to

him and, crawling partly into Akil's lap, proceeded to lick his face until Akil could hardly breathe. "Draco was worried about you," Maria said, laughing. "It's O.K. Draco, I am here," Akil said. "Papa?" Jason sat next to his father as Akil put one arm around his son and his other on Draco's head. "Are you alright, Papa?" Akil smiled. "I am fine, son. Don't worry about me."

The peace of the evening was only interrupted by the ongoing discussion between Akil and Maria about whether he should go to the hospital. "I'm fine; it is just a cold" Akil said. "Let's make sure, husband. They will just do some tests and send you home," she insisted. Akil saw his wife's concern but he also hated hospitals. So they went back and forth over the issue until it was time for bed.

Draco was anxious to head out the next morning but he wanted Akil to come with him. The dog tried to lead the man to the door but Akil was still in his pajamas. Akil bent down to talk with Draco: "Draco, you go to the shop with Jason now. I promised Mama that I would see the doctor today; if everything is O.K. then I will come to the shop later. Will you do that for me, Draco?" The dog looked at him in the eyes with a wrinkled forehead. "You will be O.K. Draco," he said. "Son! Can you take him to the shop with you?" A few minutes later Jason was heading towards the Plaka with Draco pulling him forward on his leash.

Cynarra was already at the flower shop before Jason and Draco left their house. She wanted to get everything set up so that she could devote her morning to studying. "Kalimera! Good morning!" she heard outside. Hearing Alex's voice, she smiled. "I am working!" she called out. "O.K. I will be back at 9 o'clock to get a coffee. Bye!" he said. "But…" Cynarra began, walking out of the shop. Alex had already left.

Jason had almost finished setting up when Alexander showed up. "Hello!" he called out. Draco ran to him and Alexander threw him a piece of steak that the dog caught in his mouth. "Is your father here yet?" Alexander asked. Jason shook his head. "He was going to the doctor right after I left so I don't know if he is coming in," the boy responded. "Yes, he called me from the doctor's office and asked me to meet him here," Alexander responded. The boy's heart missed a beat, for this was unusual behavior for his father. "I will make you a coffee while you wait," Jason said.

When Akil arrived a half an hour later, Draco acted like he hadn't seen the man in weeks. "It's O.K. Draco," Akil said as the dog jumped up and down on him, leading him to his chair. When the man sat down, Draco began to whine. "Draco is worried about you," Alexander said, sitting across from Akil. "No need to worry. No need for anyone to worry," he said in a loud voice so that Jason could hear.

"What did your doctor say?" Alexander asked in a low voice, once Draco had settled down next to Akil. "He said that my blood pressure is so high that if I don't change my ways I could have a heart attack and die," Akil said, looking at the ground. Then he continued in a whisper: "I am scared, my friend. But I don't want my wife and son to know because they will become more worried. I have to change my diet and I have to get more exercise. I have many bad habits...." He trailed off. Alexander looked at his friend, head and shoulders down. This was not the Akil he knew. "We will do this together," Alexander said. "For lunch, come over to the restaurant; you can eat what I have. For coffee in the morning, now I only drink decaffeinated. For dinner only raw vegetables. And for exercise, I walk all the way up the Acropolis every evening, most of the time with Draco. You can come with us, or perhaps walk home rather than take the bus," he suggested. Akil looked up and nodded.

"Are you ready for our coffee?" Alex asked cheerfully outside of Cynarra's shop. "But I can't leave...." Cynarra started to say, but stopped when she saw Alexander standing outside, a large tray in hand with steaming coffee and sweets. "The coffee has come to you, my lady," he said, bowing. She laughed and they both sat down under the nearby tree to enjoy a moment."My father speaks highly of you," Alex began. "Well, your father speaks so little about his family!" Cynarra replied with a laugh. "That's my father!" Alex said, rolling his eyes. "He is all about the business. But maybe that is starting to change..." he continued.

"Do you like working at your father's restaurant?" Cynarra asked, after taking her first sip of the dark coffee. "I like helping my father. As far as the restaurant, I am grateful to have work. What about you in your flower shop?" he asked. Cynarra rolled her eyes. "I hate it. Like you, I must help my parents, for now. But I don't want to work in a flower shop for the rest of my life," she said. "What would you like to do?" he asked. "I want to travel; I want to study in England. Then I want to get my degree in business and decide where I want to live. I want a life bigger than the Plaka," she said. "There are many," Alex began, "who would love to work in the Plaka, with tourists coming all the time. Are you unhappy here?" Cynarra paused. "I would not say I am unhappy. It is just not enough for me."

"What about your future, Alex?" Cynarra asked as she sipped. "I wish to help my father. The restaurant is hard work and he can no longer put in all the hours. For the future, I do not know. Sometimes I wish I was far away..." Alex trailed off while looking beyond the Plaka. Then he turned to Cynarra. "But now we are here in this moment, and I am glad that you are here with me." Cynarra smiled.

It was approaching lunch time and Akil was busy at the shop with customers. Only when things settled down around 2 o'clock did he make his way to Alexander's restaurant with Draco at his side. "Welcome my friends!" Alexander called as the two approached. "Come in back!" Circling around the building, Alexander led Akil to a table set with a white tablecloth, shiny silverware, and crystal glasses. "You don't have to do this," Akil said. "You are my friend. Plus, it won't be like this every day. But Draco likes it." The dog had placed himself besides one of the chairs next to the table. Once they had sat down, Alex served them a lunch of sliced cucumbers and tomatoes, grilled fish with exactly three olives on the side. "My doctor says no more than three a day," Alexander said with a wink. Then Alex brought some grilled vegetables to eat with the fish. "You see my friend, we can eat healthy and still be happy. And tonight, if you like, we can go up the Acropolis with Draco."

Draco was looking up eagerly at the two. "I wonder if Draco likes carrots?" Akil asked, as he handed one to the dog. Draco had never seen a carrot before; he took it carefully in his mouth and dropped it on the ground. Sniffing it, he took it in his mouth and bit it. A few seconds later he was munching on it and then asking for another. "Draco can share our healthy diet also!" Alexander said.

"Any customers while I was gone, son?" Akil asked Jason on his return. "Only two Americans. They wanted a hamburger. So I used the frozen patties that you showed me. They seemed to like it but they asked for 'relish'. What is 'relish'?" Akil shook his head. "I have no idea, son. But I heard it tastes terrible!" Both of them laughed. "Son, I can take over now; why don't you go home? Draco is here with me." So while Draco stayed curled up under the tree, the boy made his way home and Akil went into the shop to prepare some dough for the next morning.

Towards evening Alexander stopped by. "Walk with me up the hill?" he asked Akil. "Today I have to clean the shop but I will walk home instead of taking the bus," Akil said as he put the coffee on for both of them. He smiled and said: "Don't worry; decaffeinated." Akil continued, "I sent Jason home; the boy has become so helpful and is always here working and playing with Draco. I want him to enjoy himself outside of here also. Before Draco, I couldn't drag him here. Now I can't drag him away!" and he laughed. Alexander smiled and reached down to the dog. "Yes, our Draco is like a human magnet!"

The sun had set by the time Alexander and Draco reached the area of the Parthenon. As usual, Alexander bent down and gave Draco a treat and bid him goodnight. The dog ran to his usual place where there was a hole in the fence, ducked through, then dashed across the open space to the Parthenon steps, treat in mouth. Once there he turned and watched Alexander until the man waved and turned to go back down the hill. Draco ate his treat as the sun turned red and disappeared.

The Return

Daria stretched her legs and yawned as she woke up next to Adelino. "I sat down, then I fell asleep," he called out to Diana, who was preparing food. Diana smiled. "I better get up and walk. I have to get myself fit again so that I can return to work. Our son shouldn't have to do this. He is too young, too much responsibility." Diana stopped what she was doing and approached Adelino. "I know he is too young, Adelino. It sorrows me also to see him have to work. And his mistake in going to the workshop bothers him; I can see it in his eyes. But what can we do? Perhaps I can take some work as a washerwoman," she suggested. Adelino shook his head. "No, we will find a way, but not that," and he kissed her on the cheek. Daria barked, since she was ready to go out. "Back soon," he said, and they left.

Before he knew it, somehow Adelino, using his stick for support, found himself climbing the Acropolis with Daria by his side. When he reached the work area, one of his former co-workers called out "Adelino!" In an instant he was surrounded by his friends and other workers. "When are you coming back to work?" one said. Another: "Your son does a fine job!" And he also heard: "We miss you Adelino." He looked around at the faces of his friends. "I wonder if the foreman would let me...." He paused; one of the workers broke in: "What, Adelino?" Adelino shook his head. "Do you think he would let me come here to start small, without getting paid, to build up my strength? Then when I am able to cut the stone, do you think he might let me return to work?" A few of the workers started clapping.

"Don't worry, Adelino. We will take care of it. Just return tomorrow and we will work it all out." At that moment Tiro approached the group. "Papa!" The boy hugged his father as Daria jumped up. "Tomorrow your father is coming back to work!" someone in the crowd said. "Does Mama know?" Tiro asked. At this the men backed away. "I will speak with Mama. We will talk tonight, son," he said, kissing the boy on the forehead.

When Tiro walked home from work later that day, he could hear his mother's voice as he approached the house. "And if you injure yourself?" he heard. Before opening the door the boy took a deep breath. "And...." his mother began, but stopped in mid sentence on seeing Tiro. "Welcome home, son," she said in a very different tone. The boy looked at his father, who had a wrinkled forehead. Looking in the corner, he spotted Daria, huddled in a ball and trembling. His mother, though speaking with a calm voice, had an intense look in her eyes. "You're scaring Daria and you are scaring me," Tiro said looking at them both. "I'm sorry, son, but your father...." she began. "I know about Papa. He wants to see if he can do some work. He wants to see if he can help. You're worried about him and you're worried about me. I know that. Why don't you let Papa come to work with me, just for a few hours every day. That would make him happy and me too," he said. Tiro walked over and picked up Daria; he sat down and put her on his lap. His mother looked at him. "You're right. I'm such a fool..." Adelino rose from where he was sitting and embraced his wife. "You are no fool. You just love so much..." Diana leaned on her husband's shoulder and closed her eyes.

The next morning Daria was in an especially good mood, jumping and running in circles, while the entire family walked towards the Acropolis. Diana insisted on speaking with the foreman in charge before allowing her husband to do any work, Adelino was smiling as he reflected on the possibility of providing for his family once again, and Tiro and Daria were enjoying the company of the family together. When she began to bark, Diana scolded the dog. "But Mama, she is just so excited!" Tiro said in her defense. "Son, some are still sleeping at this early hour. Can you make her be quiet?" she asked. At this, Tiro scooped the dog up and carried her in his arms until they reached the bottom of the hill.

Adelino turned to his wife: "Let me speak with the foreman. He is a friend of mine. I promise I will not do any heavy work. After all, he is doing me a favor by letting me take on a lesser job. I will work it out with him and I will not put myself at risk. I promise." Diana reluctantly agreed. "Then I will see you later today. You said you will only put in half a day today, and you, son, I will see for dinner." They both agreed and Adelino kissed his wife.

As the group separated, Daria pulled at her rope, wanting to go with the men but Diana tugged her the other way. "Come, Daria. We have to stick together today," she said. Soon the dog was trotting happily by her side on the way to the food stalls.

Adelino knew that he was unable to lift the stones so the foreman, grateful that Adelino was back, put him on lighter jobs. "Can you sand and smooth the rock after the rough work has been done?" the foreman asked. "They will be smoother than a baby's bottom!" Adelino said. The foreman smiled. Tiro, meanwhile, was doing heavier work with chisel and hammer. He checked in on his father after a few hours. "I can't earn as much as before by doing this work but I can provide something," he said to his son. "Papa, just don't hurt yourself," the boy said. Adelino was annoyed at this comment, but, glancing at his son's face, he understood. He stopped what he was doing and pulled his son's head against his shoulder, giving him a half hug. "Now get back to work, son, before we both lose our jobs!" he said laughing.

Having returned from the food stalls, Diana was beginning to prepare the evening meal at home. Adelino said he would return at midday so she also had a lunch ready for him. At a certain point, Diana noticed that Daria had disappeared. Looking around the house, she found the dog sitting, looking at the front door, waiting. Diana laughed. "Daria!" she said. "I know you miss him and you are concerned. I'm concerned too. But Adelino says he will be careful and we have to trust him. Now come with me and I will give you something." Daria grasped the meaning of the words and followed Diana back into the kitchen area.

When Adelino returned home, Daria was beside herself. She had become accustomed to spending the entire day with him so she didn't understand his absence. Adelino laughed as he went to the kitchen and kissed his wife. "Both of us were worried about you!" she said as Adelino sat down and Daria jumped in his lap, licking his face. "They have me on menial jobs but I am grateful to be able to do some work for the family," he said smiling."I do want you to be careful, husband. We almost lost you, we almost lost Daria. Truly Athena is watching over us, but I don't want you to try her patience."

Alex and Cynarra

When Draco opened one eye, lying on the steps of the Acropolis, he had one thought: Cynarra. He hadn't been to visit her in a few days, and Cynarra had not come by Akil's shop. He missed her; as he got up and stretched his legs and wagged his tail, he thought of Cynarra's face, laughing, as she squirted him with water. After a big long yawn, the dog began trotting down the hill towards her flower shop.

Cynarra arrived about an hour after sunrise. She was startled when she found Draco there, lying curled up in front, waiting. "Draco!" she said. The dog leapt to his feet and stood against Cynarra's leg. "I missed you too, Draco," she said as she reached down to pet his head. "Let me see if I have something for you," she said as she opened the door of the shop, the dog following her in.

After his treat, Draco wanted to play, so Cynarra got the hose and sprayed the water as Draco tried to dodge the spray. Cynarra then turned off the water and sniffed the dog. "Draco! Bath time," she said. Draco put his tail between his legs as Cynarra got the soap.

"Kalimera! Good morning! What are you two up to?" Alex called out as he approached Cynarra's shop. Draco ran towards him, barked, then ran back to Cynarra. "Draco!" she said, reprovingly. "Draco doesn't want a bath, and I have to open the shop soon. Can you help me get him washed? He smells like dog," she said. Alex laughed. "I would be worried if he smelled like me! Yes, I can help." Alex held him by the collar as Cynarra came at the dog with bucket and soap.

By the end of the bath, Cynarra was laughing, Alex was soaked, and Draco was running in circles, shaking off the water as he barked. It was still early and there was a chill in the air. "I will get both of you towels," she said as she entered the shop. Draco wanted to play, so he dared Alex to try to catch him. "Dracooooooooooo!" Alex called out as the dog darted around him. Cynarra handed Alex a towel, then headed towards Draco, who was not in the mood to be dried but to be chased. So Cynarra darted this way and that, trying to catch the dog as Alex laughed. She finally gave up. "If you catch a cold, Draco, it will be your own fault," she said as she threw the towel inside her shop.

"I have to go to work," Alex said, ducking his head inside the shop. "After the lunch crowd leaves I will bring us lunch, about two o'clock," he said. Before Cynarra could reply, he was gone.

Draco stuck his nose in the door, looking up at Cynarra. "Draco, what are we going to do with this Alex?" she asked.

"Where is Draco, Papa?" Jason asked. "He is a free spirit, son. It is still early. He will come by, you will see," Akil said. "Alexander asked me to bring him some rolls this morning, Papa. I will be back soon," Jason said.

It was a few minutes later that Akil heard whining outside his shop. "Dracooooooo!" he called out. The dog barked and wildly wagged his tail as Akil came out. "Where have you been, Draco?" he asked. Then he smelled the shampoo. "And how was Cynarra this morning?" The dog barked and whined. "O.K., Draco. I will sit with you for a bit but then I have to finish preparing the food inside." The dog followed him to his chair, putting his nose under Akil's hand to make sure that the man remembered to pet his head.

"Papa! Draco!" Jason said, as he rounded the corner, returning to the shop. Akil laughed. "I told you he knows where his family is, son," Akil said.

Akil had made a small bed for Draco out of blanket and pillow and there Draco lay that day, keeping one eye on Akil and the other on the activity around the shop. When Alexander came by that evening to walk up the Acropolis, Draco was ready to play. "Akil!" Alexander called out, as Draco ran beside him, licking Alexander's hands. "Hello, my friend!" Akil responded. "Draco wants some attention. There is a ball over there if you want to throw it," Akil said, pointing. Alexander picked it up and kept Draco running back and forth for the next twenty minutes. "I'm almost ready," Akil said to Alexander, as he moved some crates of drinks and food inside the shop.

As the sun was setting the two men, Akil and Alexander, made their way up the Acropolis, led by Draco. "Why does he love it up here so much?" Alexander asked. Akil looked at Draco, happily trotting in front of them. "There is something here that is part of him and I don't know what that is."

Alexander brought some food up with him to the Parthenon and he handed it to Draco before descending. The dog gobbled it up, brushed against Akil, then scampered over to the hole under the fence. Before slipping under he waited and watched the two men. "Let's go," Akil said. "He won't go under the fence until we leave," he said. The two men turned and descended down the hill.

Lost Again

Daria sprang to her feet as soon as Adelino got out of bed. She followed him into the kitchen area as he started to get ready for work. It was still dark out when Tiro, rubbing his eyes, wandered in. "I'm tired, Papa," the boy said. Soon the whole family was up, as Diana entered and addressed them all: "Give me just a little time and I will have your food ready for your work today; bread and cheese for right now. Go get dressed," she said as she turned to prepare the meals. Daria followed Adelino, intending to not let him out of her sight, should he disappear for the entire day again. "Daria, don't you want to stay home here with Mama?" he asked. The dog wagged her tail.

The sky was still gray when father and son were ready to set out. Since Adelino still walked with the help of a stick, they left a little early so that he could make his way up the hill slowly. "My wife, what are you doing?" Adelino asked, as Diana exited the house and closed the door behind her. "Daria and I decided to walk with you today," she said, smiling. "I am glad, Mama," Tiro said, as he reached down to pat Daria on the head. "But why?" Adelino asked. Diana put her hands on her hips. "Well, believe it or not, husband, we enjoy your company!" Adelino laughed and kissed his wife on the forehead. She then put her arm in his and the four walked towards the Acropolis while most of the town still slept.

When they reached the base of the hill, Diana said: "Now you two take care of yourselves. Tiro, make sure your father doesn't hurt himself. And husband..." Adelino stopped her. "I know, wife. I love you too," he said kissing her cheek.

When the two men continued on, Daria followed them until Diana slightly tugged her rope. "Daria, we girls are together today," she said. The dog turned to look at Adelino moving away. "I know you want to be with him, Daria; he will be back tonight. Come along now; let's go to the market." So the two made their way down the road, Daria scampering ahead.

"Are you alright, Adelino?" his coworker asked, as they scraped away at the stone. "You look like you are suffering!" he continued. "I am fine!" Adelino replied. In reality, his leg and his back caused him pain, and this was aggravated by the bending and stooping necessary for his work. Adelino, however, was determined to support his family to the best of his ability; he took his focus off his aching body and kept it on the stone.

"Here!" his young coworker said, handing him some water later in the morning. "We both need to take a breath," he continued. Adelino continued to work, ignoring the water. A few minutes later he paused and stopped what he was doing. Turning to his coworker, he said: "I am sorry. I am a stubborn man. I am returning from an injury and I am trying to prove myself...." He took up the cup. "Thank you for the water. We can rest a few minutes," he said. His coworker put down his tools and smiled, sipping from his cup.

While Daria was fascinated by the smells of the market, Diana was trying to figure out how much she could spend for dinner since, even with both men working, their wages were less than Adelino's before the accident. She would look for what was on sale today, as Daria followed behind. "Fish or cheese; I can't buy both," she said out loud. She followed her nose. Diana found a fish for dinner, so she began to negotiate for the price. "It's a beautiful fish," the seller said. "Just caught this morning by my own son!" he said. "You can prepare it any way you want..." he said, interrupted by Diana. "I know how to prepare it; I just need a better price," she said. "I can always go to the other fish sellers," she warned. The man stopped her. "No no no no, I will give you a good price." When he named the price, she offered him half. They negotiated a bit further and before long, Diana had the wrapped fish in hand. She looked down at Daria. She still had the rope in her hand, but the dog was gone.

Adventures

Akil was the first one awake. He crept into the kitchen so as not to disturb his wife and son. He quietly filled the coffee pot and put it on to brew. It was misty outside the window as he gazed out down the road. As the smell of fresh coffee filled the house, he knew that wife and son would soon gravitate to the kitchen.

Maria was the first to smell the coffee and appeared. "Thank you, husband," she said as she wandered in, put her head on his shoulder, then went to fill her cup. "I will do that, Maria," Akil said as he poured the cups and sat down. After a few sips Akil noticed Maria looking at him. He smiled. "Maria..." he said reprovingly. "What is on your mind?" She laughed. "Can't you read my mind by now, Akil?" He laughed. "I just want you to take care of yourself, Akil. I want you to be well and happy and with us for a long long time..." Akil moved his chair and sat next to Maria, taking her hand in his own. "I will my love," he whispered, kissing her hand.

"Kalimera! Good morning, Papa, Mama," Jason said, yawning as he came into the kitchen. "Will you come to the shop today, son?" Akil asked. "Sure Papa," the boy replied, plopping himself down in a chair. "A little coffee, son?" Maria asked. The boy nodded as he put his head on the table. "I will go on ahead to the shop," Akil said finishing his coffee. "Always the first one in the Plaka," Maria said laughing. She continued: "I will try to come by around lunch. We can all have a healthy meal together." Akil kissed his wife's forehead, gathered his things, and set out.

It was still early when Akil arrived at the edge of the Plaka; he was startled when, out of nowhere, Draco ran up to him, then sat whining, looking at Akil in the eyes. "What's wrong, Draco?" he asked. The dog whined again, walked over, and pressed against his leg. "Oh Draco, my complicated friend! I wish you could tell me what is going on with you. It is alright," he said as he bent down to pet the dog. "Do you want to spend the day with me, Draco?" he asked. The dog looked at him. "Come on, Draco! Let's go to the shop together," Akil continued. The dog followed him by his side, while continuously looking up at him.

Arriving at the shop, Akil went inside to unpack his supplies while Draco waited. After a minute or two he heard the dog whimpering; first lightly, then insistently. Akil stuck his head out. "Draco! You're O.K. Draco! I will be there in a minute," he said, ducking his head inside. The whining continued. "Draco! What can I do with you? What are you thinking?" he said, coming outside as the dog licked his hand. Sitting in his wooden chair, the dog came beside him then tried to crawl into his lap. Akil laughed. "Not all your weight, Draco!" he said, caressing the dog's head and preventing him from jumping up on him. The dog seemed to relax. "That's a good boy, Draco. I am here," he said.

"Coffee!" Alexander called out, as he rounded the corner, tray in hand. Akil moved to get up, but Draco put his paw on his leg. "I am being held down!" Akil said laughing. When Draco saw Alexander, he wagged his tail but didn't budge. "What's up with Draco today?" Alexander asked. "A complicated emotional life," Akil whispered. Alexander sat down. "I should call my son," Akil said, "to help me set up the shop." Alexander put his hand up. "Don't bother. I can help you. My son Alex is at the restaurant," he said. "Just tell me what you need done; give Draco a few moments. I think he needs it," Alexander said, finishing off his coffee and rising from his chair. "I need the ice moved from the ice maker to the freezer. Can you do that, my friend?" Akil asked. Alexander nodded and went into the shop while Draco kept his head firmly in Akil's lap.

"Alright, Draco," Akil said gently. "You can stay with me

today but we can't let Alexander do all the work." The man rose to his feet, Draco following him closely behind. "Alexander! You are my guest! You sit here while I finish opening up the shop," he said. "We can do it together," Alexander replied. So the two men first put the dough out to rise for the rolls, then unloaded the sandwich materials, snacks, drinks, and other light foods that Akil sold; they then put the snacks on the racks where customers could see them from the road. Alexander glanced at the doorway, seeing Draco curled up outside with a wrinkled forehead. "Our friend doesn't look too happy today. Maybe you should bring him home tonight," Alexander suggested. Akil nodded. "Sometimes Draco seems so afraid to be abandoned, and yet he wants his freedom. Maybe that is hard for him." Alexander nodded. "I want my freedom too!" Alexander whispered. Akil laughed. "I will see you later my friend. I am going to take over for Alex and give him a break at the restaurant," he said, leaving the shop.

When Jason came he found his father working with Draco following behind him. "Son," Akil said as Jason entered. Draco wagged his tail but didn't leave Akil's side. "What's up with Draco?" he asked. Akil rolled his eyes. "He is having one of those days. Can you take him for a walk or maybe an adventure?" Jason smiled. "Sure, Papa. And Mama said to tell you to not eat anything you're not supposed to and that she will bring us lunch." Akil laughed. Since Draco didn't want to leave, Jason put on his leash and the two headed towards Cynarra's flower shop.

When Draco saw Cynarra and Alex chatting outside her shop, he hid behind Jason's legs and sat down. "Don't you want to see Cynarra?" Jason turned and asked the dog. "Come on, Draco! Maybe you won't get a bath today!" he said, as he pulled on the leash and Draco reluctantly followed. Alex was the first to see the boy and dog. "Kalimera! Good morning to you!" he said bowing. "Draco!" Cynarra called out. Rather than running, the dog approached her with head down. Cynarra turned to Jason. "What's wrong with Draco?" she asked. Jason shrugged. "I don't think he wants a bath today," Jason continued. "You don't have to get a bath today, Draco," she said soothingly. "What are you two up to?" Alex asked. "Draco's acting funny, so Papa told me to take him on an adventure. Do you want to come?" he asked them. Alexander and Cynarra looked at each other. Before Cynarra could speak, Alex said: "You go, Cynarra! I have to take care of lunch preparation at the restaurant. How often do you get an invitation to an adventure? Look! I will make a sign and put it on your shop. It will say 'Back at noon.' Your parents will never know unless they show up. You can blame me if they do. I will buy some flowers for the tables from you when you return, so your parents won't suspect a thing." Cynarra hesitated. "Come on, Cynarra! We never get to go on an adventure together!" Jason insisted. Cynarra laughed. "I must be crazy!" she said, as she went into the shop, changed her shoes, closed the shop window and door, and stood looking at Alex and Jason. "O.K., let's do this adventure!" she said. Alex smiled, Draco grew excited, and Jason laughed. In an instant, the three were off.

"Where are we going, Cynarra?" Jason asked as Draco trotted ahead of them. "Well, I was thinking...with Draco we can't take the bus. And the streets are so busy...what about the National Garden?" Jason nodded. "Have you been there, Jason?" The boy shook his head. "You haven't been to the National Garden?" she asked incredulously. "It's amazing, Jason. You will love it. Draco will love it. And there is an interesting story behind it; in that garden the course of history was changed when a monkey bit a king." Jason laughed, then looked at Cynarra. "Oh, you're serious. That really happened?" Cynarra nodded. "Well, tell me the story!" the boy exclaimed as Draco glanced back at the pair.

"Around the time of World War I....hmmm...have you studied that war in school?" Cynarra asked. Jason nodded. "Yes, Hitler and all of that." Cynarra frowned. "That was World War II, Jason." She paused and began again. "It was around 1920 that Greece was on its way to becoming a great world power. We were expanding our territory. Our military was strong. Turkey was afraid of us. We were respected. The king was Alexander and

141

his statesman, who was the mastermind of creating a greater Greece, was named Eleftherios Venizelos. Greece was fighting Turkey to expand its territory. Then one day in 1920, King Alexander was walking in the gardens where we are going now, and someone's pet monkey ran up and bit him. I know it sounds ridiculous, but the king died a few weeks later. With his death, Alexander's father, Constantine, became king, and he was a disaster for Greece. Our country lost power and allies, Turkey rose in power, and it was a catastrophe for our position in the world. And all because of a monkey." Jason laughed. "Do monkeys still live in the garden?" he asked. Cynarra shook her head. "Actually, no monkeys ever lived there. The one that killed the king was somebody's pet that got away. Just think, Jason. If that monkey had not run away that day, our history would have been different," she concluded. "I wonder if Draco could change history," Jason joked. "Well, maybe he already has. We wouldn't be on our way to the National Garden today if it weren't for Draco, would we?" Cynarra responded. Draco turned when he heard his name, but kept trotting ahead.

Upon entering the National Garden, Draco stopped in his tracks, staring into the distance. "What's wrong with Draco?" Jason asked. "I forgot to tell you that here there are a lot of ducks. I do mean a lot. So keep a tight grip on Draco. I don't know if he has ever seen a duck before," Cynarra replied. For his part, Draco had to be dragged forward; approaching the area of the ducks was an adventure on which he was reluctant to embark. "Come on, Draco. They won't bite. But you don't bite them either," Jason said. Draco's ears perked up when he heard the quacking. He sniffed the air, trying to understand what these birds were but he could not relate to their sound or smell. "Maybe we shouldn't take him too close?" Jason asked Cynarra. "We better be careful. Let's just walk by the ducks. We will see others here and perhaps Draco will get used to them," she said.

There was another pond, surrounded by a fence, where the three stopped. "The parliament building is over there," Cynarra said, pointing. "We are in the heart of Athens, where the king walked and spoke with his advisors and now where our government rules," she continued. Suddenly Draco began barking. Looking down, Jason laughed. "The turtles!" he said. In the pond, in fact, there were many turtles, stacked on top of one another, sharing the sun. One had moved and had jumped into the water; this alarmed Draco, who had never seen these animals before either. "Draco! They are just little turtles. Look!" Jason said, as he pulled Draco closer to the enclosure. Draco, however, dug in his feet, determined not to approach. "Awww, he is scared. Don't force him, Jason. Let's just watch the turtles for a few minutes," she suggested. Draco sat down at a safe distance while they all watched the barely-moving reptiles.

"Come," Cynarra said, leading the two down another path away from the pond. "I want to show you something else from our ancient history," she said. After walking through a lane lined with palm trees, the three came into a clearing; among the grass and shrubs were some ancient ruins, Corinthian columns and fragments, strewn on the ground. Draco hopped up on the base of one. Cynarra and Jason sat down on a column lying on its side. "Imagine, Jason, that thousands of years ago someone may have been leaning against this column. Perhaps it came from a temple, where they were imploring their gods for some favor. Perhaps it came from a palace of a powerful leader; maybe he put his hand where you are sitting and wondered about the future of this land. The ruins are signs of the greatness of Greece and they still breathe our history for those who listen," she said dramatically. Draco scooted himself into a lying position on top of the column base and put his chin between his paws, looking first at Jason, then at Cynarra. He then closed his eyes.

"Draco feels right at home here," Jason whispered. "Let him dream a little bit," Cynarra suggested. A gentle breeze blew across the area as Jason and Cynarra savored the moment in silence.

After a few minutes Jason whispered: "Maybe we should

wake him up." Draco, in fact, was whimpering in his sleep.

"Sounds like a bad dream," the boy continued. "We should continue anyway," Cynarra replied. So Jason called out gently "Draco! Draco!" The dog looked up, stood, stretched his hind legs and then wagged his tail; he was ready for the next adventure.

"Where shall we go now, Cynarra?" Jason asked. "There is a place in this garden that few people know about. I haven't been there in years. But I will only show it to you, Jason, if you promise to not show or tell anyone about it. In fact, you have to swear to it. It's a secret only for very special people. We don't want tourists going there; we don't want your friends going there. In fact, we don't want anyone going there who might ruin it. Do you swear, Jason?" Now the boy's interest was peaked and he nodded. "You have to say it," Cynarra said firmly. "I swear that I will not reveal this secret place to any living person," Jason said. Cynarra smiled, then turned and set off down a narrow path towards an overgrown area of the park. Boy and dog followed.

Once in the general area, it took Cynarra a few minutes to find the mouth of the cave since it was completely overgrown. "It looks like nobody has been here since I was a child" she said, peering inside. "Cynarra, we can't go in there!" Jason objected as Cynarra took a step into the entrance. Draco whimpered and sat down. "There could be bats, or spiders, or a wild animal!" Jason continued, alarmed. "Aren't those all the things that boys like?" Cynarra asked, smiling. "Whoever told you that was not a boy!" Jason said, sitting down next to Draco. "O.K., you two stay here and I will just go in a few feet, just to see if it is safe," she said, taking out a small flashlight. "Cynarra...." Jason said, disapprovingly. "I'll be fine; this is our adventure!" Cynarra replied, stepping into the shadows. Soon she disappeared.

Minutes seemed like hours as Jason stared at the dark opening and Draco whined and became restless. "Cynarra, are you there?" Jason called out, but there was no answer. "Don't make us come in and get you!" Jason called out, having no intention of stepping into the cave.

After another fifteen minutes had passed Jason could stand it no longer. "Draco, I think we should go in. Maybe something happened to her. I don't have a flashlight so we will have to go in together, O.K?" Draco looked up at the boy with a wrinkled brow. Jason got up and dragged the dog towards the cave opening. Draco stopped at the entrance and sniffed. "What do you think, Draco?" Jason asked. Slowly, carefully, the boy and dog stepped in and disappeared into the darkness.

Jason stopped to let his eyes adjust. "Cynarra!" he called. "Cynarra, are you alright?" But there was only an echo in response. Draco, for his part, stood with his ears erect, staring straight ahead as he sniffed the air. The boy took one step forward. "Cynarra?" he called again. "O.K. Draco; there is no way but forward. I wish I had a flashlight!" Jason said. His eyes began to adjust to the darkness; he could see that the cave turned a corner. "Let's go over there and call for Cynarra," the boy said to Draco. "Cynarra!" he called, but no response. Once around the corner, Jason could see a faint glow in the distance. "Look, Draco! There's something there in the cave! Maybe she is there," he said. Just as he was taking a step, however, he heard an echo in the chamber: "Jason.......Jason......" the voice called out. "Where are you, Cynarra?" Jason called out. But there was silence.

"Draco, now I'm starting to get scared," the boy confided. He pulled the dog next to his leg and took another step forward towards the glow. "Jason....." the echo came again. Draco whined as they both froze. "Cynarra! Where are you? Are you alright?" Silence again. "O.K. Draco, let's go find her!" the boy said. Again a voice: "Go towards the light!" Jason shook his head. "Are you kidding me, Cynarra? 'Go towards the light???'" There was another echo. "Go towards the light and you will find your friend...." At this point Jason and Draco walked as fast as they could towards that faint glow.

Jason was unsure now whether Cynarra was joking with him

or in real trouble. Draco, sniffing the air, now pulled the boy forward. "Slow down, Draco! We don't know what's in here," the boy said. Draco, ignoring him, pulled Jason forward still. The dim light grew. "Cynarra?" Jason called, but there was no response. Suddenly Draco stopped in his tracks, his ears perked, and listened. He then barked and pulled the boy towards the light with all his strength. After turning several corners, they spied an opening at the end of the cave. As they approached, it seemed to grow in size. "Look, Draco! An exit! Maybe she is outside!"

When they finally left the cave, Jason had to shade his eyes since the light seemed so bright. Draco started to bark and pull on his chain. He dragged Jason behind him as he made his way across one path, around a hedge, and into an open area. There, on a bench, sat Cynarra.

"Cynarra! We have been searching for you everywhere!" Jason said, irritated. "I've been here the whole time," she said. "No you haven't. We heard voices in the cave," Jason insisted. Cynarra shook her head. "I walked through the cave, I remembered the exit, I came out here, and I sat on this bench. I figured that you would do the same so I just waited for you. And look, you did!" she said smiling. "Come on! You were in the cave! You were teasing me in there! At one point you said 'go towards the light.' We heard you. Even Draco had his ears up." Cynarra laughed. "'Go towards the light'? That sounds like a bad movie! Jason, I walked through the cave, came out, and sat down. I don't know what you heard in the cave, but it wasn't me," she said. Cynarra continued: "I'm sorry if I gave you a scare." Jason shook his head. "I wasn't scared." Cynarra glanced at his face and smiled.

"Perhaps we've had enough adventure for today. If my parents discover I haven't sold any flowers they will disown me," Cynarra said. "Pass by our shop for a coffee on the way?" Jason suggested. They both turned and looked at Draco. "Are you ready to go home, Draco?" Cynarra asked. Draco lifted his ears and looked eagerly towards her. "I think so," Cynarra said. So the three got up and headed back to the Plaka.

"The three adventurers are back!" Akil called out as they approached. Draco pulled Jason towards Akil, who stooped down to pat the dog's head. "Draco is drooling all over! And he has some cobwebs on him! That's a sure sign that all of you had fun! Tell me all about it over a coffee," he said as he went into the shop to prepare it. As the coffee smell wafted through the breeze, Draco let Akil know that he wanted a treat. The dog stuck his nose into the shop and sniffed. "O.K. Draco; we will have coffee and you can have something too," he said. A few minutes later Akil came out with a loaded tray: coffee, sugar, milk, and a small plate with a chew bone on it. He put it on a small table as the three sat in a circle with Draco looking on. "What's going on today?" a voice called out. Alexander turned the corner and approached as Akil scooted out and pushed in an extra chair. "You're just in time, friend," Akil said. "Come for a coffee and to hear about an adventure," he said laughing. Draco, feeling he had been forgotten, started to whine. "Ohhhh Draco, I could never forget you," Akil said as he handed him a bone.

"Can I tell them, Cynarra?" Jason asked eagerly. "You can't reveal where. You promised," Cynarra replied.

"We found a cave in the National Garden," Jason began. Cynarra rolled her eyes. "Very good at keeping secrets!" she said, but Jason continued. "Cynarra walked right in and disappeared. While we waited outside I started to wonder if something happened to her, since she was taking so long. So after a long time Draco and I went into the cave to look for her. It was so dark that I couldn't see my hand in front of my face! So we were in the cave and suddenly I heard this voice. It was a quiet voice and an echo..." Akil and Alexander were eager to hear the rest. "What did the voice say?" Alexander asked. "It said to follow the light. You see, there was this faint light at the other end of the cave. But I think the voice was Cynarra playing a trick on me," Jason said, looking at Cynarra. She shook her head. "It wasn't me! I walked straight through that cave and sat on the bench," she insisted.

Jason shook his head. "Anyway, so we saw this light and we walked towards it. Draco kept sniffing as if he sensed something. So the light became an opening and we headed towards it. The whole time I was calling for Cynarra but she didn't answer. That's why I think she was playing a joke. So we found the exit to the cave, went through it, and Draco dragged me down a path where we found Cynarra sitting in the sun. Now doesn't that sound suspicious to you?" the boy asked. Cynarra shook her head. Akil looked at Cynarra and looked at the boy. Alexander said: "I don't know what to think."

Cynarra looked at her watch and almost jumped out of her seat. "My parents ...!" she said. "It's alright, Cynarra. Alex spoke to me and we are ordering flowers from you today for the tables. Plus, we will put a basket of roses by the exit and have them for sale. So your parents should be happy with your earnings today. If you like, I can walk with you to the restaurant to make the arrangements," Alexander said. "That would be great. But my parents will still complain; you don't know them," she said, shaking her head.

As Cynarra and Alexander got up, Draco did also; the dog shook himself, then stood by Cynarra's side. She looked down and said: "Now Draco, I am O.K., I didn't get lost in the cave. You have to stay here with Akil because we have work to do now." The dog looked at her inquisitively. When the two began to walk away Akil held onto Draco's collar. "Stay here with us, Draco. You can go visit Cynarra later."

"How was your adventure?" Alex asked as Cynarra entered the restaurant with Alexander. "She disappeared into a cave and then appeared on the other side with no possible explanation!" Alexander answered. Alex left the kitchen to join them. "Now how did you accomplish that?" he asked as he reached over to remove a cobweb from her hair. Cynarra laughed. "I remembered a cave at the National Garden from when I was little. So when we found it, I walked through it. Everything else was Jason's imagination." Alexander looked at her. "Even the mysterious voices?" Cynarra smiled. "Well, that was part his imagination and part me, but don't tell him anything! Let him think that the cave is magical. That's what I used to think and I'm sorry that I grew out of that. You have to promise," she insisted. Both father and son raised their hand and said together: "I promise." Cynarra changed the subject. "Let's make arrangements for the flowers. I know my parents have come by to check on me so I want to have something to tell them," she said. "Why don't I come with you to the flower shop. Papa can watch the restaurant and we can decide on what we need." The three agreed and Cynarra and Alex set off.

Alex was the first to see Cynarra's parents standing in front of the shop. "Please let me do the talking," he said to Cynarra as he motioned in their direction. Cynarra seemed anxious. "Don't worry," he said.

As they approached the shop, Alex greeted the parents warmly. "Good day to you!" he said. "There is not much left of the day!" the mother snapped back. Ignoring the comment, Alex continued. "I am so grateful to your daughter. My father's restaurant is placing a large order and Cynarra has been helping us today. We have a lot of work ahead of us. Would you like to have a coffee with us once we return to the restaurant with our first load of flowers?" Cynarra smiled at Alex's ingenuity. "Oh, we don't want to get in your way. We just thought…." the mother's voice trailed off. "It's nice of you to stop by, Mama and Papa," Cynarra interjected. "It's been a busy day. Shall I see you tonight after my classes?" she asked. Both parents nodded and scurried off. Once they were some distance away both Alex and Cynarra began laughing.

"Well, we better get to work if we are not liars," Cynarra broke in. Alex took a deep breath to stop laughing. "O.K., I am ready. I have my father's list. We can get the flowers for the tables first and then decide on the rest. What do you have the most of?" he asked as they wandered into the shop. Alex looked around. "I wouldn't know where to start; you have so many flowers," he said. "Let's start with flowers for the tables outside since those need to withstand the most heat," Cynarra suggested. Alex counted the outside tables in his head, and they started to gather bunches of flowers and foliage. "We can't afford to buy flowers every day. If we could, I would be here every day buying them from you," Alex said. Cynarra looked at him, saw the expression in his eyes, and blushed.

Draco was sleeping outside Akil's shop. "What did you do to poor Draco, son? He's all worn out!" Akil exclaimed. "I don't think Draco is used to adventures outside the Plaka and the Acropolis. He was so excited at the garden and so scared in the cave. I think that took all his energy away! Look Papa, his leg is shaking. I think he's dreaming...."

Answered Prayers

Diana returned to the fish seller. "Can you keep this for me?" she asked. He obliged her, putting the fish back in cold water. Diana was so upset that she was shaking. "Let me think. Where would Daria go? What would make her run off? Athena, guide my thoughts and my steps please!" Diana started walking as she began to choke down tears. She spoke to herself in a low voice: "Calm down and think..." She took a deep breath. She then turned and looked in all directions. She saw the town, the streets, the trees, the Acropolis, the Areopagus, the gardens, the... Diana froze as a thought occurred to her and she ran off in the direction of the Acropolis.

By the time she reached the construction zone on the top of the hill, Diana was sobbing out of exhaustion, frustration, and worry. She stopped to gather herself before speaking with the foreman. "Could you please tell me where my husband Adelino is working today? I must speak with him for a moment." The foreman saw the tears in her eyes. "I hope everything is alright. He is working on the other side of that wall," he said motioning. Diana thanked him and set off.

When Adelino looked up and saw his wife and the state she was in, he dropped what he was doing and hobbled over to her. Diana fell into his arms. "Daria ran away in the marketplace," she sobbed. "I don't know where to find her...." Adelino said: "It's alright. She is here." Diana stopped crying. "What do you mean 'she is here'?" Adelino laughed. "I mean, she is here. She came running up that hill a little while ago. I looked up and there she

151

was, running towards me. She just jumped up and started licking my face as if she hadn't seen me in years. But then I grew alarmed because I thought that something had happened to you. So I sent Tiro out to look for you, so we will have to find him now. But as far as Daria, she is tied up firmly next to where I am working. Let me show you." Adelino put his arm around his wife and led her to the area where Daria was. The dog, seeing Diana, crouched in the corner, knowing that she had done wrong.

"I don't know whether to be angry, or grateful, or happy, or furious...." Diana trailed off as she looked at Daria in the corner, who was shaking out of fear of being punished. "Everything is alright, my wife. Why don't I keep Daria here today and we can deal with this situation at home? For now, we must find Tiro, but the foreman will not allow me to leave the job site also. Tiro said he was going to go the house to check on you and then to the market if you weren't there." Diana had calmed down by now. She laughed and looked at her husband. "I feel like a little girl, crying about her lost puppy." Adelino kissed her head. "My love, Daria is much more than that. She is family. I completely understand. Why don't you take a day for yourself and I can cook when I return home." Diana laughed again. "The thought of you cooking the fish I bought – which is still sitting at the market– would not give me a restful day! I will take care of dinner. The walk to the house and market will help me clear my thoughts," she said.

Diana made her way down the hill and returned to the fish market. The experience of losing Daria and its consequences had badly shaken her. "What is the matter, Diana?" the fish seller asked her as she approached his stall. She leaned against the stall. "Something terrible almost happened, but it didn't. Athena answered my prayers" she said. "Well, that is a cause for a celebration. Here, along with your fish, I am going to give you some of my fresh catch. Do you eat *kalamari*?" Diana smiled. "I have, but we cannot afford it." The fish seller smiled. "Today you will eat kalamari since the gods have smiled on you." He prepared a package for Diana, who thanked him profusely. "Just ask the goddess to smile down on me also. She hears your prayers," he said, bidding her good day.

Diana made a stop on her way home to see her sister, Kalliope. "What a pleasure, sister," Kalliope called out. "Let me help you with those packages," she said, sniffing. "This is fish! We need to put it in cold water while we visit," Kalliope said. Diana kissed her sister and said: "I can't stay, sister. But I wanted to invite you and your family to our home for dinner tonight. The fish seller gave me some *kalamari*, which we rarely get to taste, and Tiro has never had. Come share it with us, and help me figure out how to cook it! Plus, it's a little celebration." She paused, looking at her sister, wondering if she would laugh. "What?" Kalliope asked. Diana smiled. "Daria ran away again..." Kalliope took a breath in, knowing how much the dog meant to them. "But thank the gods, she ran straight up the Acropolis. So another tragedy of the lost dog was averted. So we are going to celebrate," she said. "We will be there. And I will bring some bread and wine," Kalliope said, hugging her sister.

Tiro was coming down the street when she left her sister's house. "Mama!" he called out, and ran towards her. "Daria..." he began. "I know, son," Diana interrupted. "I have been up the Acropolis and down again. Now be on time for dinner," she said. "We have something special." Tiro smiled and ran back towards the hill.

"You were a bad girl today," Adelino said to Daria at the end of his shift. "Diana was so upset and tired and we all would have been so worried about you," he continued as he untied her rope to walk home. "Have you forgotten what happened last time we lost you?" he asked. Daria looked up at the man with her tail between her legs. "What's wrong with Daria?" Tiro asked, when he rounded the corner to gather his things. "She's a bright girl. She knows she ran away and did wrong. We just have to make sure it doesn't happen again," he said. "But Papa," Tiro objected. "Look how scared she is!" At this point Daria was trembling as both were talking about her. Tiro handed his supplies to his father and picked the dog up. "I will carry her down the hill so she doesn't think we don't like her anymore!" the boy said. Adelino laughed, patted his son on the back, and the two started out for home.

There was a sense of excitement in the air as Diana and Kalliope were preparing the dinner. Kalliope's husband Cisseus and their two small children were in back tending the fire to reduce it to charcoal. "We should do this more often, sister," Kalliope said. "You are right. It took Daria running away for us to celebrate together." She laughed. "Now that's a situation that we need to deal with later; I don't want to think about it now. Adelino will know what to do. That dog wants to be with him every minute of the day and night! Even I don't want to be with Adelino that much!" she said, laughing again. "Let's begin to prepare the vegetables," Kalliope suggested as she carried over the cabbage and cucumbers to start slicing.

"Mama, the fire is almost down!" the boy said, running into the house. Kalliope replied: "Tell your father to keep it hot until Adelino arrives since the fish will cook very quickly and we want to eat it fresh." The boy was excited. "Is Tiro coming too?" he asked eagerly. "Yes, your cousin is on his way, son," she said, and the boy dashed out.

Even at some distance away, Daria sensed the excitement at the house and began pulling on her rope, dragging Tiro behind her. "What is wrong with Daria?" the boy asked, laughing. The dog was sniffing the air. "I think she smells the dinner your mother is making," Adelino said. "Daria, be good!" Adelino reprimanded her as she tugged on the rope even harder. When the three got close to the house they heard voices and laughter. "I think we're having a party, Papa!" Tiro exclaimed. "Adelino!" he heard from inside. "Adelino and Tiro are here!"

Diana came out the door to greet her husband and son. "I invited my sister's family to come celebrate with us! Athena hears our prayers, I have a wonderful family, and the fish seller gave me *kalamari* to brighten our day!" she said. "What's kalamari, Mama?" Tiro asked. "If I describe it, you may not eat it. If you taste it, you will love it," Diana replied.

A moment later both families were gathered together behind their house while Adelino and Cisseus tended the fire. Suddenly, there was barking. "Daria thinks that nobody is paying attention to her!" Tiro said laughing. "Come on, girl," Adelino said, swooping her up in one arm as he chatted with Cisseus. The dog immediately relaxed, enjoying the scene from her secure perch.

A Journey Ends

Draco slowly opened his eyes and looked around as if wondering where he was. "Finally you woke up, you sleepyhead!" Akil said. By this time it was late afternoon and Alexander was sitting with Akil under the tree. "Are you hungry, Draco? I brought you a treat from the restaurant!" The word "treat" made Draco approach Alexander, tail wagging, tongue hanging out, gazing at him. "Just a minute my friend," Alexander said as he rose from his seat. "It's on the top shelf in the refrigerator," Akil called after him. A few moments later Draco was devouring the stew which was left over from the night before. "Draco knows who his friends are!" Akil said, laughing. "Or rather," Alexander responded, "who he can get a good meal from!" Akil nodded.

"Are you walking with us up to Acropolis this evening?" Alexander asked. Akil chuckled. "I don't want to but I need to," he said. "It will get easier," Alexander replied. Just then they heard: "Good evening!" Both men turned as Cynarra greeted them. "Come visit with us, Cynarra!" Akil said, pulling out a chair. "Can I make you a coffee?" he said, rising from his seat. Draco, for his part, stopped eating his stew and ran towards Cynarra. "I can only stay a minute. Maybe a quick cup," she said as Akil entered the shop. "Where have you been, Draco?" she asked, bending down to scratch his head. "I think he can't take himself away from Akil," Alexander said chuckling. "Well, this dog needs a bath!" she said. Draco, grasping the meaning, ran to Alexander and crawled under his chair. "Not today, Draco!" Alexander said. "What's wrong?" Akil asked, the tray of coffees in hand. "Our friend doesn't want a bath, just like our children when they were small," Alexander said. "I will send Jason around with Draco tomorrow so our friend can get his b-a-t-h," Akil said, spelling the word. "Come on out, boy," Akil said as Draco began to crawl out from under the chair.

"How are your studies going?" Alexander asked. "As long as my parents don't nag me, I can focus on passing my courses. When they come around the shop and ask me how many sales I have made, or why I don't want to stay in the Plaka, or why I want to study overseas, they make me upset and then I have trouble concentrating," she replied. "Does Alex support your studies?" Alexander asked pointedly. Cynarra knew this was a loaded question so she chose her words carefully. "Your son is a good man and he is very supportive," she said. Alexander nodded, wanting to ask more. Akil sensed this and gave his friend a look to say: "don't." Akil switched the conversation. "What a wonderful day with friends! Cynarra, you know you are always welcome here," he said as he filled her cup again.

"Well, I have a class in an hour so I have to go," Cynarra said, rising from her seat. "Thank you for your hospitality, both of you," she said. "Are you going to hike up the Acropolis with Draco?" she asked. Akil nodded. "If I want to live a long life my doctor said I must exercise. This is the easiest way, with my friend Alexander and Draco." The dog's ears perked up. Cynarra whispered: "Don't forget to bring our friend by tomorrow so we can give him a b-a-t-h." Akil laughed. "I won't forget."

A few minutes later the three of them, Akil, Alexander and Draco, set off across the Plaka for the Acropolis. "So what do you think of Cynarra and Alex?" Akil asked. "I've never seen the boy like this, my friend. He really likes that girl. But Cynarra is unusual. She doesn't want to stay here. She wants to go to university in England, she wants to travel, she doesn't want to settle in the Plaka. She's not like us. Alex, on the other hand, is content where he is. He would be content here or anywhere. But the problem is the business. I can no longer run the restaurant alone, so, more and more, it is falling into his hands. So though he likes Cynarra, he is engaged to the Plaka." Akil shook his head. "Too bad. Two nice young people. Who knows how it will unfold," he said as they continued towards the hill, Draco walking ahead.

"Are you alright?" Alexander asked Akil, who was huffing and puffing when they reached the top. "I'm just trying to keep up with you and Draco. I'm fine. I will get used to it," he said. "Now Draco," Akil continued. "Do you want to go to sleep already?" The dog sat down, tail wagging, looking at Akil. "Do you know I brought you a treat?" he continued as he took a small sandwich out of his pocket. Both men laughed when they saw the longing in the dog's eyes. "O.K. Draco. Let's sit a moment over there and you can have your meal," he said, nodding to Alexander. So the two men sat on a bench as Draco happily ate his snack.

As the sky turned from gold to gray, Akil stood up. "If I am late for dinner I will never hear the end of it! Shall we go, Alexander? Draco, are you going to be O.K.?" The dog looked up at him, wagging his tail. "Yes, let's head down my friend. Draco, I think it is time for you to sleep," Alexander replied. Akil rubbed Draco's head, the two men turned, then started down the hill. Draco watched them disappear, ran to his secret passageway under the fence, and onto the steps of the Parthenon. He looked out at the setting sun, eyes squinted, sniffing, content to be in his safe place.

Three Years Later

Draco was sleeping later these days and when he woke up the sun was already in the sky. He stood on all fours and stretched, first his back, then his hind legs. Like every morning, the first thing on his mind was Akil. A little more slowly than before, the dog made his way down the hill towards the Plaka.

Jason now worked with his father full time, having completed high school. The boy didn't yet know if he wanted to go to the university or eventually take over his father's business, so helping out at the shop seemed like a good idea for now. Akil smiled as he watched his son unload crates of water and soft drinks; the boy was becoming a man. Jason was inside the shop, putting the drinks into the refrigerator, when he heard his father call "Drrraccccooooooooo!" He laughed, knowing that the dog was now within sight and that a tail would be wagging. Pouring water into a bowl, he brought it out and put it on the ground. Draco was already at Akil's side, pressing against him, looking up at Akil, tail wagging wildly. "Did you have a good sleep, Draco? Did you have nice dreams?" the man asked. The dog whined, tongue hanging out, and jumped up. "You're too big, my boy," Akil said, bending over and embracing Draco's head.

Jason approached with a bowl of food. "Breakfast time, Draco!" he said. Draco ran to the water first and drank almost all of it; then he set upon the food.

"Cynarra is back in town, Alexander tells me. She finished her term at Cambridge and is home for the summer," Akil said. "Will she come see us?" Jason asked. "Awww, you know she will, and

159

Draco too. Maybe we better give him a bath before she comes, so she won't think we have been neglecting our friend," Akil continued. Jason nodded. "What about Alex?" Jason asked. Akil shook his head. "Cynarra is following her dream while Alex is working in the Plaka. I don't know what they are thinking..." he trailed off.

"Good morning!" Alexander called out as he approached the shop. "Hi, Uncle Alexander!" Jason answered. Over the years they had become so close that Jason now called him "uncle."

Draco ran to Alexander, his tail wagging wildly. "Remember the days when our friend used to jump all the way up and lick my nose?" Alexander said to Akil. "We're all getting old, my friend," he said, sitting next to Akil. Jason soon came with steaming cups of coffee. "Soon Jason will have grandchildren running around here and I will be just a useless old man!" Akil said. Jason piped up. "Papa, I don't even have a girlfriend!" Akil winked at Alexander. "You will soon enough, son," he replied.

Turning to Alexander, Akil asked: "And how are you my friend? How are things at home and at the restaurant?" Alexander laughed. "Alex is so excited that Cynarra is home for the summer. He's like a little boy. I keep telling him that Cynarra is a career woman and that he shouldn't think of her so much, but he says he can't help it. For weeks at the restaurant all he talks about is when she is coming home. And this morning he keeps talking about seeing her this afternoon, between the lunch and dinner shifts. So there it is. Feelings running high, but I still don't know what the boy and Cynarra are thinking."

Jason appeared with two plates; he had made breakfast without the men noticing it. "Son, you didn't have to do that!" Akil said, accepting the plate. "Look at this! You are better than my chef," Alexander exclaimed, accepting the plate of egg whites, black olives, fruit, and raw vegetables. "Come join us, Jason!" Alexander said. "I have to finish setting up here. You go ahead; I will come in awhile," he said. Alexander looked at Akil. "This son of yours has become very responsible. I remember when you were worried about him; he was running around the streets and failing his classes. Then things began to change. That was about the time that Draco appeared, no?" he asked. Akil nodded.

It wasn't long before Cynarra came by. Alexander had returned to the restaurant to help his son and Jason and Akil were in the shop making sandwiches. "Kalimera! Good morning!" she greeted them from outside. Draco was the first to greet her, running up to Cynarra, whining, wagging his tail and jumping up and down. When she bent down to pet him, Draco planted a big lick on her face."Dracccooooo!" she said, laughing. "I love you too! I miss you too, boy!" she said as the dog continued to jump and whine.

"Cynarra!" Akil called out, approaching her with open arms. Soon Jason joined them with Draco growing even more excited. When the dog started to bark, Akil reassured him. "Don't worry Draco. Cynarra didn't forget you!" Cynarra asked, "And how is our four-legged friend?" Akil looked at the dog and nodded. "He is here every single morning and stays all day; he follows me around everywhere. He is very attached to Jason also. But sometimes I worry about him. He is getting older; he sleeps longer and walks up the Acropolis slower than before. But his appetite is good and he knows he has a home here." Realizing he was being spoken of, Draco looked back and forth between Akil and Cynarra. "And how are you, my friend?" Akil asked, motioning to a chair. Jason disappeared into the shop to prepare coffee and snacks. "How is Cambridge?" Cynarra smiled. "Cambridge is wonderful but not easy. I have to study day and night just to keep up. But I love it!" Akil then asked: "Do you ever miss us in the Plaka? Draco often drags Jason to the flower shop to look for you." At this, Akil noticed that Cynarra's eyes teared up. "Yes, I miss it," she said.

"Coffee is ready!" Jason announced. "I've missed the Greek coffee," Cynarra continued. "You wouldn't believe how bad the coffee is in the U.K.!" Jason poured her cup. "You can have all the coffee you want; you can come here every day if you can," Akil said. After a few sips, Akil asked, "Have you seen Alex yet?" Cynarra took a breath. "Yes, and I will see him later. But it is difficult…" she trailed off.

It wasn't long before Akil's wife, Maria, showed up. "Maria!" Cynarra said, rising from her chair. "I heard you were back home and I was hoping you were here!" she said, handing Cynarra a plate of sweets. "You're going to get me fat!" Cynarra said. Akil rose to his feet. "What a joy to see you here," he said to Maria. For his part, Jason was in the shop preparing more coffee. "Where's Jason?" Maria asked. Akil tilted his head towards the shop. "He is a better shopkeeper than me!"

Maria sat down next to Cynarra. "Tell me about your adventures!" Cynarra paused and looked into the distance. "There is so much to tell; it is like another lifetime over there. I don't know what to say," she replied. "Well, tell me about the other students," Maria insisted. Cynarra smiled. "I lost count of the countries that other students are from. Africa, Asia, Europe, America, all gathered in one place. But they are not like the tourists like we see here in the Plaka; the students want to learn and progress and they seem so happy to be at Cambridge, just like me!" she said. "Is there anyone else from Greece?" Maria asked. Cynarra nodded. "There are two from Thessaloniki, but I am the only one from Athens," she replied. "What are you studying, Cynarra? I know you told me but I don't remember." "Business administration," she replied. "Tell me about your classes," Maria asked. Akil interjected: "Don't make it sound too good, Cynarra! I may come home from work someday and find a note from Maria saying 'Gone to Cambridge. Back whenever!'" They all laughed.

"What is England like?" Maria asked. "It is gray, it is historical, it is like a garden dotted with towns, it is beautiful," Cynarra replied. Maria wrinkled her forehead. "You will return to Greece, won't you?" she asked. Cynarra frowned. "I want to. But what if there is no work?" Akil interjected: "There is always the flower shop!" They all laughed. "What about the people?" Maria continued. "What is amazing about Cambridge is that there are people from all over the world, in the same rooms, at the same time, every day! In my study group there is a girl from India, another from Africa, and a boy from Germany. The British are very polite, unless you go to a soccer game, of course. It feels like such a big world there!"

Maria looked at her husband. "We should go to the U.K. and visit Cynarra sometime," she said. Akil didn't reply. "I know what you are thinking! Money! Well, let's go anyway, or I will just go alone!" Akil laughed. "Yes, we can go, if Cynarra wants visitors. After all, she is a student," he replied. Cynarra smiled. "Of course you can come! You are like family. My parents still criticize my decision but you have always supported me. But what about Draco?" she asked, looking down at the dog who was looking at her. Maria broke in: "Yes, Draco will be confused if he comes here and doesn't find Akil. He may go wandering off. We will have to think of a solution to make sure that he is safe." Draco whined so Cynarra stroked he head as he rested his chin on her leg.

"Well, I have to go!" Cynarra announced. "Stop by later here and I can bring dinner," Maria suggested. "I can't; Alex and I are going out," she replied. Maria raised her eyebrows. "I see we have to have another conversation," Maria said. Cynarra laughed. "Tomorrow morning I will make breakfast here for us," Akil suggested. Cynarra nodded, Maria smiled, and Akil gave a thumbs up.

Draco followed Cynarra as she departed. "Dracooooooo," Cynarra said. "I'm not at the flower shop today so you have to stay with Akil; otherwise you won't be safe. Akil! Can you make sure Draco doesn't follow me?" she called out. "Draco! Draco!" Akil called, and the dog trotted over to him. Then Cynarra turned the corner and was out of sight.

"Now you go ahead; I can take care of everything. I already told Akil that I won't be walking up the Acropolis with him this evening," Alexander said. He could see that Alex was excited and eager to leave. "This is the first time I am taking Cynarra out since she returned!" he replied. "What if she has changed?" he asked. "Of course she has changed, son. You have changed also, whether you realize it or not. Why don't you head home and get ready. Everything here is prepared for the dinner shift; don't worry about the restaurant! You don't have to return this evening. Don't worry!" Alex replied, "It's not the restaurant that I'm worried about!"

Some hours later, Cynarra and Alex were outside of Athens in a quiet restaurant far away from the Plaka. Alex had resolved to not pressure Cynarra about returning to Athens; in fact, he would not bring it up at all. Tonight would be a special time to enjoy each other's company, he thought, and not to worry about the future. When he looked at her across the table, with her flowing black hair and sparkling dark eyes, she seemed the most beautiful woman who had ever lived. "I'm happy to be here with you," he said smiling.

"I have an interesting piece of news for you, though it is by no means certain," Cynarra began. "My professor in Cambridge is friends with the head of the business department here in Athens. He said that he has spoken highly of me and that there is a chance I could get a job as an associate professor at the university in Athens. But this would be after I finish my studies at Cambridge, which will take one or two more years." When she finished she looked at Alex and laughed. "I have never seen you smile so widely! I didn't know your face could make such a huge smile!" Alex kept smiling as Cynarra also noticed that his eyes had watered up.

Draco, for his part, was ready to go up to the Plaka but he was hesitant. "Oh, you're waiting for Alexander, my friend. He isn't coming this evening but you will see him tomorrow," Akil said. "Jason, would you like to walk with us?" Akil called out. "No, Papa, I want to see if we get any more customers; then I want to clean up so I don't have to do it in the morning. I will see you at dinner. Take care, Draco!" he called out. Then Akil motioned towards the Plaka as Draco began to trot besides him towards the hill.

"Are we getting old, Draco?" Akil asked, as they climbed the stairs. He noticed that Draco, who had a few white hairs now on his chin, used to run right up to the top but now took one stair at a time. "You keep well, my friend," Akil said with a bit of worry in his tone. For his part, Draco walked alongside the man, sometimes stopping to sniff along the way.

When they finally reached the top, the sun was sinking below the horizon. Akil sat down on a bench; Draco hopped up and sat beside him. "Draco, when will you come home with me? You're getting old!" Akil said, patting his head. " I understand that, my friend," the man continued. Draco laid down and put his chin on Akil's leg, looking up at him. "What is it about this place that is so important to you, Draco?" the man asked. He looked down and Draco had closed his eyes. "Oh, I see. It is a place of peace," Akil whispered.

Simple Joys

Daria woke up when she heard Adelino stirring in the kitchen area. As he was putting some bread and cheese into a cloth sack, he noticed the dog below, looking up at him wide eyed. The man smiled, cut a small piece of cheese, and handed it to her. "Don't tell Mama!" he whispered.

As he continued preparing to go to work, the dog followed him around. "We have to wake up Tiro now," he said in a low voice. Man and dog crept into the boy's room. "It's time to get up, son," he said. Tiro opened one eye. "Alright Papa," he replied. Daria licked his hand. By the time Adelino returned to the kitchen, Diana was up also. She always wanted to start and end their day together.

Tiro rubbed his eyes as he sat down to a breakfast of barley bread dipped in watered-down wine with some sliced cheese on the side. "Will you come to the Acropolis today, Mama?" Tiro asked. "Daria and I may walk up around lunch time after I go to the market," she replied. Daria had long since settled into the routine of spending the day with Diana; several times a week they made their way up the hill to share lunch with Adelino and Tiro. "Make sure Daria is fastened in that harness that Tiro made," Adelino said. "She has gotten loose too many times," he said, winking at the dog. "She's so attached to you! What would Daria do without you?" Diana said. "Well, I hope you would also say: 'what would I do without you!'" Adelino said, getting up from his chair and kissing his wife on the forehead. Diana laughed as Tiro rolled his eyes.

Once the men left for work Diana started her chores with Daria following her wherever she went. "I wish you could help me clean the floors," she said. Daria sat down and looked at her. "After we straighten up the house we can go to the market," she continued. Daria, recognizing the word, wagged her tail. "You go lie in your bed while I wash the floors," she said as she spread the soapy water. Daria dashed off into her corner.

As they made their way up the Acropolis later that day, Daria pulled on her rope to try to arrive before Diana. Occasionally the dog stopped to sniff the air; Diana had prepared a warm dish with fish from the market that morning and the aroma was surrounding them. It was a strenuous climb to the top but Diana made the effort to spend some time with her husband and son during their work day because she enjoyed their time together and also because she wanted to keep an eye on Adelino and Tiro, to make sure they didn't injure themselves.

"My favorite girls!" Adelino called out when the two were within sight. Diana let the rope drop and Daria ran to Adelino as if she hadn't seen him for months. As she jumped up and down, trying to lick his face, Adelino bent down to receive her kisses. When Diana approached, he rose and opened his arms. "My queen," he said. Diana laughed.

The three sat down on some marble blocks, using another stone for their table. Daria sat next to Adelino, her eyes following his hands as he unwrapped the bread and cheese. When Diana looked away he snuck the dog a morsel. "How is your morning, son?" Diana asked Tiro. "Today they let me work on one of the outer columns," he said with pride. "Until now they haven't trusted me with important pieces," he continued. Diana wrinkled her forehead. "Are you being careful?" she asked. The boy nodded. "What about your father? Is he being careful?" she asked. Adelino said: "Why don't you ask me?" Diana continued to look at her son. "Because you always say: 'yes, I have been safe! I haven't done anything all morning! No cause to worry,'" Tiro looked at his mother, then at his father. "Papa has been safe;

everyone here likes him. They all come and say hello to him every day. The foreman likes Papa, so he doesn't give him anything to do that would be a risk for him," he continued. Diana nodded. "That's what I like. Details!" she said. There was a little whining next to Adelino's leg. Daria wanted to join in; if not in the conversation, at least in the food. "Why don't you give Daria a little bread?" Diana said. Adelino replied, "I thought you would never ask." He handed the dog some bread, and when Diana wasn't looking, another small piece of cheese.

Diana opened the pot that she had brought up the hill and the odor of freshly made fish stew filled the space. Daria began to sniff the air; Adelino smiled and Tiro' eyes grew large. "Mama, how did you find time to make this?" he asked. "Well, I almost tripped over Daria doing it; she kept following me around. The pot was heavy; can you carry it down after work, son?" she asked. "Sure Mama. I feel bad that you have to climb this hill..." he trailed off as he loaded the stew on a dish. "I come because I want to," she replied. Again, next to Adelino's leg, there was whining. "Just a little bread dipped in the sauce," Adelino said, as he handed another morsel to Daria. "Where does she store all that food?" Diana asked, as they looked at the long-legged slim little brown and white dog. "I think she burns it off by worrying," Adelino replied.

"Have you seen Pheidias? Does he still come up there to check on progress?" Diana asked. Tiro shook his head. "I don't think he likes the sun..." The boy trailed off when Adelino put his finger to his lips. "The stones have ears," his father whispered. "It is the statue of Athena that holds his attention, from what I hear from the other men," Adelino said. "His planners come up to see us sometimes but they don't come to our area. Since we have been working here for years, they know they can trust us. They spend more time looking at the work of the newer men and at the more detailed work over there," Adelino said as he pointed to the other side of the construction zone. "Do you think Athena will bless us since we are working on her temple?" Tiro asked. "Oh, I think she already has," Adelino replied. There was a whining from below; Diana laughed. "Someone thinks she has been forgotten," she said, tilting her head towards Daria. "Athena has blessed you also, Daria. She rescued you from being lost. Athena has blessed all of us. She brought me back to work. She gave us a wonderful son. She gave me a wife who is my queen…" "If you don't stop I am going to start crying," Diana said. Adelino took her hand, looked her in the eyes and said, "Thank you for coming today, my wife."

Daria had a keen sense of time and, sensing it was the hour for them to go, she started pulling on her rope. "Someone wants to go home," Adelino said laughing. "She knows that you have to get back to work. She also knows that her dark corner in the house is the perfect place for a nap this afternoon. So we will just gather our things and be off. I will see you both at sundown for dinner. Tiro, keep an eye on your father. If he tries to lift something too heavy, stop him. If he becomes cross with you, he will have to deal with me later." Tiro nodded. Adelino said, "Yes, Mama," and laughed.

A few minutes later, Daria was yanking on her rope, eager to quickly lead Diana down the hill so they could settle inside their cool home.

Fear

"Why is Draco not here yet, Papa? It's already ten o'clock. I haven't seen him anywhere in the Plaka. Should I go look for him?" Jason asked. Akil looked at his watch. "The last time he was this late was when he got a thorn in his foot," the boy insisted. "If he is not here in an hour then I will go up the hill, if you can handle the lunch crowd, son." Jason nodded.

Akil found himself repeatedly looking in the direction of the Acropolis for any sign of the dog. Jason could sense his father's unspoken worry. "Papa, I have everything here ready. Why don't you go get Draco?" Akil stood up. "I think I will, son." Alexander rounded the corner at that moment. "Kalimera! Good morning! Heading off somewhere?" he asked. "Draco hasn't shown up so I am going up the Acropolis to find him. Would you like to come with me?" he asked. Alexander nodded. "Can Jason call the restaurant and tell Alex that I will be delayed and to keep doing what he is doing?" Jason called out: "I am already calling!"

The two men set off.

Alexander knew Akil well and he could see the concern on his face. To try to get his mind off speculating about Draco, he asked "Have you seen Cynarra lately?" Akil nodded. "Yes, she comes by almost every day. My wife wants to give her a party, but I don't know..." Alexander broke in. "That's a great idea! We could have it at the restaurant; a surprise coming-home party for just her friends. Oh, and her parents also. We could have it in the afternoon, when the Plaka is less busy, so Jason and Alex can leave their work for a few hours. Why don't you tell Maria to come by the restaurant so we can talk about it." Akil laughed. "What have I unleashed! I will tell her, my friend," he said.

It was about thirty minutes later, after climbing the hill and looking around, that they came upon the dog, who seemed unable to walk. "Draco!" Akil called out, a lump in his throat. "What happened to you? Did you hurt your foot again?" he asked, sitting down on the step next to the dog. Draco licked his face, then buried his head under Akil's arm. "Something is wrong with his leg," Akil said as he stroked the dog to calm him. "I think we need to get Draco to the veterinarian. This is worse than the last time. He can't use his leg at all!" Alexander added. "There is one I know who comes to the restaurant. We can bring Draco to him; I will ask Alex to make the appointment. But first we have to get Draco down the hill." Before he had finished speaking Akil was already picking up the dog. "But he is heavy and there are many stairs. You might hurt your back," Alex objected. "I would rather have a bad back for a few days, my friend, than Draco doing more serious injury to his leg. I am O.K., we can make it down together and make a few stops." The three set off down the hill.

"Akil, my friend," Alexander said, as they paused for a breath. "Let me head down before you. I can ask Alex to contact the veterinarian and to have my car ready. Unless you want me to stay with you," he asked. "Thank you so much, my friend. Yes, please make the arrangements. If you have your car at the edge of the Plaka, then I will head straight there. And if you could tell Jason that I will at the shop later, but try not to alarm him." The two men agreed and Alexander headed down the hill.

Draco was not a small dog, and sometimes Akil struggled as he took one step at a time. Draco squirmed since he wanted to walk down the stairs himself, but Akil knew better. "Be calm, my friend Draco. You have to let me carry you down." His voice calmed the dog as Akil went down a few more stairs. "We will stop at that landing and rest," he said. Once he made it there, he put Draco down. The dog held his back leg off the ground. Akil looked down at him and his heart melted. He sat next to the dog who began to lick the sweat off his face. "Alright, Draco. Let's try to make it all the way down to the Plaka this time," Akil said as he picked him up.

When they arrived at the bottom of the hill, Akil found Cynarra waiting for him. "Alexander asked me to meet you here; I was at the restaurant. I will show you where the car is. How is Draco?" she asked, looking first at the dog, who was struggling to get down to greet Cynarra, and then at Akil, who looked distraught. "I don't know who is worse off, you or Draco!" she said. This made Akil smile. "Do you want me to come with you, Akil?" she asked. Akil shook his head. "I think we will be too many; we will go and find out what happened to our friend Draco," he said. "Then we will see you back in the Plaka." "Cynarra?" Akil asked. "Can you stop by the shop to see if my son is doing alright?" Cynarra nodded.

Draco had never been to a veterinarian before, but the smell of antiseptic alarmed him; he squirmed to get out of Akil's arms as they walked into the front office. "Draco, I am here, Draco. Don't be scared," Akil said. Alexander touched Akil's arm, understanding that Akil was anxious and the dog was sensing that. "Who is the dog's owner?" the woman behind the counter asked. "I am," Akil said and signed all the papers. "Have a seat and the doctor will be with you shortly," she said, motioning to the waiting room. Akil set Draco down and both men sat. Draco put his head on Akil's leg and looked up at him with the saddest eyes Akil had ever seen. "It's O.K. boy," he reassured him.

After a few moments the doctor stepped out and greeted Alexander. "Thank you for seeing us on short notice," Alexander said. "This man comes to my restaurant at least once a week," he continued. "This is my friend Akil and this is his dog Draco. Draco can't walk on his leg. If I may add, he has also been more tired these past few months, as if he had half the energy of before. It may be his age or....we don't know." The doctor looked at Draco, then at Akil. "We can give him a complete examination, but first let's see what the problem is with his leg. Can you have him walk on it so I can see?" Akil got up and Draco followed him, hopping to avoid putting his back leg down and whining. "Alright, I understand. I believe the problem is in his foot, not his leg. Let's bring him back and check him out. Akil, can you carry him to the back area?" With that, man and dog disappeared while Alexander waited.

The minutes seemed like hours as Alexander wondered how the dog was doing and how his friend Akil was. About half an hour had passed when Akil came out of the back area. "What did the doctor say?" Alexander asked. "Our friend stepped on a piece of glass, which was still embedded in his foot. Then it got infected. Poor Draco. The doctor got the glass out; I had to hold Draco firmly and I needed the help of the nurse to keep him steady. Now the doctor is treating the wound and putting a big bandage on it. Draco will have to wear a cone on his neck, and won't be able to go outside for a week. In a few days we need to have his bandage changed; after one week we will bring him back to see if he is healed. I also have to give him an antibiotic pill for the next few weeks; but that's the easy part. I can hide that in his food..." Alexander nodded. "Draco is used to his freedom. He isn't going to like staying inside for a week, and he will hate that cone. How will he eat?" Akil responded, "We can take it off when he needs to eat, but we can't let him take his bandage off. The doctor said that the medicine needs time to work. Since we haven't brought him in before, the doctor is giving Draco a complete check up."

A few minutes later the doctor came out and motioned for Akil to come to the back room. "How old is Draco?" he asked. Akil shrugged. "He came to us from the Acropolis so I don't know," he answered. "If I had to guess, I would say he is between eleven and thirteen years old. He is in amazing health for that age. I can see that you are very attached to him as he is to you. Now for his leg, we know how to treat it. Just prevent him from chewing off that bandage, keep him indoors until he heals, and that will be fine. But I found something else. Let's sit down here," he said. Akil's heart began to race. The doctor took Draco off the table and put him down next to Akil. "Do you feel this bulge on Draco's side?" the doctor asked. "Yes; I just thought that Draco was getting fatter, just like me as I become older," Akil said. "Well, I would think that also, but this is only on one side. I took some blood work and did some more tests; I will have the results when you return in a few days. But I suspect that Draco has cancer…" The doctor kept talking but Akil could no longer hear him. He just wanted to take Draco and go home. After a few minutes he tuned in again in time to hear the doctor say "…and we will talk about this more thoroughly once I have the test results."

When Akil left the back office, Draco in his arms, and entered the waiting room, Alexander saw that his face was white. "What is wrong, my friend?" he asked, but Akil did not reply. When they were near Akil's house, he told Alexander that the doctor took some tests. "He found a lump on Draco but he doesn't know what it is. In a few days he will have the results," he said. Alexander reassured him. "I am sure it is nothing. Draco has a long life ahead of him." Akil smiled. "Please don't say anything to anyone about the lump. We don't know anything yet." Then after a pause, he continued: "I don't know which is going to be more difficult: waiting for these test results, or telling my wife that she will be babysitting Draco for the next week or more." Alexander laughed. "I think your wife will be the greater challenge." After thanking him, Akil got out of the car, lifted up Draco, and carried him to his front door.

Maria was an organized woman and she shunned surprises. Akil knew this, and was prepared for his wife to put up a fight when he brought Draco into the house unannounced, but there was no other alternative. He didn't have time to call her since all of this had happened so fast; he prepared for the worse. He opened the door and walked in as Maria was coming out of the kitchen. She opened her mouth, but then she paused. She saw Draco with the cone on his head, his hind foot wrapped in a large bandage and, most of all, she saw the distraught look on her husband's face. Immediately she dropped her defenses. "What happened?" she asked. Akil took a deep breath; he put Draco down on the carpet, sat down on the sofa, and looked down, closing his eyes. Maria sat down next to him and put her hand on his leg. Akil took a deep breath and said, "Just give me a minute," keeping his eyes shut. "You're all sweaty. I will get you some cold water and a treat for Draco." Hearing his name, Draco tried to get up but Akil reached out and pulled him next to his leg.

Once he had gathered himself, Akil sipped the water while his wife sat next to him. "I need your help, Maria. Draco has an infection in his foot and we have to keep him off it as much as possible for a week. He has to have the bandage on for a week; after that he may be able to return to his normal routine. I want us to keep him here this week. I know it will be hard for all of us, including Draco, because he loves to sleep at the Parthenon. But if we don't cure the infection it could get worse," he said. To Akil's surprise, Maria didn't offer any objections. "You go to work this week and I will watch Draco. That is not a problem. But there is something else. What is it?" she persisted. Akil took a breath. "The doctor found a lump on Draco's side. Here, you can feel it here," he said as he guided her hand to the lump. "The doctor said that it might be c..... I can't say the word. It's the word that starts with a 'c.' In a few days we will know for sure. I don't want anyone to know until we are sure," Akil said. Maria looked at her husband with great affection; to some he seemed a hard man on the outside but his capacity to love was so great that it pained her at this moment. "Draco is family. We will do everything to make sure he lives a long and happy life." Akil leaned over and kissed her as Draco whined.

"I must go and help Jason at the shop. Can you watch Draco?

He will probably be restless and will want to come with me." Maria responded confidently, "I will handle Draco, you go to work. But let's not let him see you leave. I will give him a treat in the back bedroom while you slip out," she said. Akil squeezed her hand. "I will pick him up and put him on a pillow in the corner. For the treat, make sure he doesn't drop it inside his cone, and…." "Husband," Maria broke in, "I can handle this. You go to work and help our son. Draco is safe here." Akil laughed at himself and once Draco was munching on his treat in the bedroom, Akil slipped out the front door.

Jason peppered his father with questions all day. "What did the doctor say? How did his foot get infected? Can't we keep Draco at home always? What kind of tests did the doctor do? Why did the doctor take a blood test? Is Draco going to be O.K.?" With every answer Akil tried to reassure his son, but Jason sensed that Akil was holding something back. "Are you worried about Draco, Papa?" the boy asked. "Son, Draco will be fine!" the man replied. Jason looked at his father skeptically, then went back to work in the shop.

Later that afternoon Maria called Akil at the shop. "Is everything alright?" Akil asked, alarmed. "Yes, everything is fine here. I just wanted to let you know that I still want to give Cynarra her party; Draco will be fine, but let's not say anything to her about his tests until afterwards. And can you tell Alexander the same? He will tell Alex who will tell Cynarra." Akil nodded. "Already done; I swore Alexander to secrecy. I am sure he will come by later today and I will repeat it…" After the call, Jason asked "Secrecy about what?" Akil patted his son on the shoulder. "Now what kind of a secret would it be if I spread it around, son?"

It was a few hours later that Alex showed up with Cynarra. "Welcome! Welcome!" Akil said, pulling out some chairs next to an outdoor table. Cynarra studied his face. "Akil, how is Draco?" she asked. So Akil sat them down and recounted the doctor visit, but he left out the part about the tests to diagnose cancer. "So he will be alright in a week?" Alex asked. Akil nodded. "It will be so funny to see Draco with a cone around his head," Cynarra said laughing. She then grew serious. "But poor thing! He is such an active dog; how will he stay inside for a week? And how will you get him to sleep at night? He always wants to go up to the Parthenon. What is it about that place and this dog?" she asked, not expecting an answer. "We will manage somehow. There are three of us; Maria is watching him today." Cynarra grew pensive. "Draco needs us now."

Jason showed up with coffee for everyone. "Alex, can you help me with something in the shop for a moment, please? Jason, you can visit with Cynarra if you like," Akil said rising. Alex followed him into the shop. "Maria wants you to contact her about the party for Cynarra. She wants to have it on Friday afternoon, so we can close down the shop for a few hours. Can you speak with her later today to make arrangements?" Alex nodded and smiled. He started to turn but Akil stopped him. "One more thing. Did your father tell you anything about Draco?" Alex shook his head. "Just that he injured his foot but he didn't tell us any details. Why? Is something wrong?" Akil shook his head. "No, nothing. I was just wondering if I was repeating the same story." He patted Alex on the shoulder and the two walked out of the shop.

Akil skipped his usual walk up the Acropolis because he was concerned about how his wife was getting along. "Son, why don't you head home and see how your mother is doing with Draco? I will see if we have any last customers then close up the shop." "Sure Papa," the boy responded, as he finished wiping the counter. "This dog has more energy than all of us put together!" Maria proclaimed as Akil walked in a few hours later. "Thank you for sending Jason home early so I could get dinner started," she said smiling. Maria looked into Akil's eyes. "How are you, husband?" Akil looked down and responded, "I am good. I am great!" As he moved out of the hallway, Maria stopped him and whispered in his ear, "Tomorrow morning I am going to the church to say a special prayer to the Virgin for our Draco. You say a prayer also because she will hear both of us." Akil, never a religious man, replied: "I will make the same prayer," and he kissed his wife on the cheek. Jason had taken the cone off Draco and was playing with him on the carpet while the dog was lying on his side. But when Draco saw Akil, he got up on three legs; Akil put his hand out. "Stay there Draco. Stay off that foot. I will come to you," he said as he sat on a chair next to the dog, who scooted up against him. "I'm going to let you two play while I help your mother," he said, as he got up. "Papa, can Draco stay in my room tonight?" Jason asked. "As long as his cone is on for the entire night and you try to keep him off that foot. And you will probably have to take him out once to go to the bathroom. Can you do that, son?" Jason nodded.

Draco lay in the corner as the family ate dinner that night. "Draco looks confused, Papa," Jason said. "He doesn't understand why he isn't on the Parthenon or why he has that cone on. He probably thinks he is being punished; maybe after dinner we can take his cone off and you can play with him again. With your mother's permission, we can also give him some table scraps." Akil looked at Maria with eyebrows raised; she nodded.

When it was time for bed, Jason brought Draco into his room and made a bed in the corner with a blanket. He shut off the light and lay down but soon became aware that Draco was sitting in front of his door, waiting to get out. "Draco, come and sleep," Jason pleaded. The dog whined, so Jason got up, put him next to his bed, and patted his head to try to calm him down. The boy dozed off, only to be awoken again by Draco's whining and pawing at the door. This happened over and over again until morning.

Akil was up early making the coffee. Soon Maria joined him and started preparing breakfast. She touched Akil's arm: "Listen." They paused and heard Draco's whining. "Maybe Draco needs to go out. I will take care of it," Akil said. When he opened the door, Draco hopped to the front door. "I think we have a bathroom emergency!" he said laughing. He put on Draco's leash, picked up the dog, and disappeared out the front door.

When he returned a few minutes later, Maria told Akil that Jason got little sleep the night before because Draco was so restless. "Let's let Jason sleep," Akil replied. "I can manage the shop; he can catch up on his rest. Tonight I will take Draco; I can sleep on the sofa. We will take turns so it's not too difficult for one person." Maria looked at her husband skeptically, but only nodded. "Have your coffee, husband. We will manage here fine and I will keep Draco off that foot as much as I can. He has so much energy!"

News

When Jason got up later that morning, Maria called Akil at the shop. "I am going to keep Jason at the house today, unless you need him there. He can take care of Draco and keep him from walking on his foot." Akil agreed. "That is a very good idea. I think I will bring the car this week; that way I can bring Draco and Jason with me. We can tie him up here at the shop, put a blanket down, and put some chairs nearby for visitors. That way you can get your preparations for Cynarra's party done and you won't have to worry about Draco or Jason."

Over the next few days this plan worked well, until the day arrived when Draco needed his bandage changed and Akil would get the test results. "Papa, let me come with you!" Jason said, but Akil shook his head. "Son, someone has to tend the shop." Maria then stepped in, "I will come with you!" but Akil insisted, "It isn't necessary. Everything will be alright." Even Alexander stopped by the shop to arrange coming along. "You have to help Alex with the party preparations. After all, it is tomorrow!" Akil said.

In reality, Akil wanted to go alone so that whatever the news was, he would have time to digest it.

Akil left early for the appointment that morning, carrying Draco in the car with him. Without telling anyone, he first drove to the local church, which he hadn't stepped into in years; he parked his car, lifted Draco, and walked in. It was dark but he could see the shimmer of the golden icons and he could smell the faint odor of incense. Akil sat in back and put Draco on the floor next to him. Spotting the icon of the Theotokos, the Virgin Mary, he made the sign of the cross, knelt down, and prayed.

"Now it is all in God's hands," Akil said to Draco as they got back in the car. Draco tried to lick him, but the cone got in the way.

Draco began to shiver out of fear once he smelled the antiseptic in the veterinarian's office, but Akil held him tight. "How is our friend?" the lady at the front desk asked. "He is a handful, but the foot doesn't seem to be bothering him as much," Akil responded. Just then the door opened. "Kalimera! Good morning!" the doctor said, motioning them in. "Let's take a look at that foot, clean it up again, and give Draco a fresh bandage. If he is walking normally in two days you can take the bandage and cone off but keep him indoors until Monday. After that, if everything is healed, he can resume his normal routine," the doctor said. "But what about the test results?" Akil asked. "We will talk about that once we take care of Draco," he responded. "Why don't you go ahead and hold Draco while I take a look at this foot," he continued.

After his wound had been washed and the new bandage was in place, Draco was at the door and ready to go. "Sit down for a moment please," the veterinarian said, motioning to a chair. "I don't know how to word this to make it better, but here it is: Draco has cancer. It is on his liver. These are the three options: surgery, radiation, or do nothing. As far as surgery, it is risky and he may not survive. But if successful, it could give him a few more years. The second option is radiation. This could diminish or eliminate the tumor and could also give him a few more years, but it would greatly reduce his quality of life. Just like humans, dogs also suffer the effects of radiation therapy. But they have the disadvantage of not knowing what is being done to them and why. The third option is to let nature take its course, to continue to give Draco the great life he has with you, and to be with him as he goes through this. You see, Draco has no idea he has cancer. The only thing on his mind right now is going home with you.

Maybe it is best that way. In any case, it is your decision. Think about this and let me know." Akil asked, "If we do nothing, how long does Draco have?" The doctor glanced at the dog. "He gets a lot of exercise, and other than this, he seems in very good health. It could be months, it could be years. If you choose this route, watch for any behavior changes: loss of weight or appetite, sleeping abnormally long, loss of energy or any other behaviors that you haven't seen before. These could be signs of the progression of the cancer."

After thanking the doctor and paying his bill, Akil carried Draco to the car. He put the dog next to him and stared straight forward. "Let's not go home yet, Draco," he said as he started the car and drove towards the center of the city.

Akil parked as close as he could to the National Garden, took off Draco's cone, picked the dog up, carried him through the front gate and across the grass, until he found a bench in front of one of the fountains. He put Draco on the bench, sat down next to him, and gazed into the spraying water. Draco whined for attention; Akil patted him on the head. Draco scooted down and lay on the bench, putting his chin on Akil's leg and closed his eyes. Akil closed his eyes also, trying to push down the emotions that were bubbling up from his heart.

They stayed there for a long time. Akil thought about his prayer that morning. "Please take care of our Draco," he repeated. Draco opened one eye, looked up at Akil, then closed it again.

Akil, not being one to show emotion, waited until he felt in control of his feelings. Then he stood up, picked up the dog, and said: "Now it is time to go home, Draco."

Maria and Akil had been married over twenty years. She knew Akil so well that she could read what was on his mind from the expression on his face. So when he walked into the house after the appointment, carrying Draco, she knew what the veterinarian had said. "How long does he have?" she asked. "With surgery, maybe two years; without surgery, maybe years or just months. But he may not survive surgery. I can't take that chance. I have to tell the doctor that we will not do the surgery. Also, I don't want anyone to know, not Jason, not Alexander, nobody." Maria thought a moment. "I think it is a good decision to not do the surgery, but I think it is a bad decision to not tell anyone. They have a right to know," she said. Akil shook his head. "How would you feel," Maria began, "if Alexander found out that Draco was sick and he didn't tell you, and you only found out after Draco was gone? I would feel upset and betrayed. You have to remember that they are attached to Draco also. They have a right to know. But not until after Cynarra's party; I don't want her to be sad tomorrow," Maria said. She looked at her husband, still a handsome man with some grey hair now around his temples. Akil took a deep breath. "You are right," he said.

"I am going to go to the shop in the car and I will bring Draco." Maria interjected: "But what will you say to Alexander? He will come and ask you, you know that..." Akil thought. "Ummm, I can say that I have to talk with the vet in a few days and then I will have all the information. It is partially true," he said.

Secrets

When word got around the Plaka that Draco was at the shop, Jason found himself running in and out for most of the afternoon, making and serving coffee. Cynarra and Alex were the first to arrive. "I convinced my father to take care of the restaurant for a few hours since this is more important," Alex said. "How is our little friend?" Cynarra asked as Draco pulled on the rope to approach her. "Well, this is tough week for him, with his foot and the cone and sleeping at my house when he wants to be out in the open. So company will do him good," Akil said. "How are both of you?" Akil asked, noticing that they were now holding hands. "The university here is interested in hiring Cynarra next year. She could finish her doctorate from here as she starts as an assistant professor. Isn't that wonderful?" Alex said. Akil smiled since he knew what that meant for him. "Yes, that truly is wonderful," he said. Draco whined. "Can I take his cone off?" Cynarra asked. "As long as we make sure that he doesn't chew on his bandage," Jason responded as he set down a plate of baklava. "And how is Alexander?" Akil asked. "Oh, you will see. He wants to come see you as soon as we get back," Alex said.

Soon Alex left to relieve his father at the restaurant while Cynarra and Akil remained seated under the tree, sipping on their coffee. "I know that Maria is going to have a lot of questions," he said motioning in the direction of Alex's departure. Cynarra laughed. "Nothing is sure except for the fact that I will not get trapped in the Plaka for the rest of my life!" she said. "But Draco misses you," Akil continued. After a pause, he continued, looking down: "We all miss you." Cynarra began to respond, but a surprising emotion leapt to her throat so she stopped short. "I miss you too," she said quietly. "How is Draco?" she said. "He seems to be getting old. He doesn't move as fast as he used to. Apart from his foot, is he alright?" Akil remembered his wife's words, so he reassured Cynarra, "He is getting old, just like me!"

"Well, just as we were talking about them!" Akil called out as Alexander and Maria approached the shop. The two were deep in conversation but stopped short when they spotted Cynarra. "Cynarra!" Maria said as she kissed her on both cheeks. Draco was up in an instant, looking up at Maria and waiting for her greeting. "And you too Draco!" she said, patting his back. Then the dog followed Alexander to his chair, hopping on three legs. "Yes, I brought you a treat, Draco!" he said, taking a cracker and cheese out of his pocket.

Jason suddenly appeared with a bowl full of freshly cut watermelon. "Son, you're a good man," Akil said, kissing Jason on the head. The appearance of the watermelon made Draco excited; he started to try to trot around. "Draco, stay!" Akil said as he got up to get a paper plate. He put a few pieces of watermelon on the plate, cut them into smaller chunks, then put them next to Draco. After sniffing them for some time, since he had never had watermelon, he hesitantly licked one. Finding it agreeable, he tasted one. Then, in an instant, his plate was empty. "Papa, Draco ate all of his before you even started!" Jason said laughing. Draco, of course, was waiting for another helping.

Alexander also didn't want to spoil the joy of Cynarra's party the next day; so, finding no opportunity to ask Akil in private about Draco's test results, he headed back to the restaurant to help Alex prepare for the dinner shift. Cynarra also rose. "I better go spend some time with my parents, otherwise....well, you know them...." she said, and bid her goodbyes. When they were alone, Akil asked his wife, "Are the preparations for the party complete? Does Cynarra suspect anything?" Diana shook her head. "She thinks she is going out on a date with Alex. He will take her out but then will tell her that he forgot his wallet and needs to return to the restaurant. When they return we will surprise them. We will be behind the restaurant where the tables will be set up. We will even have some music," she said. Draco was curled up at Akil's feet. "Do you think we should bring Draco, Papa?" Jason asked, as he approached his parents. "Yes, son, I think we should," Akil replied, giving his wife a knowing look.

The Party

The next day arrived and Maria was up even earlier than usual. Akil was still on the sofa, sound asleep, while Draco was already following her around the kitchen. "Quiet, Draco," she said as she put the coffee on the stove to brew. She looked to see if her husband was awake, then gave Draco a bit of cheese from the refrigerator. She heard Akil stir; he sat up on the sofa and shook his head, as if trying to rouse himself. "How did you sleep?" she asked. "Up and down a lot; Draco kept wanting to go out and he kept shaking, trying to get the cone off. But I think I got a bit more sleep than Jason did the other night. I will be fine," he said, rising to his feet. Draco walked over to him and tried to lead him to the front door. "Now do you need to go to the bathroom or are you trying to go to the Acropolis?" he asked. "Better to be sure than sorry," Maria said. "But come, have a bit of coffee before you take him out," she said, handing him a cup. "My queen," he said, leaning over and giving her a kiss on the cheek.

When Akil and Draco returned, they found Jason up and at the table. "Why are you so hungry today, son?" Akil asked, laughing. Jason had a mouth full of bread and cheese, and two hard boiled eggs on his plate in front of him. The boy shrugged as Akil sat next to him. "I am going to the Plaka early today to set up," Maria began. "Cynarra's parents agreed to keep her away; they're going to ask her to do something, I don't know what. Alex has already told her that he is picking her up at her parents' house at 2:00p.m.; after that he will drive her to the edge of town, tell her he forgot his wallet, and be at the restaurant between 2:30 and 3.

187

So you two, and Draco, have to be there by 2:00. Can I rely on you to do that?" she asked. Jason nodded. Akil seemed to be dozing off as he bit his bread and cheese. "Akil, do you understand?" she repeated. He nodded. "Jason, can you give your father lots of coffee today, especially after lunch? I don't want him sleeping through the party," she said. Jason nodded again. "Yes, Mama, I will make sure he is there and awake." Then Maria sat down to finish breakfast with them.

Draco had no dreams the past few nights, but, rolled up in the corner of the kitchen, as he struggled to keep his eyes open, he looked up at Akil sipping his coffee and at Maria cutting a piece of cheese. He felt at peace as he dozed off. He then awoke when Akil called him. "Draco! Draco! Come over here, boy! Let's see how you are doing today!" he said. Akil then held out a treat for the dog.

Though his bandage was still on his foot, Draco seemed to be walking better. Akil, however, decided to follow the doctor's orders and keep it on for the full seven days. So when it came time to leave for work, he picked up Draco, called his son, and the three went down to the car.

At the shop Draco was settled under the tree while Akil and Jason tended to customers. The morning sped by until it was time to leave.

Draco wasn't sure what was going on as Akil picked him up and carried him over to the restaurant. It was nearly two o'clock and Jason walked beside him, carrying a huge bowl of fruit salad. "You didn't have to bring anything but yourselves!" Alexander called out of the kitchen as they circled around in back of the building. Maria looked anxious as she put flowers on the table. "She will probably notice that these are not expensive flowers," she complained. Akil put Draco down. "My wife," he said, "Cynarra will be overjoyed because what you have done is wonderful. Now let's finish with the flowers and have a toast together before they arrive. I don't think she suspects a thing!" he said. Maria stopped and thought a moment. "Yes, the work is done. Now it's time to start celebrating. Let's call Alexander out of the kitchen and have a toast." As they raised their glasses a few moments later, Draco looked up at Akil with fixed eyes. "Draco! You can have water to toast with us," he said as he got a bowl and filled it for the dog.

"I am going to watch for them," Alexander said. "When you hear me say: 'Alex!' in a loud voice, you will know that they are near. I have the music on very low. Once we surprise Cynarra, Maria, can you turn it up?" "I think we are all ready," he said. "Now Draco, you have to be quiet too," he said as the dog tilted his head and looked at the man.

It was only a few minutes later that they heard Alexander call out: "Alex! What are you doing back here?" There was a pause, then Alexander's voice could be heard again: "I think I saw your wallet on the table outside in the back." Maria motioned to Cynarra's parents, who had been waiting inside. A moment later, as Cynarra and Alex turned the corner, they all screamed, "Surprise!" Draco picked up on the excitement and started to bark, Cynarra's parents clapped their hands, and Akil and Maria pointed to the banner above, which said: "Welcome home Cynarra!" Maria then turned up the music as Cynarra continued to stand there speechless. Maria then approached her, took her by the arm, and led her towards the beverage table. "We want you to know that you are missed and loved," she said to Cynarra. "Can't you say something?" she asked. "Thank you; I am so surprised. How did you do this?" Cynarra's parents then approached. "Welcome home, daughter," they said as they handed her some white orchids.

"I know it's a strange hour of the afternoon, but you all have to eat!" Alexander said, as he brought out the dishes with Jason's help. Alex sat down next to Cynarra; she turned to him and asked, "But why?" Alex looked her in the eyes and said: "Because you deserve this and more." Akil then came over, holding a squirming Draco. "He wants to be close to you, but he still has his bandage on. Here, I will take his cone off so he can lick you also," Akil

189

said, chuckling. Cynarra reached over to stroke his head, but Draco intercepted her hand and licked it front and back. "Oh Draco," she said, "I love you too!"

It was a happy afternoon. Alexander and Jason were serving the food, Greek music played in the background, Draco feasted on his special plate of leftovers, and the others were gathered around Cynarra, who was telling stories about her life in Cambridge. "You should come back and stay here," her mother interjected. Cynarra was wise enough to leave that comment without a response, as her father continued: "The flower shop is a good business. You could expand it if you want...." Seeing where the conversation was headed, Maria stepped in. "Whatever you decide to you, we support you. Your friendship is important to us. Plus, we get to experience the outside world through you!"

As the afternoon wore on, Akil said: "We should get going; we have to open the shop for the evening crowd and you have to get ready for your dinner shift." Alexander nodded. "Akil, can you come with me inside for a moment?" Alexander asked. Once separated from the others Alexander asked: "Akil my friend, what about Draco? His test results?" Akil responded: "Can you come tomorrow morning, at about ten o'clock?" Alexander nodded. "And bring Alex and Cynarra if they are around." With that he turned and left. Alexander waited inside, looking at Draco playing with Cynarra. "I hope it is good news," he said to himself.

"You did a wonderful job," Akil said to Maria over dinner that evening. "Cynarra didn't suspect a thing. And you, son, also did a wonderful job. You worked so hard preparing the fruit salad and helping Alexander serve. Thank you." "Do you think Cynarra will return to live here?" Jason asked. "Part of that may depend on Alex," Maria responded. "But it also depends on if she finds a job here. One thing for sure: Cynarra would not spend one more day working in her parent's flower shop. She is meant to do greater things." Akil agreed.

After Jason went to bed, Akil sat on the sofa with Maria as Draco curled up at his feet. Akil took a deep breath. "Tomorrow I will tell the others about Draco," he began, "including Jason. I would rather keep it to myself, but you are right. They have a right to know. And I am going to tell them about my decision to not do surgery or chemotherapy; I hope that they agree. After that, I don't want to talk about it again." Maria squeezed his hand. "Will you stay out here with Draco again?" she asked. Akil nodded. "I better; he will drive both of us crazy if I bring him into our room. But he is worth it. Tomorrow we can take off his bandage," he said. Diana rose. "Let me get your some sheets," she said. Draco lifted his head and followed her movements; then put his head back down when she returned. "Good night, husband," she said. "Good night, my queen," Akil responded.

Challenges

Jason noticed that his father was pensive the next morning at the shop. Akil was silent as they took the rolls out of the oven and put sugar on them. After a few minutes he said to his son: "I invited Alexander to stop by at about ten o'clock. Perhaps Alex and Cynarra will come. We can offer them some coffee and something to eat. Perhaps we can have some sandwiches ready." "Yes, Papa," Jason said. Draco, meanwhile, sat outside the door of the shop, his head on his paws, keeping an eye on father and son.

"Kalimera! Good morning," Alex called out. "Good morning, good morning!" Akil responded. "Thank you for that amazing surprise yesterday!" Cynarra said. Alex laughed. "She really was surprised. I am glad that she didn't see that I had my wallet all along!" Akil laughed. "Come and have a coffee with us," Akil said, motioning to some seats set in a circle around a small table under the tree. Draco was nearby; Akil took his cone off, untied his rope, and brought him over to the circle. Jason then appeared with the coffee and sandwiches.

"Kalimera! Good morning!" Alexander called out as he rounded the corner. Akil pulled out a chair for him. "I am so glad that you enjoyed the party," Akil began. "Son, come sit here next to me," he said to Jason, pulling a chair beside him. "Besides my family here," he said, putting his hand on Jason's shoulder, "and Maria, who is at home, you are my family. Families talk about things, happy things and sad things, no?" Alexander nodded. Cynarra put her coffee down, focusing on what Akil was saying. "Draco is part of this family, no?" Akil paused and took a breath.

192

"I have some news about Draco," he began. Akil then explained the visit to the veterinarian, the cancer tests, and the bulge on Draco's side. "So the results of the tests came in, and our Draco here has cancer on his liver." Alexander started to interrupt but Akil motioned to him. "Let me say all of this so I only have to say it once. They can operate, which could prolong his life for a year or two, but Draco may not survive the surgery and the recovery would be long. They could also do radiation but our Draco would be miserable and the outcome is uncertain. If we don't do the surgery or the radiation, our Draco could live for months or years, but we don't know. I believe that the best choice is to not do the surgery or radiation, but I would bring him to the veterinarian regularly to monitor his health. In the meantime, we could make sure that the rest of his days are as happy as he has made ours. That is what I wanted to tell you."

There was a silence as these words sunk in. Draco, who had been sitting next to Cynarra, whined as he looked up at her, tears streaming down her face. He put his front paws on her leg to try to lick her face. Jason was looking at the ground, motionless. "He's like family; of course we will take care of him," Alexander said. "He's a very sensitive dog," Akil began with a lump in his throat. "He senses when we are sad or upset. So we have to try to be happy for his sake and ours," he said. Draco whined as he tried to console Cynarra by licking her. "I'm sorry," she said. Akil shook his head. "No, that is alright, Cynarra. This has to sink in. I didn't want to say anything until after your party. I am sorry for upsetting you," he said. "It's O.K. It's just a shock. I thought Draco would always be here. The Plaka and Draco; whenever I returned they would always be here. This is just a shock," she said. When Alex put his arm around her, she began to cry. Alex held her while Draco looked up at both of them and whined. "Come on, Draco!" Akil said. "You let Cynarra have a little bit of space. We are going to have a wonderful day today, and tonight you get to have your bandage removed. Then, if you are all healed, you can return to your beloved Acropolis," Akil said, stroking his head.

"We will go take a walk and we will be back," Alex said, rising with Cynarra. Alexander rose also. "I have to tend to the restaurant but I will also return later," he said. Akil and Jason were left alone, sitting under the tree with Draco. "How are you, son?" Akil asked. "I'm scared, Papa." "So am I, son," Akil responded, pulling Jason over and kissing the top of his head. "Why don't we work in the shop together," he continued. "It will be good for us." So the two made sandwiches and rolls for a few hours until Cynarra returned. "Alex is helping at the restaurant. I am sorry for before. I am better now." Akil nodded. "I think our Draco needs a bath," she said. "If you remove his bandage tonight, let me take him tomorrow. I want to give him a spa treatment. I will get his nails clipped, a professional shampoo, and they will brush him afterwards. I can pick him up in my car. Will he be able to walk tomorrow once the bandage is removed?" Akil smiled and nodded. "Tomorrow is going to be either a wonderful day for Draco, or a terrifying day," he said. "I think he will love it," Cynarra responded.

That evening the removal of Draco's bandage became a job for the whole family. Jason held Draco and whispered in his ear, Akil cut away the bandage, and Maria was on hand to wash the foot with disinfectant. "How does it look?" Akil asked his wife as she placed the foot in a bucket of soapy water. "To me it looks normal, but let's see how he walks on it without the bandage. Hold him tight, Jason. I want this foot to soak for a few minutes." Jason asked, "When will Draco be able to go up the Acropolis?" Maria responded, "I think we should just keep him here; he would be safer." Akil nodded. "Let's let Draco decide; if his foot is healed he will let us know where he wants to sleep."

Draco was playful that evening, having both his bandage and cone removed. "He will never go to sleep if you keep getting him excited, Jason," Diana called out from the kitchen. "Papa, I can sleep on the sofa tonight and watch Draco. You had to do it the last few nights." Akil agreed.

Choices

The next morning Cynarra picked up Draco from the shop at nine o'clock. "You are early!" Akil said. "Kalimera! Good morning! Coffee?" he asked. Cynarra shook her head. "We have a nine thirty appointment at the beauty parlor," she said. "How is Draco's foot?" she asked. Akil nodded. "Good. I think he is healed. We will find out today once he walks on it all day, but it looks fine," he said. "O.K. Draco, time to come with Auntie Cynarra!" she said. "I better use the leash," she said. Jason brought it over to her. "We will be finished around noon," she said. "And Draco will look and smell like a new dog!"

Once they got to the dog salon Draco was determined not to go in, trying to drag Cynarra in the other direction. "What is wrong, Draco?" Cynarra asked, perplexed. Cynarra pulled him inside the door and made him accompany her to the check-in desk. "I am Cynarra, and this is Draco. He needs a complete makeover and we do have an appointment," she said. "This way please," the woman behind the counter said.

Once inside the doggie beautification room, a woman who wore a white smock came in and greeted them. "You look like a doctor," Cynarra exclaimed. The petite woman laughed. "I wish I was! I just need to take down what Draco needs today. You said a 'complete makeover.' Has he been here before?" Cynarra shook his head. "Has he been groomed professionally before?" Cynarra again shook her head. The woman then looked Draco up and down and to the side. "He seems to be a sweet dog. I would suggest that we clip his nails, trim his hair, then wash, blow dry, brush, and groom him." "That sounds perfect!" Cynarra replied. "Since this is Draco's first time, why don't you stay here until we get his nails clipped to make sure he understands that we aren't going to harm him. The rest of the treatment he will enjoy. It will take a few hours." "Draco," Cynarra said, addressing the dog directly, "These people are not going to hurt you. You will be O.K. and I will be right here," she said. "I will bring in my husband Kahil; he is a strong man and can handle Draco, but he is also gentle and loves dogs," the woman said as she left the room.

Draco managed to get through the ordeal of getting his nails clipped and Cynarra stayed in the room until they started to wet him down and soap him up. "See, Draco, it isn't so bad," she said as the warm suds dripped down the side of his face. "I will wait here for Draco," she said, exiting to the front room. Kahil, a tall muscular man with black hair and eyes, massaged the soap deeply into Draco's back and nodded to Cynarra that it was alright to leave. The dog put his head up and stretched his back as he enjoyed the massage.

Cynarra was still reading her book when, a few hours later, Kahil led Draco out. Her mouth dropped open. "Is this Draco?" she asked, amazed. His black hair, which was always pressed against his body like a Labrador, was now puffed out and fluffy. The hair around his ears, mouth, and feet was now neatly trimmed. Gone were the longer scraggly hairs around his face. Cynarra exclaimed, "He smells glorious!" and Kahil laughed. "I am glad that you approve. He is a great dog; after I washed him we were best friends. I look forward to seeing Draco again!" Cynarra laughed. "I can't wait to show him to his friends. We have to do this regularly," she said. After she paid the bill, the two of them walked out, Draco prancing before her with a new dignity.

Back at the shop, Akil and Jason were still making sandwiches when Cynarra called out. "We're back!" Akil stepped out of the shop and stopped, stunned. Then he started laughing.

Jason then stepped out, saw Draco, and laughed. Draco hid behind Cynarra's legs. "Oh Draco, I'm sorry," Akil said as he approached. He put his finger to his lips so Jason would stop laughing. "You're beautiful, Draco," Akil said crouching down. Draco then approached Akil, pressing his face against his. "His fur is so soft!" Jason exclaimed, stroking his back. "I can't believe how fluffy he is!" he continued. Draco started enjoying the attention. Akil rose to his feet. "Let's call Alexander and tell him you decided to get a dog and invite him to come and see it. Let's see if he recognizes Draco!" Cynarra laughed. "Call him and tell him to come after his lunch crowd," she suggested.

When Alexander came later he immediately recognized Draco, but he was also amazed at his appearance. The afternoon was spent with compliments and admiration for the beautiful dog. As evening grew near, Jason asked his father: "Papa, what about tonight? Where will Draco sleep?" Akil replied: "He has to come home with us, son. He is freshly washed and your mother will want to see him. He will get dirty at the Parthenon. Tomorrow night we will let him choose where to go." Jason agreed.

Maria was just as surprised at Draco as Akil and Jason when they first saw him. "Be careful about laughing," Akil warned her. "Believe it or not, he gets embarrassed!" Jason added. "Well, I think he looks wonderful, like a show dog!" Maria exclaimed.

The next morning, Akil, as usual, was the first one up except for Draco, who was sitting by the front door waiting to get out. "Do you need to go to the bathroom, boy?" he asked. Taking out his leash, Akil led the dog outside. He kept pulling Akil towards the Acropolis. "Bathroom now, and tonight we will decide where you will sleep," Akil said. Draco obliged him, and the two headed back home.

Akil walked Draco to the shop that morning while Jason slept in. The dog walked normally, with no noticeable pain in his foot. "Good boy!" Akil said as the dog trotted next to him. "Today I won't have to tie you up, but you need to keep out of trouble," Akil continued. As soon as they arrived at the shop, Draco, having his leash removed, dashed away through the Plaka, while Akil shook his head. "He wants his freedom," he muttered as he turned to begin preparations for the morning.

About half an hour later, Draco showed up again with Alexander in tow. "Did you send him to fetch me?" Alexander asked laughing. Akil shrugged. "He came to the restaurant barking until I gave him a treat. Then he kept barking until I followed him here. This is a special dog you have here, Akil!" Alexander said. "Come sit with me for a bit my friend; I will make some coffee," Akil said. "Just for a few minutes; Alex is not at the restaurant yet and I am doing the preparation. He works so hard but he should not have to work the morning and evening. I keep telling him that he has to make time to live, not just work. That boy! He is just crazy about Cynarra. Work and Cynarra, that's all he has...." he trailed off. "I see we have some things to talk about this morning," Akil called out as he put the coffee on.

Jason suddenly showed up. "Sorry I am late, Papa. I was just a little tired," he said. "No problem, son. Draco is a handful," he said. Then Akil called Alexander over and said: "Let's talk this evening. Will you walk up the Acropolis with me?" Alexander agreed. "Will Draco come home with us, Papa?" Jason called out. "I don't know son. We will see if we wants to stay up there or come back down with us." Though Jason didn't like this arrangement, he said nothing.

Alexander returned to the restaurant after his coffee. Later that day Cynarra and Alex dropped by to spend a little time with Akil, Jason, and Draco. Suddenly Maria showed up with a basket full of sandwiches. "Good thing I made extra!" she said as she approached. She kissed Cynarra on the cheek and commented about how good Draco looked and smelled. "I want to pay for Draco's beauty treatment next time; we can bring him to the salon again in a few weeks," she said. Akil gave her a look. "You mean I will pay for him," he said, and she nodded. Akil didn't object.

When customers began showing up at the shop looking for sandwiches and ice cream, the little party broke up, each to his own tasks. Business at Akil's shop was busy that afternoon, and before long the sun was going down and Draco was getting restless. "Now you stay here until Alexander comes," Akil said to the dog. "We will walk up the hill together," he said.

It was about a half hour later that the three of them, Akil, Alexander, and Draco, were making their way across the Plaka towards the Acropolis. The dog trotted happily before them, looking back occasionally to make sure they were following him. All the way up the hill the two men spoke about Alex and Cynarra, about Draco's health, about their families, about the restaurant and the shop, about Cynarra's parents...without resolving anything. "I wish I knew the right answers," Alexander said. Before long they reached the top, next to the fence surrounding the Parthenon, and sat down on the bench with Draco sitting on the ground and leaning against Akil's leg. The sun began to set as Alexander turned to Akil and asked: "Well, what do you think? What should we do?" Akil looked down at Draco, who was looking up at him. "I think we should stand up and head down the hill. He will decide if he wants to come down with us or stay here tonight." "But aren't you worried about him?" Alexander asked. Akil nodded. "Of course I am, but I cannot let my worry take away his freedom." At that the two men stood; Draco stood and looked at them. As they took the first steps down the hill, the dog turned in the other direction, ran along the fence, scooted underneath, and made a dash towards the steps of the Parthenon. Akil turned back. "Somehow I knew that would be his choice."

When they reached the bottom of the hill the two men parted ways. "Come have coffee with me tomorrow morning," Akil invited him. "I will bring breakfast," Alexander responded.

Akil took a long way home, reflecting on the day and the past weeks. He stopped short when he looked up and found himself standing in front of the church where he had come to pray for Draco. The door was open, so Akil ascended the steps and walked into the dark church. He looked around; it was empty. Akil felt a surge of anger in his heart; he stood in the back and focused his attention towards the iconostasis, the sanctuary, and said out loud: "Why did you let this happen? I pleaded with you to make him well! But you didn't. Why? He is just a poor helpless little creature! Why couldn't you hear my prayer? Why take it out on Draco? Why punish him? What would it have cost you to make him healthy?..." The more he spoke, the more irritated Akil became. Suddenly, on the left side of the sanctuary, a priest stepped out. Akil turned to go, but the priest called out, "Please wait!" Akil froze.

The priest sat down near Akil and invited him to do the same. "Are you angry at God?" he asked Akil. "I am sorry if it is a sin, Father, but yes, I am very angry. I came here, I said a prayer for someone close to me who may have had cancer, I asked God to take care of him, and what happens? He has cancer and may not have long to live. Does that sound just to you, Father? Does that sound loving?" The priest looked down. "No, it doesn't sound just or loving. You are Maria's husband, no?" Akil nodded. "I will make a confession to you. I have been angry at God on more than one occasion. I don't think it is wrong to be angry at him; we all get angry at those we love. But I think it is important that you keep communicating with him, even if only to tell him how angry you are..." Akil thought about his words, then shook his head. "But Father, it isn't right, it's just not right..." The priest said: "No, it isn't. But there is a positive side to this." Akil interrupted him. "What possible positive side is there to sickness and death?" The priest looked him in the eyes. "I can see that you carry this person in your heart. This person is a gift to you and that is no small thing." At that, the priest got up and left.

On his way home, Akil said out loud: "Well, I am still angry with you!"

When Akil entered the front door Jason seemed disappointed. "He wanted to stay at the Parthenon tonight," Akil said, reading the boy's mind. "Papa, Mama," Jason began; "I am going to wake up early tomorrow to meet Draco at the Parthenon and make sure he gets down safely." Maria looked at Akil, who didn't object. She was skeptical of Jason's resolution, however, since she knew that her son disliked getting up early.

Food and Humans

Daria woke up with a start as she heard the mallet hit the stone. She had dozed off in a corner near Adelino's workspace. Tiro had insisted on bringing her up the Acropolis that day. Diana was against it because of what they had been through already with Daria running away and getting lost. "Daria won't run away from Papa. If you are coming up for lunch with us, you could bring her down with you then," Tiro added. Diana looked at her husband. "Our son is becoming an excellent negotiator. Soon he will be selling me the stones on the Acropolis!" she said and laughed. "I will agree only if you keep her tied up near your father and that I come get her at lunch time." Tiro nodded.

Adelino had placed Daria nearby, behind a short wall with a stone missing so Daria could see through. He didn't want to risk her getting hit by fragments as he chiseled the rock. He had become a stonecutter who specialized in the finer details of carving, which required more expertise and less strain. It was the perfect job for Adelino, who was skilled but was still limited by his injury.

The sun was high and it was hot when Diana arrived hours later. She was loaded down with bread and cheese, olives and wine, and a jug of water dangling from her hand. "Diana!" Adelino called as he hobbled out to help her. Daria jumped up to watch as Adelino took the heavy jugs from his wife. "I do not want you to come here carrying such heavy burdens," Adelino began. "Just bread and cheese; Tiro and I can bring up the rest in the morning," he said. "But the water will be warm," Diana objected. "Better warm water than an exhausted wife," Adelino replied. "I will go call Tiro," he said as he left the area. Daria began to bark. "There you are! Hidden behind that wall! Here...." she said as she picked Daria up, who tried to lick Diana's face. "You're coming home with me today," she continued. Daria began sniffing, having caught the scent of the cheese. "Don't tell Papa," she said, as she reached inside and broke off a small piece, handing it to the dog.

Once Tiro arrived, the group sat down to lunch with Daria sitting next to Adelino's leg. "Does Pheidias come to this part of the hill?" Diana asked as she sliced some cheese. "When he comes, I hide!" Adelino said. Diana looked at him, wondering what he meant. "After that incident with the statue of the goddess we thought that it is better if Pheidias was not reminded of it. So Tiro and I focus on our work; if word gets around that Pheidias is in the area, we just keep sanding and chiseling. He never comes to this section, but if he ever would, he will find us doing good work." Diana nodded. "Yes those were dark days..." she said as she remembered the situation their son had gotten them in. "But that is all in the past," her husband said. Diana shook herself out of that thought. "Yes, and here we are. And I have a surprise, if you look at the bottom of the basket." Jason dug deep and pulled out a small honey raisin cake. "Mama! Did you make it?" Diana laughed. "Do you think I have a servant who made it for me? If I do, tell me where she is hiding!" Adelino chuckled and leaned over and kissed his wife.

Below they heard "Rrrrrrrrrrrrrr" as Daria signaled that she was there too. She too smelled the raisins and honey, and licked her lips expectantly. "She can have a bit of the leftover bread and cheese," Diana said, reading Adelino's mind.

The Future Unfolds

When Akil woke up the next morning, the first thing he did was to peak into Jason's room. He then went to the kitchen to make the coffee, shaking his head in amazement. It was a short time later that Maria got up. "Shall I wake up Jason?" she asked. Akil motioned to the boy's room with a tilt of his head. Maria looked, then came back to the kitchen shaking her head. "I never would have believed it. He got up early. He must really love that dog," she said.

Jason wanted to make sure that he got to the Parthenon before Draco headed down, so he had left home before dawn. He climbed the stairs rapidly and in less than half an hour he was on top. Peering through the fence, he saw Draco still sleeping on the steps of the Parthenon. Rather than waking him, Jason sat down on the nearby bench to watch the sun rise. It didn't take long for Draco to pick up the boy's scent; Jason could see him lift his head and sniff into the air. He then got up on all four feet and shook vigorously. Then, more sniffing. Draco then started trotting in the direction of the space under the fence; he slipped under, then bolted towards Jason. Jason stroked his fur, patted his head, and gave Draco a big long hug. When the dog began to squirm, he realized it was time to head down the hill.

Jason noticed that Draco was taking one step at a time. "Are you O.K., Draco?" he asked. The dog stopped and looked up, then continued slowly towards the Plaka.

It was still early when they got to the shop, so Jason gave Draco some dry dog food and water and started to prepare the shop for the day. Akil showed up a little later with a package wrapped in tin foil. "Kalimera! Good morning, son!" he said as he kissed the boy's head. Draco barked. "Yes, good morning to you also, Draco," he said, bending down to receive a lick. "Your mother says that you have to eat this breakfast. I will finish the preparations and put on some coffee for us," Akil said. "But...." Jason began, but Akil stopped him. "If you don't eat, your mother is going to ask me, and then ask you, and then insist that you not get up early....so let's avoid all of that, son. Eat your breakfast, and I will take care of the shop. After all, Draco wants some company." The boy took the food and sat at one of the outdoor tables, with Draco sitting on the ground next to him sniffing.

"How did it go this morning, son?" Akil asked, as he sat down and handed his son a coffee. "I got there before Draco woke up. He was so funny, sleeping on the steps of the Parthenon. It was like a painting. But then he sniffed me and woke up. I probably got there too early. Tomorrow I will leave a few minutes later so I won't wake Draco up. Then we walked down the stairs. But Papa, I noticed that Draco walks down the stairs so slowly. Do you think he is alright? Could it be his foot, or...." Akil saw the concern on his son's face. "He is just getting older, like me," he replied. Draco got up and walked around to Akil. He laid down and put his chin on Akil's shoe. "I think someone is preparing for a nap and intends to keep me captive," Akil whispered.

Cynarra showed up later that morning and was dismayed to find that Draco's hair was flattened down on the side he had slept on. "I will return soon," she said, departing. About an hour later she came back with a wire hair brush in hand. "We are not going to let you look raggedy any more!" she announced, as she called Draco to come sit next to her. When she started to brush his back, the dog looked straight up, stretching his back in pleasure. "Look how he likes it, Papa!" Jason called out. "He will be Draco the black puff ball," Cynarra said.

Alex showed up a little later. "So this is my competition now," he said, looking at Cynarra and Draco. "Akil," Alex continued, "Can you stop by the restaurant about five before you and my father walk up the hill?" Akil nodded. "Certainly." "Oh, can you bring Maria also, and Jason, if he can leave the shop for a few minutes?" This all seemed odd, but Akil agreed.

"What is it about? Is something wrong?" Maria asked on the phone when Akil called her from the shop. "I don't know; he just wants us all there. If there are no customers we can close up the shop for a half hour so Jason can come," he said.

As the afternoon wore on Akil wondered what was going on. Since Alexander didn't stop by that day, he had no other information. He began to wonder if something was wrong with Alexander and this fear built up in his mind. "Come, let's see what is the matter," he said. So the four of them, Akil, Maria, Jason, and Draco, headed over to Alexander's restaurant at the agreed upon hour.

When they arrived they were surprised to find Alexander's wife, who rarely socialized, as well as Cynarra's parents. Alex was smiling and chatting with Cynarra at his side. Alexander came out and greeted his friends. "Are you alright?" Akil whispered to him. Alexander nodded.

Alex began to speak. "We have asked you to come here today because you are our family, some through blood, some through affection, some both...." Here several present chuckled. Cynarra then added: "You are those who are most special to me in the world." Then Alex continued: "We want you to be the first to know that we are engaged." At that moment there was a "pop" as Alexander opened a bottle of sparkling wine. It was Cynarra's mother who clapped first, then the rest. "Congratulations!" Maria exclaimed. "I am so happy for you," Akil added. "I know you all want to know about Cynarra's education and future. Rather than whispering about it, I will tell you what we know," Alex began. "She still has a year at Cambridge on her way to obtaining her doctorate. She also has an offer to teach at the University here in Athens in their business department. I will never take away her dreams," he said, and he kissed her.

"When will you get married?" Maria asked. "Yes, when?" Cynarra's mother seconded. "After she finishes at Cambridge. It will be a long engagement, but that will give us a lot of time to plan," he said. Cynarra could already see the wheels turning in her mother's head. "Mama, no plans without me, alright?" Cynarra's mother nodded, then kissed her daughter on the head.

"A toast to the future married couple!" Alexander said. Everyone present drank to the happiness of Alex and Cynarra. "Let's sit for a moment," Alexander invited them. "I know we all have to get back to work but let's celebrate this moment," and he lifted his glass again. As the afternoon wore on, Akil excused himself so he could open up the shop. Before he left, Alexander asked him: "Can you wait for me? I may be about an hour late; then we can walk up the Acropolis together. I will meet you at the shop?" Akil agreed.

The two men took their time climbing the stairs to the Acropolis, letting Draco set the pace. "Children marrying, kids, grandkids, life goes on. Next it will be your Jason," Alexander said. "I hope not for awhile," Akil said. "He is so young; he is so happy without responsibilities. All of the rest will come soon enough."

When they reached the top, they sat on their bench with Draco leaning on Akil's leg and the sun setting on the horizon. "Life isn't so bad, is it my friend?" Alexander asked. "No, not at all my friend," Akil replied.

The Longing

Jason continued to rise early over the next weeks until he was able to pinpoint the exact time when Draco usually woke up. This gave him a few moments of extra rest in the morning. Every day the two walked down to the shop and greeted Akil, who had coffee, breakfast, and dog food ready, and sat under the tree as they started their day together. Inevitably, Alexander, Cynarra, Alex and Maria would stop by, spending a few moments or longer together under the same tree, sipping coffee, chatting about their day and enjoying one another's company. Draco was always in that circle also; if he felt he was being ignored he would whine, and somebody, usually Akil, would scoot him over against his leg and pat his head.

It was dawn on the first day of August. During the past week Cynarra was preparing to return to Cambridge, Alexander was secretly making wedding preparations with Cynarra's parents, and that morning Jason was walking up the Acropolis to meet Draco. When he got to the top he saw Draco on the steps, as usual, so he sat on the bench and waited. As the sky turned from gray to pink to blue, he waited, but still Draco didn't stir. Jason went up to the fence and called out "Draco!" The dog lifted his head and got up, but with difficulty. He began to walk slowly towards Jason, slipping once but then catching himself. Jason's heart began to beat wildly out of fear and concern. "Are you alright, Draco?" he asked. The boy went to the space in the fence where Draco crawled under and helped pull him through. He sat down next to the dog. "What's wrong, Draco?" he asked. The dog licked him and feebly wagged his tail. Jason reached over and hugged the dog. "Please be O.K., Draco!" he pleaded.

The boy stood up and Draco looked up at him. "Can you make it down the stairs?" Jason asked. He led Draco down, but the dog slipped on the first step. "Don't worry Draco, I can carry you," he said as he lifted the dog up. "You're heavy, Draco! But we will go slowly. Good boy!" he reassured him.

Akil was at the shop wondering why Jason was so late. He called his wife. "Yes, Jason left early today. I heard him leave. He went to the Acropolis. Should I walk up and look for him?" she asked. "No, no, no," Akil said. "I am closer. I can....." He broke off his sentence as he saw Jason carrying Draco across the Plaka. "He is here. I will call you later," he said. He walked quickly over to Jason. "What happened?" Akil asked. "I don't know, Papa. Draco isn't well. Something is wrong. We have to bring him to the doctor!" the boy said, tears streaming down his face. "O.K., son. Let me take Draco from you. We will bring him under the tree, give him some food and water, and I will call the veterinarian."

Maria came by the shop a short time later in the car and picked up Akil and Draco, while Jason minded the shop. Draco lay down on the back seat. "What's wrong with poor Draco?" she asked. "I don't know, Maria. Maybe he just ate something that was bad for him," he said reassuringly. "Did you give him anything to eat or drink?" Maria asked. "He wouldn't eat," Akil responded.

Draco put up little resistance as Akil carried him into the veterinarian's office. He was the first one to be examined that morning; both Akil and Maria went into the exam room and put Draco up on the stainless steel table. The veterinarian greeted both of them, then proceeded to examine Draco. He looked in the dog's eyes, examined the lump on his side, looked into his ears and then took his temperature (that was the part that Draco didn't like). "It is the cancer; it has spread," he announced. Maria put her arm in her husband's arm as they listened for more information. "There is nothing we can do at this point but to keep Draco comfortable and happy. He is losing strength and eventually his organs will begin to shut down. He may have days or a few weeks," he said. "What would you like to do?" he asked Akil. "I want to take him home with us; he is family," Akil replied. "If you need me, I am here," the doctor said. "I will give you some pills that relieve pain; if he shows any signs of distress you can give one to him. He may eat or not eat, but try to give him plenty of water and morsels of foods he enjoys. After that, nature will take its course."

Akil didn't speak a word on the way home; Maria knew he was deeply upset so she didn't push him. He drove directly to the shop, took Draco out of the car, and said: "Thank you, my wife." Maria cried as she drove home.

At the shop Jason asked excitedly: "What did they say? How is Draco?" Akil replied, "I will tell you everything son, but first, please prepare a bowl of water for Draco and get out some of the sandwich meat and some cheese. If we chop it up perhaps we can get him to eat. The veterinarian said that food will give him strength." Jason ran to prepare Draco's meal.

It was about the time that Alexander stopped by for coffee. When he got to the shop, he found Jason frantically chopping meat; he then spotted Akil carrying Draco to his blanket under the tree. "What in the world?" he said out loud. "Jason, what is going on?" he asked. Jason, with trembling voice, replied: "I found Draco sick this morning. Papa just came back from the doctor with him."

The two men greeted each other as Akil put Draco down. He wagged his tail slightly and looked up at Alexander. "How are you, Draco?" he asked. "That is a question that a lot of people are asking this morning," Akil responded. "Come on, boy!" Akil said, sitting down and pulling Draco beside him. Jason brought the food and water but Draco didn't touch it. "Come on, Draco, you have to drink," Akil insisted. He dipped his finger into the water and put it against Draco's mouth, who licked it. He did it again and Draco licked the water off. After a few more times he was able to get Draco to drink out of the bowl. "Now a little food, Draco," he said as he held a small piece of meat in front of Draco's mouth. He ate a few bites from Akil's hand but would not eat out of the bowl.

"Papa, what happened?" Jason asked. Akil took a breath. "It is the cancer. It is spreading. That's why he is getting weak and acting so strangely. The doctor said to keep him comfortable and happy so that is exactly what we are going to do. We all know how sensitive Draco is and if he realizes that everyone around him is sad, then he will be sad too. So let's try to be happy for Draco's sake," he said. "But Papa, did the doctor say.....how long.....Draco....." he trailed off. "Weeks or days, but you never know, son," Akil replied.

Alexander was quiet as he looked down at Draco while Akil spoke. After a pause, he said "Draco has been a good friend." He then got up. "I will come back later," he said as he turned away.

Word spread quickly through the Plaka, and soon Cynarra and Alex came, as well Maria, and other shopkeepers nearby who had known Draco over the years. Jason put a pillow on the ground for Draco and sat next to him, stroking his head. Draco kept looking around, unused to so many people together in one place looking at him, talking about him, and pointing at him. It was too much, so he put his chin on his paws and looked from one person to the other.

The discussion around him was about remedies; each one thought of an idea to make Draco well. A potion, a diet, an herb; each idea was proposed, dissected, and eventually discarded. They each wanted Draco to get well but had no idea how to achieve it.

Akil was playing host; as he walked towards the shop to prepare some cheese and snacks for his guests, he looked up into the sky and said: "I am still mad at you."

Jason, meanwhile, asked his mother: "Can we please take Draco home with us, Mama? He can't be up there alone!" Maria stroked her son's hair. "Of course we can, son." "But Papa might say that Draco should choose!" Jason continued. "I will handle your father. Draco is coming home with us," she said firmly. When Akil returned he noticed that both Maria and Jason were looking at him. "What?" he asked, setting down the food. "Draco is coming home with us," Maria said in a tone that implied: "This is not to be discussed." Akil nodded.

Jason insisted on sleeping on the sofa that night so he could more easily take Draco outside during the night. "He may have to go to the bathroom without realizing it," Akil said. "I will get up and take him outside during the night to see if I can get him to go. You can take him out if he lets you know that he needs to go again." Jason agreed.

It was a restless night for both boy and dog, since Draco kept going to the front door and Jason took him outside several times, but Draco didn't need to go to the bathroom. Instead, he kept pulling the boy towards the Acropolis. "No, Draco, not there. We have to stay at the house tonight. It's safer for you," Jason said, tugging on the leash.

When he got back on the sofa and closed his eyes, it seemed like only a few minutes had passed when he heard Akil in the kitchen making coffee. He opened his eyes and saw his father standing near him. "Are you alright, son?" he asked. "Yes, Papa. Is Draco O.K.?" he asked, turning towards where the dog had been. "Yes, he is in the kitchen with me, son. Rest."

Draco seemed weaker than the day before, so once he was ready to leave for work, Akil picked the dog up and put him in the car. "Let Jason rest; he can come to the shop later," Akil told Maria. "I will come with him later," Maria said. She returned to the house sad: sad for her son, sad for her husband, and sad for Draco. That day there were a stream of visitors to the shop just like the day before. Draco lay in the shade and wanted to be next to Akil. Jason and Maria helped in the shop that morning since the dog would get up and struggle to follow Akil around when he left his chair. Alexander spent some time at the shop, followed by

Alex, Cynarra, and the neighboring shop owners. Even Kahil and his wife from the dog groomer showed up later in the afternoon. When the day was drawing to a close and everybody had left except for Jason and Akil, Draco started whining. "What's wrong, Draco?" Akil asked. When the dog started to pull away, Akil ran and grabbed him. "Jason, can you get the leash please?" he asked. After attaching it to the dog's collar, Draco started to pull Akil towards the Acropolis, whining loudly. "Papa, we have to bring him home!" the boy pleaded. "I know, son," Akil replied. "Draco," Akil continued, "You have to come home with us. It is safer there. We can go to the Acropolis during the day." Draco whined loudly and pulled, then whined and pulled some more.

"There is something on the Acropolis that he needs," Akil said to Jason. He paused and thought about it. "I will see what Draco wants, son. If he wants to go up the Acropolis, I will go up with him. I will carry him back down later and drive him home. Can you tell your mother I will be a little late?" he asked. "Yes Papa, but don't leave Draco alone, please," the boy pleaded. "I won't leave him there, son," Akil replied. "Can I come with you, Papa?" Jason asked. "No, son. I need you to watch Draco tonight at home, so you need your rest. I will take care of this," he said, and the two parted ways.

It was with difficulty that Draco made it to the top, and in fact, Akil carried him for most of the way. But the dog seemed determined, as if an invisible force were drawing him there. When they got to their bench, the sun was dipping below the horizon and the last tourists were leaving the area. Akil picked up Draco and sat him on the bench beside him. The dog was sitting straight up, alert and curious. Then, after a few minutes, he lay down and put his chin on Akil's leg as Akil stroked his head.

It wasn't long before Draco drifted off to sleep and Akil could tell the dog was dreaming by the way he was moving his legs.

"Papa, look at that black dog!" Tiro said, as they finished the last of the honey raisin cake. "He looks like he belongs to somebody," Diana commented. "Yes, he has a collar around his neck. Poor boy looks lost," Adelino said. "He must belong to someone close by and cannot find his way home, like Daria," Adelino continued. For her part, Daria was at full alert, sniffing in the air and staring in the direction of the large black dog. She started to walk forward but Adelino stopped her. "Be good, Daria," he said as he held her.

The other dog crept forward, sniffing. "Papa, I think he's hungry!" Tiro said, but Diana broke in: "One dog, yes. Two dogs, no!" "We can just try to find his owner. If he stays around we can ask the workers on the hill or see if he belongs to someone nearby." Diana looked at her husband with skepticism. "Let's just keep him long enough to find the owner; remember how it was when we couldn't find Daria?" he asked. "I will never forget that. Alright, just until we find the owner." At this point, Tiro rose and walked over to the black dog, who was frightened. The boy bent down and offered him a piece of bread, which the dog gobbled him. "He is hungry," he said as he returned to his parents with the new dog following behind him. "We can give him a little food and water, then look for who he belongs to," Adelino said. Tiro began to laugh. "Look, Mama! He and Daria like each other," he said as both dogs lay down next to one another. Diana shook her head. "It's as if they know each other…"

"When is your father coming home with Draco?" Maria asked. "It is getting so late." Jason shrugged. "I can go look for them, Mama," Jason offered. Maria shook her head. "Then I am going to lose both of you," she said.

Jason slept little that night. He stayed on the sofa so that he could hear his father come in but he never heard the front door open. He looked at the clock; it was four thirty in the morning. "A half hour more," he said to himself. Again he looked. "Five o'clock. If he doesn't come by five thirty then I will go," Jason said to himself.

Since there was still no sign of his father as the sky turned from black to gray, the boy rose, threw on his clothes, and was out the door. He was anxious to make sure that both Draco and his father were alright. He could see the Acropolis in the distance and, having a sense of urgency, he ran all the way to the base of the hill.

As Jason ran he wondered why his father hadn't returned home. Was Draco too sick? Did his father have an injury? These thoughts and others raced through his mind in the twenty minutes or so it took to reach the top.

Once there, Jason went to the bench where his father usually sat but it was empty. The boy then heard a sound that was unfamiliar. He drew his breath in and listened; he heard someone sobbing.

Walking along the fence and peering into the area of the Parthenon, he could see his father lying on the steps, his arm around the furry dog.

"Papa?" the boy said, in a weak voice. Then he cried out louder "Papa! Papa!" His father sat up, wiped the tears from his eyes, and walked quickly towards his son, blocking his view of the dog. "Papa, what's wrong?!" the boy called out. Tears began running down Akil's face once more as he reached his son at the fence. "Draco has left us," Akil said, breaking down. Jason cried out "Noooooooo!!!!!!!!!!!" Akil reached for his son's hand through the fence. "Yes son, he is gone," he said. "Let me come see him!" Jason said, setting a foot to climb the fence. "No, son. Please do this for me and for Draco! Before the security and tourists come. Please go to the shop as fast as you can. Get the shovel in back of the shop. Also get Draco's blanket, his bone, and some plastic bags. Then come back here as soon as possible. Can you please do this, son? Quickly?" Jason couldn't get any words out. He nodded and dashed down the hill.

When he returned, Jason found that his father had cleared the rocks away from an area near where Draco was laying. "Throw me his blanket, son," Akil asked. He then covered the dog with the blanket. "Please wait here, son," he instructed. But Jason, determined to not be left on the outside, climbed the fence as Akil began to dig a hole. "What are you doing, Papa?" the boy asked.

"Draco needs to be in the place he loved the most," he said as he continued to dig. "The security must not know that we buried him here," he continued. "We only have about thirty minutes before they come on duty," he continued. "Let me help, Papa," Jason said. "Rest for a minute," the boy said. So the two took turns digging a deep hole, moving the stones out of the way as they prepared Draco's grave. "That is enough, son," Akil said. "Now I want you to stand over there while I put Draco in," he said as he placed the plastic at the bottom. "I will wrap him in his blanket, son. I want you to remember Draco as he was, not like this. Please son, stand over there," he insisted. So Jason backed away as his father lifted the dog off the steps and placed Draco in the grave. Then he began scooping the dirt on top. Jason then approached and helped with the dirt and placed the stones on top so the area would not look like it was disturbed. "What if we forget where we buried him, Papa? There is no marker." "I will never forget," Akil replied.

"The security will be here in a few minutes, son. They can't find us in here. Let's go now; we can return another time," Akil said. So the two climbed the fence and then headed down the hill as the sun rose.

Cynarra was already at the shop when Akil and Jason, covered with dirt, arrived. "What...." she began to say, then stopped as the two approached. She looked at Akil's tear-streaked face, then at Jason. She shook her head. "No; he is O.K., isn't he?" she said. Jason approached her and hugged her, tears rolling down his face. "No," Cynarra continued to say. But when she looked again in Akil's eyes, she knew that their beloved Draco was gone.

Akil was not one to show his emotions, but today was especially difficult in hiding what he was feeling. "Son, can you mind the shop for awhile? I will go home and tell your mother, then wash up and return," he said. "Papa, you don't have to come back. I can handle the shop today and I can tell Draco's friends..." He knew that would be the most difficult part for his father. Akil kissed his son's head and left.

When Akil arrived home, he couldn't look Maria in the eyes; he was trying to find the words to tell her. "I know. Jason told me. I am so sorry," she said as she hugged Akil, who, once again that day, could not hold back his tears.

Once he was cleaned up, Maria suggested he take the day off. "Jason can take care of the shop." Akil, who had never taken a day off in his life, considered her words. "Perhaps I will go in later," he said. "I think I will take a walk to think about these things," he said. After a few moments, Akil was out the door.

He walked a long time and found himself in the National Garden. Akil spotted the bench where he had sat with Draco and again sat there, thinking about the past weeks and years and everything that had happened. He also recalled his visit to the church and to the priest. Akil looked up towards the sky and asked, "Why do you always take away what you give?" He spent the afternoon on that bench, not wanting to face anyone, not knowing what to say or how to feel.

It was late afternoon when Akil left the National Garden; he started to walk through the city and somehow found himself standing at the base of the Acropolis. He stepped on the first stair as he had done hundreds of times before. The stair was the same, the stones were the same, the hill was exactly as it was, and yet everything felt different. He took another step, and slowly made his way up, drawn there by something he couldn't grasp.

The first stars began to appear as he reached the top and rounded the corner towards his bench.

Standing there, next to that bench, were Maria and Jason, Alex and Cynarra, Alexander and his wife, the veterinarian, the dog groomer and his wife, Cynarra's parents, as well as three of the surrounding shop owners. Maria walked down a few steps and taking her husband's hand, accompanied him towards the others. "See the gift that Draco has given us!" she whispered in his ear.